ME FOR YOU

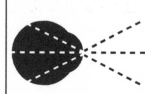

This Large Print Book carries the
Seal of Approval of N.A.V.H.

ME FOR YOU

LOLLY WINSTON

THORNDIKE PRESS
A part of Gale, a Cengage Company

GALE
A Cengage Company

Farmington Hills, Mich • San Francisco • New York • Waterville, Maine
Meriden, Conn • Mason, Ohio • Chicago

Copyright © 2019 by Lolly Winston.
Thorndike Press, a part of Gale, a Cengage Company.

Thorndike Press® Large Print Core.
The text of this Large Print edition is unabridged.
Other aspects of the book may vary from the original edition.
Set in 16 pt. Plantin.

LIBRARY OF CONGRESS CIP DATA ON FILE.
CATALOGUING IN PUBLICATION FOR THIS BOOK
IS AVAILABLE FROM THE LIBRARY OF CONGRESS

ISBN-13: 978-1-4328-6153-7 (hardcover alk. paper)

Published in 2019 by arrangement with Gallery Books, an imprint of Simon & Schuster, Inc.

Printed in Mexico
1 2 3 4 5 6 7 23 22 21 20 19

For Laurie Fox

And in loving memory of
Katherine Donner
and
Laura Geist

Farewell happy fields,
Where joy forever dwells: Hail horrors, hail
Infernal world, and thou profoundest hell
Receive thy new possessor; one who brings
A mind not to be changed by place or time.
The mind is its own place, and in itself
Can make a Heav'n of Hell, a Hell
of Heav'n.
— *JOHN MILTON, PARADISE LOST*

Life is just one goddamned thing after
another.
— *MARVIN WINSTON, EXASPERATED FATHER*

Pruning clematis sounds complicated,
but it need not be; plants are forgiving
and will quickly repair mistakes. Do
remember that dormant wood can look
dead. . . . Spring-blooming clematis
bloom only on the previous year's
"dead" wood.
— SUNSET WESTERN GARDEN BOOK

I

1

Like a fool, Rudy spoke to his wife Bethany for probably ten minutes before he realized she was dead. It was a Saturday morning and they lay in bed, neither of them having to work that day. He awoke with the idea that they should go to the beach for a long, relaxing walk.

"We can wait until this afternoon," he mused, when Bee hadn't stirred at his first suggestion of the idea. He didn't want her to feel rushed. "By then the traffic will have thinned. I'll pack us a picnic and we can watch the sun set. When it gets dark I'll take you to that little wine bar on South Main, with all the great cheeses?" He rubbed a bit of the soft cotton fabric of her nightgown between his thumb and forefinger.

Bethany slept on her back, which was unusual for her. Rudy rolled away from her onto his side, facing the wall. He backed into her, nuzzling her hip with his bum.

"I'll do everything. All you have to do is grab your sunscreen, a book, hat, and jacket for later."

They joked about it, but Rudy felt ashamed of the fact that — since he'd been downsized — Bee had maintained her higher-paying, full-time job as a hospital pharmacist, while he'd gone from CTO to a part-time department store pianist. He'd played all his life, given lessons while in graduate school. Now he wore a silly rented tuxedo and rolled out cocktail and Broadway tunes — *Plant a radish, get a radish!* — while shoppers considered the scratchiness of one pashmina over another. The only pleasant part was playing Chopin for his Hungarian friend Sasha, who worked in Fine Watches. (She made him blush. Blush! How mortifying. A married crush?) The department store was only a temporary arrangement, however, until Bethany's hospital pension kicked in.

Bee was the one who put a positive spin on everything — even his being downsized, when his tech company was acquired by a bigger company. It had been good news for all — stock, cash, T-shirts (there were always T-shirts) — and most employees stayed on. The bigger company in the merger/acquisition had wanted the "brainpower" of the little company. But not Rudy's brain-power. Bethany considered it the first step toward their mutual early retirement. "It's going to be a *great* chapter, you'll see!" They were both fifty-four, and soon she'd be eligible for her pension. Their IRAs were plump, unlike many less fortunate workers in America, she reminded Rudy.

And at least Rudy worked only with a baby grand. Bethany was strapped with training employees — some were lovely but one was downright creepy. Meanwhile, Rudy did all he could to make Bee's life easy, luxurious even, he hoped. He loved that she bragged to her friends about the lunches he packed or the extra housework he completed.

Rudy had been *made redundant* — in the words of Bee's British brother-in-law. Rudy wished his brother-in-law would stop using this phrase. It made it sound as though there were a backup, newer model of hus-band in the garage. This made Bethany giggle, but Rudy was serious — he couldn't wait for her to retire and her pension to kick in. They were almost there: long trips, short trips, staycations, the opera, entertaining — all of which they both enjoyed.

Now he took a long, deep breath and reached around to give his wife a shoulder rub. Maybe Rudy should just shut up about the beach already. Clearly Bee was exhausted from her double shift the day before.

He turned and sat up. "I'll fix you breakfast," he said softly, in case she was just now beginning to wake. Funny, because no matter how tired she might be, she was usually the first one up. She liked to rise early and drink her first cup of coffee alone at the kitchen table with the crossword. But now she lay on her back, the eyelets of her pink nightgown perfect little crescents. Rudy thought of how beautiful she would always be, even as she aged.

"Well, now aren't *you* the lazybones today," he teased, shaking her gently. A jostling caress.

Then he realized Bethany wasn't breathing.

His legs sliced through the covers as he leapt up and made his way around to her side of the bed. Her lips were dry and unresponsive as he pressed his mouth against hers. His CPR training came to him in a hysterical jumble as he blew into her lungs and pumped her chest three times below her breasts. He was gentle at first, not wanting to hurt her ribs. "Oh, Jesus!" Someone screamed. It was his voice, an

14

animalistic howl. He stumbled and fell backwards, tripping over his pleas and pajama legs.

"Bethany, honey, come on, now." He peeled back the covers. For some reason the stupid acronym PASS ran through his mind PASS, PASS: pull, aim, squeeze, sweep. Idiot: That was for using a fire extinguisher. He punched out 911 on the cordless phone. Gave the dispatcher their address. Yes, UNRESPONSIVE! JUST HURRY!

He plugged her nose, blew another three puffs of air, and pounded at her chest. Nothing. Repeat. Nothing. Her lips felt warmer. Didn't they? The room buzzed with adrenaline. The walk on the beach — the sound of the entire ocean — was in the room now. He knelt beside the bed, his eyes even with hers, waiting for the ambulance. This wasn't happening. It was one of those stupid TV dramas. Bee was as pale as the chalk-gray duvet. Still and chilly skin. He pulled the covers back up over her arms and legs and tucked them under her chin.

Right. All police cars in their town were equipped with those paddles now. There had been a fund-raiser for them. He should have called 911 sooner. His dumb outdated CPR! He raised Bee's feet and put a pillow under them beneath the covers. He spoke

15

to her, "You're going to be all right, just —"
Then the doorbell.

He did not want to leave her to let the paramedics into the house. He tugged on his khakis under his bathrobe. As quicky as Rudy charged down the stairs to the door, the ambulance workers sprinted back up. He made a U-turn to follow them.

The paramedics tried so hard for so long to revive Bethany. They were young and good-looking. Men and women with smooth, perfect muscles like Greek gods. They deftly steered her on a gurney down the hall, through the front door, and into the ambulance. Her knitting! Rudy stupidly thought he'd grab it from the hall chair; she might want to keep herself occupied while they waited for the doctors. The hospital always entailed waiting. That vest or scarf or whatever the heck it was she'd been making. She whipped through her woolly creations, plowed through novels with amazing comprehension, pruned the wisteria on a ladder all the way to the top of the trellis, and mowed the lawn herself, despite Rudy's protests. If there were words to sum up Bethany, you really just needed one: capable. But kind, and funny, and smart, too. Certainly never one to correct people or show off her many abilities.

Here's the kicker: Late the previous after-noon, Rudy had taken Bee to their family doctor, who had squeezed her in at the end of the day. She'd come home from work *feeling off* — minor chest pains, palpitations. *Just not feeling herself.* That dolt of a doctor sent her *home,* with Gas-X. And stress. Bee had pointed out that Rudy took wonderful care of her. Rudy would've been pleased if he weren't so worried. She'd had an EKG in the office that "appeared to be normal." So Einstein diagnosed her with gas. Bee didn't go to the doctor very often, and she was *not* a complainer — their guy knew that, and he should have examined her more extensively, listened more carefully. Not been so quick to wrap up his day. Gas! It annoyed Rudy that Bethany, a hospital pharmacist, had this reverence for MDs. She'd giggled on the way home, embar-rassed by her diagnosis, burping and quickly covering her mouth as she laughed, her cheeks not rosy enough, if you asked Rudy. Now Rudy recalled with anger the doctor's sanguine confidence. Could you have a normal EKG then die of a heart attack?

Bethany had held Rudy's hand in hers as she told the doctor what excellent care her husband took of her. But dinners and wine, and massages, and bag lunches brimming with fresh fruit, and twice-yearly vacations couldn't take the place of a decent doctor diagnosing heart disease.

That morning Rudy decided to follow the ambulance in his car. Maybe they'd need the car once they were at the hospital. Rudy bitterly regretted this decision. He could have been holding Bee's hand in the ambulance, stroking her forehead, whispering to her. Yet he'd been afraid he would somehow hamper Bee's rescue. Maybe he'd get in the way of these swift paramedics, who boiled over with youth and capability.

Besides which, he'd had to pee. It was the most absurd need, given the circumstances, but Rudy hadn't relieved himself since the night before. He'd traded his robe for a shirt, buttoned all wrong, and hung on to the gurney until it was in the ambulance. They'd loaded Bee with simultaneous speed and gentleness that touched Rudy. Then his bladder shot off a final warning signal. He told the medics he would follow. The woman paramedic looked at him a bit curiously — or at least he thought she did, later, going over the morning in his head. Over and over and over. All of the things he could have done differently. If only if only if only. All the way back to signs he might have missed the night before, beyond that to the doctor's office, preceded by the days and weeks leading up to Bee's death.

Some of the morning was a blur, but Rudy remained haunted by these two indignities among the events of his wife's death: (1) He may not have properly performed CPR. (They told him he'd done fine, but still, he looked it up: the method had changed. His skills stank. Pounding his wife's lovely chest!) (2) He took a whiz in his driveway. As the ambulance sped away, he clutched his car keys then stepped into the narrow passageway between his car and the neighbor's hedge and hid behind the flaps of his khakis to relieve himself. *"Good morning!"* Rudy heard another neighbor bellow. (Had the dog-walking man not *seen* the ambulance?) Rudy hollered back *"Hello!"* too loudly before finishing and folding himself into his pants, climbing into the car and driving to the hospital.

He shuddered as he recalled the ambulance screaming down their street as he followed behind, stupidly thinking of the things he would bring her in the hospital later. Recounting the hours of that awful morning would always lead him to the same conclusion: He did not save his wife. No perfectly performed Mozart sonata could erase this fact. He could pound out the piano libretto for the Fifth Symphony at the mall until the startled shoppers bought every pashmina in the place. This would not bring back his wife.

Trauma. Survivor's guilt. These words from his family doctor were meant to make Rudy feel better. But he didn't want the names of conditions or a diagnosis for himself. What he wanted was that goddamned doctor to have provided a medical explanation during their appointment for why Bee wasn't feeling well — for him to have sent her straightaway to the hospital, instead of sending her home with a recommendation for Gas-X. In retrospect, Rudy could hear a condescending *we're-all-getting-older!* tone in the doctor's voice that irritated him. He should have taken her straight to the ER. *Gas.* Rudy should have been able to save his wife. Period. He should have been a more proficient husband. A take-charge guy. Hell, he should have been a star conductor at a major symphony in a big city. A dignified shock of white hair would have sailed around his head as he led a choral group and mass of musicians in the orchestra pit, swooping into the glorious last movement of Beethoven's Ninth Symphony. Sweat would have flown from his forehead. *He* should have been the one to die . . . right there! A heart attack. Collapsing with a final slice of the baton, doubling over within the folds of a real, designer tuxedo. The women in the audience would have swooned. His wife would have beamed, not knowing he was already gone. He would have gotten one of those *real* obits in the papers. "He left us doing what he loved to do most," Bethany would quietly have remarked, all dignity and poise.

Bee would have been a content, comfortable widow, set up with all that she needed. Perhaps she'd have dated that widower in their neighborhood, the fellow who walked a golden retriever and complimented Bee profusely on her garden. He would have taken the place of Rudy on nature trails with Rudy and Bee's beautiful granddaughter, Keira, identifying rare flower species left and right. Keira had no interest in the birds Rudy could spot from a distance, but she loved the colorful flowers that her grandmother pointed out to her. Rudy hated that guy now for knowing what ceanothus was, for admiring the blue flowers, which were, in fact, Bethany's favorite, even though they hadn't bloomed until four years after the shrub was planted. He hated that this guy knew the blooms were called dark star. The flower clusters had appeared for the second time just the other day.

Cecilia, who had joined her father at the hospital, and then followed him home, sadly, tearfully, at the end of the day, had cut a branch and put it in a small vase on the kitchen windowsill. "They're not really cut flowers," she explained to her father. "But Mom loved them so."

CeCe's husband, Spencer, was a doctor. He had met them at the hospital that afternoon, awkwardly patting Rudy's back and saying that healthy-looking women, especially those who are slim and fit, were the "under-diagnosed." Bethany wasn't heavy, didn't have high cholesterol or blood pressure, and so she'd been instructed to take gas tablets, walk off the chest pain, and "drink more water."

Spencer hadn't disagreed with these suggestions. As a doctor, he wasn't particularly hands-on, touchy, or warm. Maybe that's what he and CeCe shared — that all-business manner. So serious for young people. Rudy's son-in-law was a neonatologist, a specialist in a perilous field, yet his calm was irksome. It verged on aloofness during this family crisis. Bee had loved her son-in-law, teased him for his scientific nerdiness, worked crossword puzzles with him, tousled his boyish brown hair. If you asked

22

Rudy, Spencer would certainly have to work on his bedside manner.

"Drink more water is *not* medical advice!" Rudy shouted, so irritated it felt as though something in his neck might burst. "That imbecile doctor! I should have sensed something was wrong. Taken her to the ER." He was surprised Spencer didn't chime in to defend his profession.

"Oh, Dad," CeCe insisted later that treacherous afternoon, her worried eyes searching his face, "there's nothing you could have done. You must understand. Nothing. Even if it happened *before* bed." She squeezed his hands in hers. For the first time ever — even though Rudy's thick fingers could span entire octaves of piano keys — he felt that his little girl's hands might be stronger than his. "She was asleep. She died peacefully." CeCe closed her eyes, clearly comforted by this notion. Spencer gave her a light, brotherly hug.

Peacefully, perhaps, Rudy thought. But it should have been when Bethany was ninety.

They were back at the house by then, putting off the funeral home until their nerves were less jangled. Rudy felt that he and CeCe were suddenly all alone in the room, in the world. Tunnel vision made his distracted son-in-law seem far away, a stranger almost. Spencer kept checking his phone, and Rudy was sure it was not because he was checking on the sitter who was watching Keira. His son-in-law rubbed CeCe's shoulders absentmindedly, got Rudy a glass of water. Again with the water! Then he declared there was an emergency at the hospital, and picked up his jacket.

"Seriously, Spencer?" CeCe asked. "Right now? You can't get someone else on call? Are you fucking kidding me?"

Rudy had heard his daughter swear so rarely that he choked on his water as it went down, coughing and spitting into his hand. He agreed: Going in to work? On the day of Bethany's death? While that afternoon was a blur, Rudy remembered this unusual coldness from his daughter's husband.

"CeCe." Spencer looked at his wife pleadingly, squeezed her upper arm.

What was he, the goddamned next-door neighbor? Rudy knew that CeCe felt that being married to a neonatologist meant that everyone else's children were more important than their own. That she often felt abandoned. Yet the two had always seemed so well matched. With their mutual studious, almost-solemn demeanors, they had always seemed devoted to each other. CeCe was certainly well provided for.

"I'll bring back dinner," Spencer declared hopefully, quasi-heroically.

"Right, because we're *starving* right about now," CeCe uttered in a low growl.

She crossed her arms over her chest, clenched her jaw, tears silently streaming down her cheeks. She turned away from her father and husband, wobbled and faced out toward the backyard, clearly not seeing anything she looked at.

If only Bee had been there, to settle this odd lover's spat. As the front door closed behind Spencer, Rudy took his daughter into his arms, kissed the silky top of her head, smelling the clean honeysuckle scent of her shampoo. Not for the first time that day, and not for the last time in the months to come, Rudy wished that his wife had lived rather than leaving him alone in the world without her.

Less than a week after her death, Rudy couldn't imagine ever moving away from their house. The navy-blue flowers still graced the ceanothus bush. Every time golden-retriever guy passed by, he stopped to admire the flowers, shaking his head glumly at them. Had he had a crush on Bethany? Bee, who was as friendly and chatty and beautiful as her garden? You had

25

to admire a woman who didn't mind dirt or aphids or weeds. But who was this neighbor to pine after Rudy's wife?

Rudy found himself in the upstairs bathroom, peeking out at the golden-retriever neighbor as he admired Bee's ceanothus. *Get your own damn flowering shrubs,* he thought, as he scuttled to the side of the open window.

"Get out of here!" Rudy shouted down at the man. He felt mortified, but also enraged and excited. Across the street, another neighbor rolled his garbage and recycling bins to the curb. Trash day, dog walking. Rudy's nerves were raw with resentment for these people who just carried on as though life were normal. He heard no sound from outside, noticing only that the window screen was caked with dust. Bethany always hired landscapers to wash the screens and windows once a year. Rudy didn't even know where their number was or the name of their business. *Nice husband.* He'd let his wife work full-time *and* coordinate much of the maintenance for their beautiful home. For some reason this made Rudy hate the flower-identifying neighbor even more. That guy was probably a *great* husband.

"Get out of here!" Rudy hollered again, not even sure if the man and his dog were still on the lawn. Rudy collapsed to sit cross-legged on the cool bathroom tiles, tears rolling down his face, their salt making his chapped lips sting.

■ ■ ■ ■

11 Months Later

■ ■ ■ ■

2

Rudy wouldn't play the piano at Nordstrom forever. It had been a part-time job to fill in the hours, make a little extra money, lavish his wife with employee-discounted gifts. Once her retirement began, they were to embark on the restful, yet adventure-filled, next chapter of their life. Prague. A rented cabin in Maine, where they'd make love under the weight of those gray woolen army blankets and a hand-stitched quilt.

But now, here he was, widowed for nearly a year, chubbier than he'd ever imagined, bearded — like a Russian czar — wearing a rented tuxedo and playing a department store piano. A part-time job that had somehow become his only place to be in the world. He had taken the easily given grief advice: Put one foot in front of the other. These steps had led him back to Nordstrom a few weeks after Bee's death, his black dress shoes landing on the pedals of the piano, soft pianissimo accompanying his numb dirge forward.

The baby grand was positioned beyond Cosmetics and Jewelry, tucked next to the escalator, on a wedge of carpet that defined Rudy's space as a sort of living room. His proximity to the route upstairs meant that shoppers stopped all day to ask him questions. *Where is Lingerie?* they wanted to know, as though he weren't sitting there playing the piano for crying out loud.

The first floor of the store smelled like perfume and powder, like lilies and roses, like women, like Bethany, who wore a simple, rose-scented perfume that made it impossible for Rudy to part with her clothes after she died.

In his former life, when Bee was alive, he arrived home in time to cook her dinner — his favorite part of the day. He looked forward to supper with his wife, whom he'd tell stories about the department store as he chopped and sautéed. She laughed easily at the events of the day — made them light and bearable. As she listened to his tales, she often teased Rudy gently, lovingly, in a way that helped him better understand people. Rudy lost his translator when he lost his wife. Yet he continued to report to work in a robotic, carrying-on-with-things routine. This was a new chapter, all right. The chapter of hell on earth. The chapter of why not *me* instead of her?

Rudy's piano repertoire was large and varied — everything from Erroll Garner to Broadway show tunes to a jazzy rendition of "Itsy Bitsy Spider" if smaller children hovered nearby. Women swished past him in a constant arc all morning at the department store, swooping up the escalator, often smiling down or offering a little wave. "I love that song!" they would chirp. "Oh, I *wish* I'd kept up with my lessons."

"Most do!" Rudy would reply, trying to sound as cheerful as possible. (*Smile,* Bee had always reminded him. *You have such a lovely smile.*)

The department store was smart to employ a pianist in a tuxedo. The live music promoted shopping. The sadder songs seemed to soothe customers' sorrows — encouraged them to treat themselves to a floral perfume or fresh pair of shoes. The zingier show tunes made one want to spring for a brand-new outfit for a party, with a matching new clutch and a diamond necklace. You only live once! As the shoppers spun around Rudy's corner, moving on up the escalator to Women's Dresses, he broke into show tunes and lively jaunts, *Start spreading the news!* the piano sang out. *Our lives will end soon!* A wedding, a lavish fundraiser, or even a dinner out — *Why not be belle of the ball?*

Now Rudy serenaded two naked female mannequin torsos languishing immediately to his left, by the escalator. They were made of wire and cloth, like seamstresses' dress forms, with tapered waistlines and perky breasts, although they lacked belly buttons or nipples. Long layers of beaded necklaces swept down to their sexless lower halves. The torsos had been part of Rudy's permanent audience for some time now, and although they didn't even have heads, they made him feel shy.

The gleaming glass jewelry and watch cases lay just beyond the poised mannequins, followed by the rows of sparkling cosmetics counters. Whenever Sasha was on shift at the department store — the kind Hungarian woman who worked in Fine Watches — Rudy would play her favorites — dramatic Chopin waltzes that were far too stormy for dancing. Sasha was a fair blonde with pale gray eyes, milky skin, and high cheekbones. As Rudy played, he noticed how her eyelashes fluttered, then rested halfway shut, and how she'd fold her arms and lean dreamily across the glass case. The first time they spoke, she confessed to Rudy that she liked the warmth of the case, that she wished she could lay her head down there and sleep away the ache in her back from standing all day.

The Men's Department was located directly behind Rudy, and whenever he turned around to stretch his neck, he was greeted by another headless mannequin dressed in an Armani suit with a crisp orange tie. This man watched Rudy through his entire shift, posed in a relaxed, yet businesslike manner, the arm of his suit jacket tucked into the pocket of his pants. To Rudy, the mannequin was the most authoritative figure in the store — even more so than any of the floor managers. Despite the mannequin's distinct lack of a head, he seemed to have a brain, a consciousness, and an unnerving amount of self-confidence. Today the mannequin seemed to say, *Call me, Rudy, let's make this thing work.* What thing?

Ah, his life. Since Bethany died, Rudy had been telling himself that everything was only temporary. When Bee was alive, he could mostly laugh off his job. He was just saving up a little extra for their early retirement.

But now what? the Armani mannequin

asked. *What are you going to* do?

About what? he replied. *My life?* While it felt as though he dreaded everything, what Rudy dreaded most upon waking in the morning was the constant church bells of loneliness.

Which brought him to Sasha. The strikingly lovely, yet distant Sasha, who was finer than all the expensive watches in her Fine Watches case. Before Bethany died, Rudy had had a married crush on his coworker. Since Bee left him, it bloomed into an infatuation that made his cheeks flush with shame.

One afternoon, as Rudy cleaned leaves out of the rain gutters, a chaste fantasy of Sasha came to him all at once, quickly and brightly: They lay on his sofa in front of the fire with a cashmere throw around them, glasses of wine in hand. Chopin tinkled on the hi-fi. He was so flustered by this innocent, yet vivid, fantasy of a romantic date that he stuttered the next time Sasha approached him at the piano. His fingers fumbled at the keys as he rambled on about the Hungarian composer Bartók, asking her if she'd like to hear something by her fellow countryman. Sasha smiled a bit slyly. Bartók, it turned out, had gotten her into trouble as a girl, because she spent her

36

practice time trying to learn Elton John instead of going over those stark, dark pieces her dour teacher loved.

Sasha sternly furrowed her brow, wagging a finger at Rudy. "If you don't practice the classics, you'll end up selling watches!" she hissed.

They both laughed. Sasha was funny! And kind. And pretty. Everything about her was sort of wispy — the blond hairs that escaped from her shoulder-length braid, her willowy limbs, her languid fingers. As he began the first few notes of "Tiny Dancer," she sat, almost collapsing, on the very corner of his piano bench.

He was cheating on his beloved wife!

Rudy often played the piano with his eyes closed, concentrating on all the elements of the department store's din — people talking, old men hacking, babies crying, children screaming. The phone in the Jewelry Department's unique *brrrrip brrrrip!* The squish of sneakers, the click of heels. Some heels ticked along at a remarkable pace, as though they were rushing to catch a flight. Above this cacophony was another layer of sound: the PA system. The PA had two loops, music and an announcer — a woman's voice that baffled Rudy. All she ever uttered were people's names. *Jennifer Bailey, Jennifer Bailey. Dawn Simmons, Dawn Simmons.* Her voice was at once generic and sexy — feminine and calm, yet somewhat businesslike. Maybe *Vincent Moreland, Vincent Moreland* meant that someone was stuffing a six-pack of trouser socks under their shirt or a rhinestone clutch in their coat pocket. Or maybe it just signaled that a salesclerk named Vincent Moreland was due to take his break. Perhaps Vincent was to wait until he heard the PA woman beckon, then escape to enjoy his cigarette or coffee. Was the woman in the PA a real woman or a recording? She didn't sound computerized — not like those stitched together automated voices when you called companies. She seemed to have human breath within her. But her voice was so even. Was she in a booth somewhere? Where did the PA woman live?

Now a harried young mother approached Rudy, her eyes darting around and beyond him. He kept his eye on her, fearing she might need assistance. When he realized she was breast-feeding, making a beeline for the welcoming pair of armchairs alongside the wall of the escalator — flanked by a table, lamp, and fern — Rudy felt his face redden. He bent toward the piano keys. Shoppers often paused in his little makeshift living room to gather stamina before conquering more of the mall. They didn't sit so much as collapse into the chairs, the seats whooshing beneath them, relieved sighs emerging from their lips as though pushed up from the leather cushions through their lungs. They mopped their brows, snapped their gum, rearranged their shopping bags, clicked on their cell phones, and chattered. And yes, a startling number of women settled in to breast-feed. Until today, most mothers pretended Rudy wasn't there while he gave equal concentration to not looking at them. The chairs clearly offered the mothers comfort and, Rudy supposed, some bit of privacy. His daughter, Cecilia, had been a member of La Leche League when she'd had her one child. CeCe treated breast-feeding like a 4-H Club project and chided any women who didn't do it right or long enough. He would always nod in ferocious agreement, while worrying that this was an odd natural function to be so militant about. The world never lived up to CeCe's standards, and this had concerned Rudy and Bee since she'd been a child. Not that their daughter wouldn't be fine in the world — she was the most capable person either of them knew — but that she might never be truly happy. In any case, Rudy's standby melody for nursing mothers at the store was "Brahms's Lullaby," and he switched to that now.

The woman's baby replied with a shriek so loud and piercing it was as though a pterodactyl were on the loose. When the mother magically inserted the babe's entire head into a billowing blouse with a complicated origami-like flap, it was silenced. Embarrassed that he'd looked up, Rudy bowed his face so close to the piano keys it probably appeared as though he'd play the next piece with his teeth.

Then the woman was suddenly standing *beside* Rudy, her baby's head like a melon of an additional breast under the blouse. He kept his eyes at her waist's level — dark wash jeans and a faux crocodile belt. A spray of orange freckles on a forearm. She wanted to know the time.

"I don't wear a watch, but here we have a timepiece." Rudy nodded at the small gold clock with Roman numerals beside his sheet music. Ugh. Whenever Rudy was embarrassed, he'd use far too many words to answer a simple question. A nod would have done. *You don't have to be so formal,* he heard Bethany say, giving his arm a loving squeeze. He didn't know why he fell into this odd formality when he became nervous or shy. At parties, he stuck close to Bee, happy in the shadow of her charm and ease.

The baby fussed again, and its poor mother let out a long, withering sigh of exasperation. Rudy switched to Mozart, then made an improvisational U-turn back to Brahms. What *should* one play for a woman who, no matter how discreet, was too exhausted to care about her increasingly exposed breast? The jeans, the freckles, and the belt were not going away. The mother swayed back and forth from foot to foot.

Rudy felt inadequate in the face of this poor woman's despair — in his complete inability to meet anyone's needs other than those of the songbirds in his backyard. He'd bought a "squirrel buster" feeder from a shop by the grocery since Bee died, and filled it twice a week, surprised by the attendance. He'd taken pleasure in identifying the creatures on the laminated card the store sold him. He cross-referenced the more mysterious visitors with the Audubon book. The feeder and the birds were the only new thing he'd done since Bee left him, and certainly the only remotely enjoyable activity. But it hurt that he couldn't show Bee the dark-eyed junco! How beautifully ominous he was, with his black hood and sleek brown body.

"If I don't relax, the baby won't relax," the mother explained, as though Rudy were a girlfriend or nurse.

"I'm sorry," Rudy told the piano keys. "Maybe in the ladies' lounge?" Rudy didn't mean the woman should be banished behind closed doors. Women should breast-feed wherever they wished. He wasn't judging anyone. His stupid shyness could make him such an ass.

"Have you ever been so tired you weren't sure you were going to make it?" the woman asked. "I mean, I guess, through the *day.*"

"I've been that sad," Rudy replied softly.

She nodded down at him, just as Rudy looked up a bit, trying to get past the breast to her eyes, which were filling. "Yes," she agreed.

The baby, rocked by its mother, *was* quiet now, perhaps lulled by the closeness of the piano.

"Never mess with the status quo of a quiet baby!" he whispered quietly but enthusiastically, happy to somehow be helpful. Bee had taught him this golden rule. He'd always had the urge to tickle or pick up CeCe, and later Keira, as they slept or ate peacefully in their high chairs.

"Let's try Debussy." He didn't need his

sheet music. He played pianissimo.

As the woman rocked her little one gently to the music, a cool dribble of sweat trickled down Rudy's back, under the awful tuxedo. Francis, the guy who played afternoons, wore a designer tuxedo that he *owned.* Francis also played at weddings and even as a sub with the symphony. He was a full-time musician, slowly teasing out "Jesu, Joy of Man's Desiring" as brides swished down aisles and mothers wept. Rudy's cheap tuxedo and his too-tight, absurdly shiny black shoes, rentals that he'd bought used, were a comfort to him. Who bought used rental shoes? They'd probably danced with who knows how many bridesmaids. Rudy was comforted by the fact that this clearly demonstrated that this job — that everything in his life at present — was only temporary. Perhaps even Bee's death. But she was gone, a fact worse than the Teflon frying pan feeling of the fabric of the tux, and he didn't even need this job anymore. At least it was a relief from the empty house. When Bee was alive, even when she was at the grocery store or away at a pharmacists' convention, the house had never seemed empty. Sometimes, all you needed was someone else's shoes by the door not to feel alone.

His breast-feeding friend was speaking to him again.

". . . and I'm new to the area and don't even have girlfriends yet or know where the heck I am . . . This right here is better than the dang mommy-and-me group at the hospital, though. They just make me think I'm a terrible mother."

"You're a wonderful mother," Rudy told her, for a moment feeling closer to this young woman than to his own daughter.

The woman shook her head at her shoes. "Hey, I wonder — do you think the café upstairs is baby-friendly?" She leaned in closer to Rudy, so as not to raise her voice.

Then it happened. A round white pad — like a small, conical potholder — shot out of the woman's shirt and onto the floor beside Rudy's left shoe, then under the pedals of the piano. Rudy had a perfect view of the thing as he continued to work the pedals. Why did he keep playing? His left foot could have stomped on the pad as though it were a garden snail. The woman squatted, cradling the now-fussing baby's head. Her diaper bag fell with a tug to her elbow and her unkempt blouse billowed open another notch.

Juniper TITmouse! This thought shot into Rudy's head with Tourette's-like anxiety and

44

vigor. His heart speeded up. Oh, dear. It was his favorite bird, solid gray with a little black eye and a spiky tuft of feathers at its crown quite like a hat a British woman might wear to a wedding.

"I've got it." Rudy was surprised by his own dexterity as he continued the melody with his right hand and with his left, reached down to grab the pad. His once black, salt-and-pepper curly hair brushed the piano keys. Why didn't they sew the things in for crying out loud?

His face warmed from the base of his neck to his scalp. He pressed his lips together over his teeth, causing a bit of pain as he shut himself up from this crazy recollection of that morning's birds at the feeder. He finally gave up on the Debussy, stood, and handed the poor woman the pad. Then he lifted her diaper bag and helped her back to the leather chairs, sitting beside her for a moment as she got organized. He secretly hoped she'd ask him to hold the baby. That was one thing he *could* do, though who would ask a stranger in a dime-store tuxedo?

"The café is fine, everything will be fine," he reassured the young woman. "You'll probably be its most polite customer." He felt guilty for wishing that his daughter were as sweetly vulnerable as this girl. He

45

couldn't remember the last time he'd been helpful to CeCe. She didn't even need him to watch Keira very often, having a teenage neighbor who was more conveniently located.

"Thank you." The woman's hand touched the shoulder of Rudy's suit jacket. The thing was impenetrable. Still, he felt a human touch atop the stiff fabric. "Your playing is *so* lovely." Finally, she had a good handle on the baby and diaper bag. Rudy handed her her shopping bag.

"Shopping, with a baby," the woman said, shaking her head at herself. "I'm a real genius."

"You are doing great," Rudy told her.

Rosemary Smith, the smooth, but robotic PA cooed over their heads. *Rosemary Smith.*

"Who *are* those people calling?" he asked the woman, who artfully balanced baby, stroller strapped with shopping bags, and her diaper sack. "Do you ever wonder? If those are even real names?"

The woman shrugged and laughed. "I know. Is it some kind of code? And is that even a *human* voice?" She was able to laugh the PA lady off, while Rudy couldn't shake her. "Well, thank you again." After sliding her baby back into the stroller, she gave Rudy a little wave.

Rudy bowed his head regally, grateful for the first time for a customer encounter. He might go an entire day barely interacting with another person.

And then mother and child disappeared among rounders of scarves and piles of purses, toward the elevators. Rudy felt a pang of missing them. Suddenly he wanted to tell Sasha, his best store-friend (okay, his *only* store-friend), about his visitors. About the breast pad! Was that too crass? Too intimate? Nah. Sasha had an easy sense of humor with a spark. He stood, smoothed over his jacket and hair, and headed toward Watches.

3

While Sasha's second job was less glamorous, the time certainly passed more quickly cleaning the ladies' locker room at the fancy gymnasium, which stood — like a giant peach stucco cake — at the edge of the town of Los Alnos. While she tidied and cleaned, she listened to the women chat as they changed in and out of their gym clothes. Sasha didn't understand why American women bragged about their lack of sleep as though it were a badge of honor. They had a way of complaining that was sprinkled with an odd pride. For some reason, they wrestled to outdo each other. Especially when it came to their children. The children were such a burden! Apparently few of the women who lived in the town worked. They were stay-at-home moms, although their children seemed to mostly be in after-school programs until 5. (They had bitter conversations about having to pick them up on the hour sharp — they charged you if you didn't! — and cook supper.) To Sasha, kids were a blessing, for she had lost a child of her own. Not a baby, a little girl. Stefania. Stefi: blond braids, orange popsicle–stained lips, forever singing in the back seat. This loss wasn't something Sasha had shared with anyone in America because talking about it made her disintegrate. If that was even the correct English word. She called her girlfriends back in Hungary, but the time change, the expense . . . The truth was she wished she had an American friend to tell about Stefi. She almost told Renee from Chanel at the department store, but it's not like Sasha could break down behind the Swiss Army Watches.

Sasha figured the women complained because they were ashamed of their good fortune. They couldn't say, *Look at us, at the gym, at three in the afternoon! How lucky!* Instead they seemed to feel they had to begrudge their lives — their husbands and children. *Ugh, I've got to get Billy now.* It was five o'clock. What did they think Billy was going to do, take a taxi to an after-school supper club?

They didn't marvel, as Sasha had when she first saw the enormous flower arrangements in the lobby and dressing room, towering with birds of paradise, anthuriums, red ginger, and tuberose — as though the gym were a Hawaiian resort. Sometimes the women lounged after their showers, with their hair and bodies wrapped in fluffy clean white towels — on the high-backed leather-cushioned benches before the big TV. They'd rest and watch cooking shows — aproned people cheerful about aioli- anything they were making: seared ahi tuna served on basmati rice, toasted on the bottom in a fry pan.

"How do they get the fish not to stick?" Sasha asked the semicircle of lounging women, embarrassed by her phraseology. These California foods were mostly new to her — quite unlike Hungarian fare.

"Lots of olive oil!" Two of the ladies laughed. "What do you eat at home?"

"You know, paprika, goulash?" she asked, and they all laughed.

These women undoubtedly went out for dinner many nights, probably only taking tiny bites of their food.

Meanwhile, Sasha had to tamp down her enthusiasm for how luxurious this *gymnasium* was. She treated the locker room with the same nonchalance she would have for a bus station. Still! The endless pile of bright white, sweet-smelling warm towels, fresh from the dryer. The chair masseuse in the hall. The clean smells of lotion and deodorant and hairspray. Women with rosy cheeks from exercise and a hot shower.

Rudolph, the gentleman who played the piano across the way from Sasha at the department store, called the fitness club the Peach Fortress. From the outside, the facility loomed like a giant, peach-colored stucco citadel. Why the architecture in California was so ugly, Sasha didn't understand. There was no lack of money, yet everything looked cobbled together in conflicting styles: Spanish arches, Roman pillars, stucco here, aluminum there. The cars in the parking lot were so fancy that the club continually had trouble with break-ins. Really, Sasha hadn't seen so many expensive cars in one place — like they belonged to the attendees for a ball at a palace. She parked with the other employees in a lot across the street. Finally walking into the locker room was pleasant. She'd grown to like the clean smells of chlorine and baby powder and shampoo, in contrast to the perfumed department store.

Rudy's wife, who had died of a heart attack, used to come to the gym to walk on the treadmill and to swim laps in the pool. He obviously missed his Bethany so much!

He commented that, while his wife was among the sweetest persons he knew, she could be bitingly funny. Sasha liked the idea of humor being something that could bite. It made her smile. Rudy said that the club demonstrated Bethany's ass-to-ring ratio theory about the town of Los Alnos. Rudolph's Bethany said that the smaller the women's bottoms were, the larger their diamond rings, the sleeker their cellular phones, and the bigger their sport vehicles. Sasha laughed, because it was true; they were all quite tiny and fit, with rings that you couldn't help but notice.

Given the fancy cars and giant diamonds and amount of leisure time these well-clad ladies had, Sasha assumed they'd never give her the time of day. So she was surprised to find that most of the women were actually quite nice; looking at her nametag and calling her by name — meeting her gaze to say hello. *Hi, Sasha, and how are you?* They looked her in the eye — Americans did this; they were outgoing and friendly. Most of the gym attendees picked up their towels and carried them to the hampers, and a few even wiped the counters with a paper towel when they were done fixing their hair and doing their makeup, and they often thanked Sasha. She wore her employee uniform of black slacks of any type other than denim, any type of white shirt with a collar, and her nametag.

When Stefania had been alive, Sasha would make her dinner as soon as she got home from work. Gabor, on disability, clearly wasn't too disabled to get the meal started for her, yet he never did. He could have put on the big pot of water for red potatoes. His injuries were relatively minor. They'd both taken a terrible fall together, yet Sasha continued to work despite having broken two vertebrae, while Gabor put off having a recommended hip replacement. Sasha suspected that drinking and inactivity contributed to his ailments. Still, in a way, Sasha was glad she did not have to nurse Gabor. She felt guilty about this, but it was true. She couldn't imagine working two jobs, caring for Stefi, taking care of the house and meals, and having a post-surgery husband.

Gabor was one of those people who took others down with him. He was not only impossible to help but also had a way of enmeshing you in his problems and making them yours, too. Always perceiving himself as a victim — the world ganging up on him in a conspiratorial way. Perhaps this para-noia was fueled by alcohol, but he really believed this in his skewed worldview. Even to the point of blaming those trying to help him. Gabor could ruin everything from a nice moment to an entire party, all the while convinced he'd been wronged in some way.

In fact, he had been the one to injure Sasha — to literally take her down with him. They'd been walking home from a neighbor's Christmas party back in Hungary, their young Stefi at home with a babysitter. Gabor had had way too much vodka *and* glug to drink. You were supposed to have one or the other. As they teetered, he clung to Sasha's arm, even though he was twice her weight. They slid dangerously along the icy sidewalks. "Please," Sasha pleaded. "Slide your feet, don't *lift* them." She tried to steer them, slipping along with care. She pushed her shoulder into Gabor, as though he were a heavy wind that could tip her over. He lifted his right arm to begin a rant, a continued conversation from the party, a conversation of which Sasha hadn't even been a part. His thick-gloved hand shot into the air.

"Oh, people think —" His disdain was cut off curtly by their fall. As his gloved hand scooped and clawed frantically at the air, he lost his bearings. Sasha realized in retrospect that she should have let go of him. But his grip was strong. And he made the verboten mistake on ice — he lifted his foot and then they were both cartwheeling backward, his heel high in the air as though he'd just kicked a football. All of this was in slow motion, Sasha trying again to uncurl her arm from his grip, and then they were down, on their backs, neither of them using hands to break the fall because by then Gabor had their hands entwined in a mess, and Sasha's left hand was burrowed in her pocket for warmth. She felt and heard the sudden, sharp crack that was like a long icicle snapping in half inside her. A pain shot through her abdomen. She turned her head in time to vomit into the snow, the surge of adrenaline and pain passing through her throat, burning her esophagus on the way, all their lovely Christmas dinner coming up and up and up.

Gabor, his coat thick, his drunken body loose enough to somehow rubberize in the fall, began to laugh. He had smacked the back of his head, but only after his coat and hat and hood absorbed most of the fall, so it was a light smack. (A goose egg revealed itself later, along with the hip injury.) For the moment, he just sat there, removing his woolen cap, rubbing the back of his hair vigorously, and laughing, laughing, and trying to pull Sasha up, not realizing that something inside her was very broken.

"Too much of the spirits, eh?" he asked. (She'd only had two small cups of punch.)

"I'm hurt," she sobbed, her entire body wracked with pain, the pain of the broken vertebrae — later in the hospital the X-ray showed that they were broken — but also from the awkward twist she'd quickly made so as not to throw up on herself, which seemed like the only thing that could make the situation any worse.

"Oh, now," Gabor said tenderly, realizing that she was, indeed, hurt. "Let's get you inside and put your feet by the fire."

"I can't move," Sasha said in a whisper so serious that Gabor sobered up a notch. He took off his coat and laid it over Sasha, and rushed into their house to call the ambulance as Stefi wailed in the background.

In his retelling of the tale, they'd both drunk too much, were laughing and singing, and fell together on their way home. Gabor, the sturdier one, was fine, but Sasha, his dear, delicate Sasha, broke her back. In his mind, he had truly rescued her, quickly covering her with his coat and running inside to call the ambulance, patiently waiting by her bedside as the X-rays were developed, confirming the breaks. Sasha

56

shuddered whenever she recalled lying under her husband's coat, for the first time appreciating the cold — how the sidewalk numbed the pain a bit — wishing she *had* drunk more. Before the ambulance arrived, Sasha knew that she must, somehow, at some time, get a divorce if at all possible. For her husband would forever be doing this, taking her down with him. Down, down, down, until she was buried under the frozen earth.

Just last week, Sasha received a phone call from Gabor (drunk, at 8 a.m.!) to report that he and his young, pregnant girlfriend had moved out of their house. "Their" meaning Sasha and Gabor's tiny place two houses in from the highway, the one they'd finally bought after renting for ten years in California. In the divorce agreement Gabor had yet to sign, Gabor was to buy Sasha out, but she said she'd wait until he could, figuring it was good to at least hold on to the property. Property! A house! But then Gabor had gotten laid off from yet another job and could no longer make the mortgage payments. He had asked Sasha if she would move in and take over the payments so he and his girlfriend, about whom Sasha was surprisingly complacent, could find a cheap rental. Sasha agreed.

But when she'd gotten back to their house, Sasha found the power was out, the property taxes were due, and the mortgage was two months in arrears. The bank that had cheerily refinanced the home just three years prior, even encouraging Sasha to take a bigger line of equity than she wanted, was no longer the lender. The new bank was about as sympathetic as the Mafia. Sasha had taken an entire day off from both jobs to make progressively humiliating phone calls, but wound up making no progress, except for smoking again for the first time in twelve years, after which she was sick. The sick made her cry, and the crying made her want to lie down, and the lying down made her hate herself. Why had she left Gabor in the house in the first place? Why didn't she stay and take care of the only home she'd ever owned?

Now, as she refilled the little cotton ball and Q-tip canisters in the club locker room, she worried about the long list of paperwork required by the mortgage remodification company. This company was legitimate, her friend Freda, a nurse at the dermatologist's she once visited, assured her. Still, Sasha was overwhelmed by the fact that the first thing she had to do was write the officer at the remod company a check, and a cover letter she was certain would show her limited English abilities. Then there was the pile of paperwork to collect. She had begun the search and assembly and it was overwhelming.

She sat at the counter for one of the makeup and hair dryer stations. As she wiped a counter that was sticky with hairspray, she paused to examine herself in the giant mirror. If she had one marked characteristic, it was her pale blue-gray eyes. Yet she'd never liked them. She'd always wished they were a more glamorous blue. Blue topaz. Her blond hair was well below her shoulders now. Upon close examination, the ends were brittle and the roots could use color. Darker roots made her feel cheap. She found her skin to be too thin, sometimes showing bluish veins in her forehead. She wished her eyes weren't the blue of something faded; something that once was, or could be, better. Gabor's new young wife had those bright topaz-blue eyes. Sasha's were more like stones underwater, made larger by her glasses, which she hated, too.

She remembered when Rudy first came by her station at Nordstrom. "We both wear glasses," he'd remarked. "But I like yours better." Today, he'd come by to tell her a story about a woman who had been breast-feeding by the piano. "And then her renegade nursing pad shot clear across the floor!" he'd exclaimed, blushing furiously. Sasha had never been close friends with a man before, but Rudy was such a gentleman, unlike any other men she knew. His story was funny, and they had laughed, but not unkindly, at this poor woman, who was as overwhelmed as they were. Sasha knew that Rudy had probably shown this woman a kindness that mattered, and made her feel better. Just as he made Sasha feel good about herself, even optimistic about life, for the first time in she didn't know how long.

One day he offered to help Sasha find new health insurance! He had offered up this idea as he saw her in the break room eating a box of plain Cheerios with her tea because she said her stomach was on fire. He asked why she didn't go to the doctor.

"Co-pay too much with my insurance," Sasha had explained, sitting up straighter so that perhaps it would appear that her stomach did not burn with pain. Both her stomach and her back. The two of them screaming to outdo each other. She had spread out the company's open-enrollment insurance papers on a table in the break room, unsure what to choose.

"Please, may I help you look over the options?" Rudy asked. "I'll stop by Watches later." His face reddened a bit, and he bustled out of the break room, sloshing a bit of coffee on his way.

"He wants to take care of you," Renee from the Chanel counter teased. " 'Stop by Watches.' "

They both giggled.

Later, Rudy visited her counter and surprised Sasha by politely apologizing, while making eye contact with the Swiss Army Watches. He insisted he didn't want to intrude, but did want to help.

"Oh, but I could use the help." Sasha lowered her head to meet Rudy's kind gaze.

They agreed to have coffee.

As Sasha put out new Kleenex boxes and fresh clean towels at the gym, she felt a little thrill at being single — that Rudy and she would have coffee and he might be able to help her with the bureaucratic paperwork she'd been consumed by lately.

When Gabor left Sasha for a younger woman, Sasha was surprised by the fact that she felt relief. There were times when she could not face all the personalities Gabor transformed into with alcohol. She lived with the four people that she supposed many who live with a poorly functioning alcoholic knew well. After the first two drinks there was the chatty, garrulous, sometimes amorous drunk. Bristly kisses smelling of cigarettes and vodka. It was beyond her how vodka could be so odorless in the bottle yet reek on a man's breath. Then the third and fourth drink brought the argumentative drunk. The circular arguments never worth having. Once, over how long to microwave a hot dog! Even when she didn't reply, Gabor managed to keep the argument alive himself, directing angry proclamations at her. It was an oppressive combativeness because it was directed at whatever she was doing. Cleaning the kitchen: *Why that way? Why?* She would retreat to different parts of their small house, to read, to pretend to be able to concentrate on a book. He would declare "Eh, sulking!" and then turn on the television and ask her what she would watch with him, and she would say she didn't care or would name something. Either way there was a combative answer. Then there was the passed out Gabor. You'd think it would be a relief, but he was always fully clothed, facedown, head tipped to one side, glasses on but askew, shoes on, hanging off the end of the bed, large and heavy and immovable so that Sasha could barely peel back the covers to get into bed herself, as he was usually stretched diagonally across the center. She would put on her pajamas and curl back what covers she could, then roll up earplugs and stuff them in her ears, because Gabor's drunken snoring kept her awake. (The doctor diagnosed his snoring as apnea, worsened by drinking.) The next morning's light always exposed the fourth personality: the cranky, hungover alcoholic. The crankiness was certainly worsened by the apnea, which the doctor explained interrupts the sleep pattern as many as sixty or seventy times a night. Combined with the booze, it made Gabor succumb to gurgling choking bursts of louder snorting snores every few minutes that frightened and woke Sasha even through the earplugs.

It was the quiet time at the gym, after the morning rush, and before the early afternoon ladies-who-lunch-then-StairMaster crowd. Sasha hugged the warm, sweet-smelling towels as she helped the laundress fold and shelve them.

Sometimes Sasha used to rise in the night and shuffle to her daughter's room to slide under the Aladdin quilt, spoon Stefi's small, flannel-clad body, and sink into a few hours' sleep that were clean and delicious. Sometimes during their mother/daughter morning ritual of dressing and breakfast before their walk to the bus, Gabor would bark from the bedroom, "What kind of woman doesn't even sleep with her own husband?"

It was so ridiculous — his complete lack of self-awareness, especially when marked by an octave-lower hangover gravel — that Sasha just laughed. That made him angrier, giving way to shouting, then coughing, like a huffing, puffing monster in one of Stefi's stories.

"Daddy! Don't be mad!" Stefi would holler out from the breakfast bar. This would soften Gabor. His daughter always did. If he made it down to join them for breakfast, he'd cut Stefi's toast into toast fingers and accent them with Cheerios eyes and mouths and raisin noses.

The apnea, smoking, coughing, made him spit up things into paper napkins, which he threw at the trash, missing. One morning he coughed so suddenly toast crumbs shot out of his mouth and onto the table. Stefi stopped chewing.

"Attractive," Sasha commented, immediately wishing she hadn't. She did everything she could to quell arguments in front of their daughter.

That is when Gabor shoved her. It was

not a hit. It was a shove. She was by the kitchen door, getting up to clear the dishes. He leapt up and elbowed her into the doorway while closing the door on her at the same time, muttering, "I don't want to see your *face.*" Sasha's hands weren't free, so she couldn't push back. Yet a free finger was extended from one of the mugs she carried and it caught in the doorjamb, making her yelp like an animal. Stefi had seen it all.

On the way to the bus stop, Sasha explained to Stefi that Daddy didn't want to hurt Mommy, he was just sad, and angry, because he couldn't find a job in America right now. Sometimes men, and boys — like mean boys at school — are sad, but they don't express sadness well, so they end up mad. Stefi nodded her blond head above her Pooh knapsack, taking this all in. In her head, Sasha heard *I don't want to see your face.* Perhaps this was what had perfected her self-loathing during her marriage. Age crinkling her fair skin into patchy dry spots, circles under her eyes from the chronic interrupted sleep and long work hours — Gabor's need to drink made Sasha believe there was something fundamental about her that wasn't lovable.

And then Stefi had drowned. That terrible afternoon — the screen door slapping

65

behind Stefi as she ran outside, her little feet in red sneakers, a yellow seersucker sundress pulled over her bathing suit. So excited to go swimming with her American friend and her mum. The mother appearing to be perfectly competent. Sasha not even worrying. It wasn't like her not to worry! But then Stefi was gone. Sasha's whole life. Gone in an afternoon.

4

As Rudy played the *Moonlight* Sonata, he considered the prospect of getting another part-time job. Was this putting one foot in front of the other? He could work as a butcher at the upscale grocery by his house. During high school and college, he'd worked at his father's butcher shop. He'd certainly feel more necessary at this second job. Chops, ribs, filets. People needed to eat! There were an array of vegetarian and vegan meat-substitute mixes these days, though the only vegetarian burgers Rudy had had were like cardboard coasters. He imagined laying out the loin chops pink and fresh, and preparing the meatloaf mix, veal, ground beef. He'd find a way to create a moist, flavorful veggie burger. Punching in during the afternoon rush, he'd work until the dinner hour came and went. Instead of cooking and eating dinner alone, he'd help others gather their dinners. Returning home with items from the deli to eat in front of the TV, Rudy would be too exhausted to be lonesome. Would exhaustion replace or exacerbate loneli— Suddenly someone *sat down* beside Rudy on his piano bench.

Startled, Rudy jumped and turned his head without removing his hands from the piano keys.

"That's okay, keep playing," a man in a charcoal-gray suit and purple tie said softly but firmly. He had the same confidence and authority of the headless mannequin, and Rudy felt compelled to follow his directions. Worried he might have played the sonata at least twice, he transitioned into "Für Elise."

"I'm Detective Jensen," the man declared.

Rudy tried to think of all the bad things he'd done recently. He had put celery in the garbage disposal. The threads of the celery caught in a knot and clogged the thing up. Last weekend he had glided through a stop sign while listening to an aria that made the hairs on his arms tickle. An awful sick feeling struck him when he saw a child on a bike teeter out of a driveway just beyond the intersection. He had written off the rental of his cheap tuxedo on his taxes, unsure whether this was allowable.

"I need to speak with you about your wife," the detective said in a low voice.

"She's passed on." Rudy hated these euphemisms, but they seemed polite. She died, god damn it, for no reason at all!

"Yes, sir, I understand, and I would like to discuss with you the nature of her death."

That's it. Rudy killed his wife. With his ineptitude. This man was the minister of feeble husbands.

"We have reason to believe she was murdered."

"What?"

Rudy lifted his hands from the piano, ditched Beethoven, and slammed the piano lid down over the keys. He turned to face the man, who had slick black hair, pointy features, and oily skin — like one of the bad guys out of the Nancy Drew stories he used to read CeCe before bed.

Murdered? No. First of all, why would this man tell Rudy this at work of all places? Why not make an appointment? Rudy remembered uneasily that there were several messages on his answering machine at home. The light had been blinking for days, the number of messages stacking up to seven, eight, nine. Rudy hadn't listened to them, because he'd assumed it was the Sandals resort returning the merlot-driven call he'd made one night to possibly book a vacation. That night, after finishing the

69

merlot, he'd dipped into a bottle of Bailey's Irish Cream — awful sticky, sweet stuff that coated his teeth with a moss he couldn't get rid of the next day — he'd phoned the resort to cancel, but instead got a catalog selling lawn ornaments. Now he feared both were calling.

"I need to see some kind of identification," Rudy insisted. "A badge and a business card, if you please."

"Certainly." The man rose, pulling a badge from inside his coat pocket and moving toward the armchairs by the piano. He flashed the badge at Rudy and dipped into his pants pocket for a business card from his wallet. He sunk into one of the leather armchairs and motioned to the other.

"Please, have a seat."

Rudy complied.

"A coworker of your wife's at the hospital pharmacy has been charged with two murders, and he has also confessed to murdering your wife with a lethal dose of chloral hydrate."

"But. Why? No." Rudy could only form one-word sentences. What motive could anyone possibly have for hurting Bethany?

"Motive," he said to the detective. A vexed murmur, rather than a question.

"This is what we need to investigate," the

70

detective said. His eyes were so dark they didn't seem to have pupils, yet Rudy thought he saw a glimmer of empathy there. "Sadly, there's often no motive in these types of serial cases."

Rudy squeezed two of his fingers with the fist of his other hand, until his knuckles hurt. So he wouldn't . . . He wasn't sure what. Punch a mannequin. Whoever this confessor was, he would murder him right back, with his bare hands. Rudy had chopped heads off chickens and severed and quartered the entire side of a cow. He could probably wring a man's neck, and he would.

"I need to make an appointment with you to come down to the station," the detective added, laying a hand on the shiny sleeve of Rudy's coat jacket. It was a surprisingly intimate gesture. "Please give me a call." The detective nodded at his business card, which Rudy plucked from his lap and inserted into his wallet. Then the man stood and quickly vanished through the Men's Department — his suit a gray, sartorial miasma.

What on earth? Was this some sort of practical joke? Rudy did not return to the piano.

A new perfume was being sampled today, and it smelled — after so many sprays into the nearby aisle — sickeningly sweet, like a too-old Hawaiian lei and burned butter cookies. Rudy gagged a little, his throat dry. He wanted to escape the bright bustle of the store, get out of this damned tuxedo. Meet Sasha for an early-afternoon drink and tell her about this ridiculous nonsense. Oh, this topped a flying breast-feeding pad! He would *not* tell CeCe. He would not bother his daughter with such upsetting and potentially false (probably false!) news. For the love of God, would he have to go through the five stages of grief again? Denial, HYSTERIA, *anger.*

The department store woman's oblivious voice started to coo over the PA.

"Rupert Simms, Rupert Simms." Oh, for the love of God, Rupert Simms was probably at the Canadian border by now.

"Rupert Si—"

Rudy pounded his fists on the arms of the leather chair, stood, and bellowed at the ceiling: "SHUT. UP. SHUT UP SHUT UP SHUT UP!"

5

Bethany would have told anyone that she wasn't nearly as fault-free as her sweet husband imagined her to be. Case in point: Once upon a time — when CeCe was little — Bee stole a casserole from their neighbor's stoop. At first she'd taken it, *rescued* it, and later she stole it. Scooped it up off the young couple's porch next door when she'd dropped by with a get-well card for the husband, Gray, who'd been admitted to the hospital for an appendectomy, then gotten saddled with blood poisoning. Bethany also brought Violet and Gray an arrangement of roses and hydrangea from her garden. She knew how everything in life could change with just a doctor's appointment or an emergency room visit.

The couple was new to the neighborhood, and Bethany had only spoken to them in passing as they brought in their newspapers or garbage cans.

"I think we need a new roof," Gray worried after they'd moved in, shading his eyes to peer at the wooden shingles above.

"Aw, as soon as you buy a house you go from elated to certain the whole place is going to cave in. Not time to worry yet," she reassured him. When they shook hands, Gray's was pleasantly warm and dry. He had the tousled brown hair of an overworked programmer, red-rimmed blue eyes. She wanted to dab away the little bit of shaving cream at the edge of his jaw with her thumb. Gray, Violet. Their names were colors.

Hormones. Bethany blamed hormones for the swiped casserole. It was back when she was pregnant with a second baby and then had a sudden, second-trimester miscarriage. For the first time in her life she felt insane. The next thing she knew she was a turkey tetrazzini thief.

She set the flowers on the porch in a corner of shade — *pink roses for a girl, blue hydrangea for a boy — Bethany was to have had a boy. They told her this after a pathology report. Boy boy boy wagon Lego boy. Stop!* She chided herself. Obsessive thinking. This time off from work was allowing her too much rumination. Which was why she made the arrangement for the neighbors in the first place. Working at a hospital got you

74

into the habit of at least *trying* to do things for others.

She'd ferried the casserole back to their house for safekeeping and refrigeration. You could *not* leave perishables out in the California sun! The Pyrex dish was still warm, providing relief against Bethany's tender, still-cramping abdomen. A get-well note from a woman named Cindy was tucked into the towel wrapped around the dish. *Don't leave food on a porch, Cindy.* Even if the couple was home, and a dog didn't ravish the food, it might cool to a ptomaine temperature by supper. Wouldn't that be great? Lovely Violet sick with worry for her husband, doubled over with food poisoning. As Bee closed the door to her house, grateful to be inside — the miscarriage had made her not want to see anyone — she realized she'd never made or perhaps even eaten a casserole in her life. She must have *tasted* one. Didn't they involve cream of mushroom soup? (*Bent cans: botulism. Violet, with her tiny hands and feet and spray of freckles across her nose, curled in a ball on the kitchen linoleum, unable to reach her phone.*)

Bethany removed the casserole from the basket and wrapped it in an extra layer of tin foil to keep it fresh, then stowed it in the

75

refrigerator. As soon as she saw Violet's car in the drive, she'd carry it back over.

She rearranged the two extra stems of hydrangea she'd put in a vase on the kitchen windowsill above the sink. Her favorite flower, this batch wasn't as blue as she'd have liked. She hadn't had time to add acid to the soil. The soil wasn't acidic enough in Silicon Valley. Too many millionaires, not enough bitterness. These blooms were in between blue and pink — a flecked, light purple. *Boy, girl, in between — she'd love a gay child! Bring him back. Stop. It.* She washed her hands.

After sorting the day's mail, she returned to the refrigerator, wondering what to have for dinner. Rudy was away at a weekend off-site for his tech company. ("Flip charts, flip charts, flip charts," Rudy had texted. "How much Kool-Aid can you fit into a flip chart?" "Good one," Bethany had texted back. She could always rely on Rudy to make her giggle.) CeCe was away at a Girl Scout sleepaway; collecting the long list of "MUST HAVE!" items had delighted her. Sometimes Bethany thought her daughter might be more conscientious and diligent than the grade school teachers.

"It's super-simple and old-fashioned," Cindy's feminine script said on the little card tucked in a linen napkin inside the casserole basket. "A taste of the Midwest. Hope you don't mind potato sticks!"

Bethany did not mind potato sticks.

When she opened the refrigerator door again and peered in, she knew she was going to eat the casserole, just the way you know you're going to cheat on a diet or start smoking again. As she took down a plate from the cupboard, she wasn't sure whether she would bake a replacement dish or bury the Pyrex and Red Riding Hood basket in the backyard, but she had her supper mapped out, and she was hungry.

Thank you, Cindy; there also was a little slip of paper tucked into the Saran with instructions for heating: "15 minutes in the mic or 30 at 400 degrees in the oven." Bethany didn't even know this thoughtful friend of Violet's. Why was she irritated by her little notes? She felt completely out of character. The way a photo is out of focus, or a radio only partially tuned in. Sad, crabby thoughts seeped into her brain like static from another station. Focus: "400 degrees" . . . she chose the oven.

The oven door warmed her hips as she leaned against it. An intoxicating savory smell filled the house. The smell said dinner, home, family. It was a smell that called for a place mat, cloth napkin, fork, and knife. Salt and pepper, the newspaper dry and chalky from the driveway, unfurled across the table. As she laid out these items, she knew how lucky she was to have a husband who both cooked for her and with whom it was always nice to share meals. Friends of hers complained of husbands who leapt up from the table even if they were the only ones finished eating, or of meals spent looking at the back of cell phones or laptops. No such behavior from her Rudy. *The crying again, dammit.*

Oh, the casserole was good. A glorious crunchy buttery crust of potato sticks and crushed cornflakes. Steam billowed out as Bethany dug into it with a serving spoon. ("Totally Midwestern!" Cindy's cursive winked on the instruction card.) The grief said, *go ahead, take another dollop.* She poured herself a glass of wine (no longer pregnant, she could have coffee, wine, crack, sniff glue . . .) sat down, and tucked in. The turkey and noodles were just the right combination of bland and flavorful. There were peas, which somehow weren't mushy. She detected thyme. Not dried, but fresh chopped. When she decided to heat up and eat her neighbors' casserole, she did not know how much she was going to *enjoy* it.

As she took a sip of wine, Bethany re-engineered a replacement supper in her head, deciding that she could easily find a turkey tetrazzini recipe. She'd ask Rudy for advice. Wait, would she tell Rudy? She told her husband everything. But since the miscarriage, dark thoughts had moved in like foreboding storm fronts she didn't want him to worry about. As she considered this, she heard the neighbor boys explode into the backyard. After supper was "no screen time," their mother had explained. Twins, the boys wore sweet, lopsided, mischievous grins, and were always a bit dirty around the knees and elbows. Bethany loved their grubby imperfection. But they were polite! Little boys. She'd wanted one. That was a selfish, perilous wish — to hope for a certain sex of baby. Bad luck! Since when did she believe in luck?

Bethany forced her mind back to the creation of a replacement casserole, and a story for what had happened to Cindy's dinner. It was a warm day, and she had picked up the basket, but then dropped it. She didn't realize until she lifted the dish out of the pie basket at home that it was cracked. Not just cracked, broken! Three jagged shards of Pyrex. So she'd poked a spoon in to see how badly the casserole had been affected, and decided she'd better toss it and make a replacement. "Please, tell Cindy I am SO sorry. I owe her a Pyrex casserole dish!" Not the truth: *I stole and devoured your comfort food! I made off with your comfort.* Fibbing. Nice. She'd been a thief, and now she was beefing up on being a shameless liar.

Bethany imagined eating broken Pyrex glass. A cut across her tongue, bright red blood staining the noodles. Those sanitary pads from hospital recovery that were unlike anything in thickness you'd ever get from the store. Like walking with a roll of paper towels in your pants. *Enough,* she sternly chided herself. *Rudy!* God, how she wished she were eating dinner with her husband. Since the day she was married, she'd looked forward to it every day: eating supper with her husband.

Even in college, that man could cook. It hadn't mattered if they were poor, or comfortable in later years — he always came up with something filling and delicious for his family.

Bee's favorites were his dishes mixing savory meats (or spiced tofu when CeCe was vegetarian) with sweet figs or apricots. But the best part of dinner was sitting down at the kitchen or dining room table — even at the picnic table outside under the birch trees — Rudy transformed every place into a dining haven. Even CeCe would relax into the meal, the stress of her day deflating.

"Who has a funny story?" Rudy would ask. He liked to start dinner on a light note. When teenage CeCe found this irritating, Rudy added the criteria of beautiful — any beautiful thing one of them had seen that day. Sure enough, this little game defused the more serious topics they discussed next. Perhaps Bee had cheated during this second step. She never told Rudy or CeCe how sometimes her heart fluttered arrhythmically, like a bird that had crashed into a window and needed time and a few fluttery flaps to get back up and into the sky.

6

The day after Detective Jensen visited Rudy at the store, jolly show tunes were impossible to muster on the piano. He played Sasha's more melancholy Chopin, and Beethoven sonatas. *Murder.* An inscrutable act. Rudy's stomach dropped and his legs weakened, so that it was hard to operate the piano pedals on the baby grand.

And the suspect, the confessor, was a coworker at the hospital? A place where his wife was so clearly beloved? Whenever Rudy went inside to pick Bee up after work, it took them forever just to get out of the place. Winding their way through the halls, every *single* nurse, doctor — anyone with a hospital badge — greeted her so merrily it was obvious that her easy, kind, lighthearted presence brightened that stressful and often sad place.

Rudy was not biased by the fact she was his wife. Well, he was in that he adored her.

But since the day he'd met Bethany in the grocery store parking lot by their college (okay, they'd officially met in class, but she didn't remember him, didn't remember a single thing about him, even though he'd complimented her on her photographs *and* her critique of other students' work; she only remembered the moment when Rudy offered to carry her groceries in the Kroger parking lot, so they counted this as their first-time meeting), from the moment Rudy met her, very early in the school year, Bee already had so many friends. She was funny, smart, sociable. Yet she was not a Goody Two-shoes. She had faults. Sure she did. She was very orderly and neat about some things, but messy about others. Her school-work, art classes, and later her pharmacist studies and everything about the way she did her job: tidy, tidy, tidy. Oh, but her dorm room that freshman year: a snarl of sweaters and notebooks and drawing pads and charcoal boxes and loafers and slippers that made Rudy's head hurt. At home, he and CeCe were always finding a book or cooling cup of coffee of Bee's that she'd absent-mindedly set down and forgotten. But Rudy counted himself lucky, because his wife wasn't a slob — she made their house gorgeous — and she never got after him about chores or fix-it projects. She was never a nag.

"Ronald Waters, Ronald Waters . . ." The PA lady, the unnerving calm of her cashmere voice. *"Ronald Wa—"*

Rudy shut her out of his consciousness. He realized he had played the same frenetic Haydn sonata twice now, picking up the pace as he thought of some lunatic poisoning his wife — of the unholy piece of information this Detective Jensen had delivered.

He breathed slowly through his nose to calm himself. They would get to the bottom of this. He and this Detective Jensen and whoever else was assigned to the case. He turned his mind to the piano, an instrument that had always taken him out of a dampened mood or troubled time. But not now. He looked up, looked for Sasha, but she'd slid away from the watch counter.

Rudy burrowed into the music, into his mind, away from the store, away from his scratchy stiff jacket and pants, the women at the counters cooing about foundation and herding the line of customers there for a promotional offer into a proper queue. Everyone wanted one of the little brightly flowered bags with some sort of treasures within. It was only after Bethany's death that he discovered she, too, bought those gift kits, yet she never used the little black mascaras. "Because of her contacts," CeCe had explained matter-of-factly. "Plus, she was a crier. You know. Couple layers of this gunk and you've got raccoon eyes." CeCe had tossed the tubes in the trash. She moved to throw away other things from her mother's bathroom drawers, but Rudy had stopped her. This was only weeks after Bee's death. After CeCe left, Rudy had picked through the trash, retrieving the unused tubes and organizing them in the drawer on Bee's side of their double sinks.

It was true, Rudy thought now, starting, then stopping himself from playing "Take Five." He was in no mood for happy music. He wanted to play Mozart's requiem. Bee's eyes filled with tears easily, even at advertisements, but she would always wipe her cheeks quickly and smile, laughing at herself. She never wallowed. It was poignancy that got to her. He admired his wife for finding beauty and poignancy in so many things — small things. Sometimes this made Rudy feel a bit dim-witted, but ultimately he felt gratitude for her attention to detail.

CeCe called the evening that they'd picked their way through the bathroom items, to announce that she and Spencer would go

85

through her mother's things for Rudy — which she understood was too much for him. They didn't know he planned to never give up anything of Bethany's. That he'd agree to their coming over, then cancel that day, feigning illness. People seemed to think that after the first anniversary of his wife's death it would be easier for Rudy. But now he couldn't even bear to turn the pages of the calendar — all those birthdays and holidays and anniversaries looming. Did anyone honestly think he was going to get through them? The day after Bethany died he had looked at the kitchen calendar, saw her upcoming dentist appointment noted in her clear, cursive handwriting, ripped the calendar from the wall, and stuffed it in the trash. He was self-pitying and childish and his daughter was the adult now. Well, she'd been the adult since kindergarten, frankly.

Suddenly, Rudy realized he wasn't even playing the piano at the store anymore. He was just sitting on the piano bench, with his trembling hands in his lap. *I'm on break,* he told himself. *In my mind.* No one noticed or cared. In the middle of a Lancôme gift gala, he was invisible. Completely alone. Lonely. He couldn't recall ever being lonely while Bethany was alive. Yet he had taken his wife for granted at times. Certainly he had. Early on in their marriage, before he really knew how to be a better half. During the few times Bethany grew cross, she would point out Rudy's minimalist conversational skills by carrying out entire conversations on her own. *Good morning!* Bethany would exclaim sarcastically. *How are you? Fine,* she'd answer, before Rudy could utter a word. *How did you sleep? Fine thanks, and you?*

You didn't even give me a chance to answer! Rudy would contest, looking up from his paper. He loved the presence of his wife. Sometimes she insinuated that he loved her presence more than he loved her. Which was not the case in the least!

"I hate it when you're not home," he'd confessed when she called from her annual pharmacists' convention. "I can't sleep without you."

"What? Rudy, that's ridiculous. When I'm there, it's like I'm an appliance."

That had been so far from the truth! He'd loved her more than anything, but his love hadn't been demonstrative enough. Once, early in their marriage, she'd cut out a cartoon from *The New Yorker* that hurt him deeply. Without showing it to him, she stuck it to the refrigerator with a magnet for a migraine medication. It pictured a woman in her coat, her purse on her arm, standing by the front door, ready to go out. Speaking to her husband, who sat in a chair reading the newspaper. The caption read, "I'm in the mood for love. I'll see you in a few hours." It was the only vaguely mean-spirited thing he could recall his wife doing. When she got home he said, "You know, Bee, this is funny and it isn't, because I feel like I'm a good husband. And if I'm not, all you need to do is tell me." Bee apologized. But Rudy took the episode to heart. From that day on, he became more demonstrative. (In his heart, in his mind, he already was!) Suddenly he understood how arranged marriages could work. Part of marriage was learning to fall in love. That afternoon he had pulled the cartoon off the fridge and taken it to the florist and bought Bee a dozen double-delight roses with a lavish bow, and at the bottom of the bow he'd attached the cartoon and written *sorry* as the new caption, and *I love you.* And they'd talked all through dinner. In the years to come, they had spells of finishing each other's sentences, and became equally comfortable sitting together quietly without talking, feet entwined in the center of the sofa.

Now, as a widower, Rudy turned up his opera louder and louder in the evenings, and drank more and more red wine. With a simple supper of frozen French onion soup or tri-tip from the deli. No vegetables, the volume knob his friend. Then he'd have a nightcap of cognac or something from one of the many untouched aperitifs on their bar until sleep finally blanketed him.

Today he was hungover from the previous night's cabernet, still stunned by Jensen's revelation. He continued playing the piano, but with little bravado, irritated by the shoppers as they committed their usual transgressions: tossing gum wrappers, spilling coffee on the floor.

Yes, madam, Yes, sir . . . Rudy heard the clerk's voices coo as he closed his eyes and transitioned into "As Time Goes By."

When he opened his eyes, he looked up and over to the Jewelry Department on the other side of the shoe-sale circus and caught a glance at Sasha back at her station behind the glass case of glittering watches. She seemed entertained by the cosmetics frenzy. She waved to Rudy and smiled, then gave a thumbs-up, which he took to indicate that she liked his playing.

Lunch. Was lunch with a coworker a date? Not really, he decided. They all had to eat, and the shopping mall was filled with choices of quick food for the hurried shoppers and harried workers. Maybe she'd have lunch with him today. The adrenaline of the Detective Jensen business made asking Sasha to lunch easy. He simply finished the piece he'd been playing and strode over to the watch cases to ask her. Soup, a salad, something quick. A rest for their feet. He'd love to hear about her home country.

"Yes!" Sasha said when Rudy asked her.

For a moment he was silenced by her enthusiasm. "Great," he replied. "Noon?"

"Noon." She nodded. One firm nod and a smile that revealed her straight teeth, except for the one slightly overlapping front tooth that Rudy found so endearing. On one side of her face her one cheek had a deep dimple. The other cheek's dimple was much diminished, a small scar crossing her laugh line up onto her cheek where the dimple probably used to be deeper. So many mysteries about this lovely woman. Sasha crossed her arms over her sweater set and leaned toward the warm watch case.

"And Chopin and Beethoven and Elton John, I'd like to hear how you came to like them."

"Ah, remember, I have forty minutes only."

The forty minutes went by like four. Rudy

learned that Sasha was just now trying to get a divorce, but her husband, an alcoholic, was AWOL, making it impossible to move forward. Meanwhile, his former unemployment and credit card abuse wasn't helping her any.

Rudy told Sasha briefly about Detective Jensen, brushing the conversation off as a minor procedural step, not mentioning the word *murder*. He didn't want to talk about what he hadn't even be able to process.

"Do you have children?" Rudy asked Sasha, pushing aside his plastic sandwich basket.

Sasha looked from the table to the floor. "We had a daughter . . ." She trailed off, then looked up at him, her eyes glassy with tears. She'd stopped eating her baked potato stuffed with broccoli and cheese. "Stefi." She blotted her cheeks with her used napkin, not noticing a bit of paper that latched onto one cheek. Rudy fought the urge to brush it away for her. "We lost her."

"I'm so sorry," Rudy said. "She died?" He was almost whispering now.

She nodded, unable to speak.

Rudy did not pry. He reached over and dabbed away the fluff, squeezed her hand. Then he squeezed his own hands together in his lap. Had he been too forward? It was a Bethany or a CeCe motion. When you lived with women most of your life, you weren't going to let a friend go back to work with something on her face.

"Sorry. De-schmutzifying you without asking."

Sasha sniffled, smiled. "And you lost your lovely wife."

"Bethany." Rudy was glad the food court was too loud, boisterous, and crowded for anyone to notice a guy in a tuxedo and a pretty Nordstrom employee fighting back tears over their fast-food lunches.

As they finished their sodas they chatted quickly about music, and the store. They had plenty to talk about without getting into the details of an AWOL husband, potentially murdered wife, and lost child. Yet that invisible thread of grief connected them now. Rudy felt as though it had been there all along — stretching from the piano to the Rolexes — a connection that had perhaps initiated their friendship in the first place.

"I'll tell you more about Stefi another time," Sasha told Rudy. "Next time."

There was going to be a next time. Rudy reached across the table to stack her items on her tray and clear them both. "I understand."

As they walked back to work, Sasha asked

about Bethany — impressed by her job, smiling at the guff Rudy said his wife had often given him, saying she was sorry for such a loss after the number of years they'd been married. The lunch, to Rudy's delight, was, above all, *easy*. The thing that surprised him most about Sasha — given how hard her life had been — was how quick she was to laugh. She giggled at his silly jokes, poked gentle fun at him, and laughed at herself. This made her seem younger than she probably was. Not silly. But lighthearted. Lovely. Kind. Fun. Everything that Rudy's wife had been. And yet a world apart.

They returned to their stations and Rudy launched into Sasha's favorite Chopin waltz. Rudy realized — with a twinge of guilt for his betrayal of Bethany — that the only thing he wanted to do was cook dinner for Sasha that night. For a moment he fretted about the foolishness of this fantasy, about his assumption that she, too, always ate dinner at home alone. Maybe she had a slew of girlfriends who buffered her from loneliness. Rudy hoped so. He certainly didn't want his own loneliness to seep out of him like the store's bad aftershave and suffocate her.

7

Perhaps the thing Bethany had liked least about her job was managing young employees. She hated to be bossy, yet there is no room for error at a pharmacy. The new young pharmacist assigned to work for her was precise and fast for someone who'd just moved up from being a pharmacy tech. Unfortunately, he had the personality of a mollusk. An angry mollusk. His customer service skills were somewhere between lacking and belligerent, and she found herself trying to keep him from ringing up patients and customers at the front window. His name was Waylan.

"Your name's nice. Like the singer?" she asked on his first day.

"Ugh. Blech. Different spelling. Still sucks!" He capped a bottle, bagged it, and put it in the "waiting" tray. While some medications, such as loratadine and lorazepam, were easy to confuse — both a small white tablet to boot — Bethany could tell already that she wouldn't have to worry about Waylan's pharmaceutical skills. But she needed to gently but firmly work on his service attitude. The hospital, though not in the business of making big bucks, was a business nonetheless, and it wanted patients and family members to feel comfortable using the on-site pharmacy. Convenience. *Compassionate* advice.

"Not your favorite musician, I'm guessing?" Her neck was stiff from a long shift. She tilted back her head, taking in the pockmarked acoustical tile above.

"My parents wanted to give me a *cowboy* name." Waylan threw the next order into the bin with too much force, and it overshot the basket, plummeting over the high counter to the floor below.

Bethany was glad she had to bend down out of sight to retrieve the bag because she had to stifle a burst of laughter. This kid was the least cowboy-looking character you could imagine. Instead, a classic nerd. Too thin, with wrist bones bearing little knobs that protruded under his pale skin, thick glasses, wiry red hair that didn't seem to want to conform to any style. She skipped up the three steps that led behind the pharmacist's station, behind which were the rows of shelves with bottles. Handing Waylan the bag from the floor, she asked him to recheck the order to make sure neither the cap nor any of the tablets had broken.

"I'm sorry," he said, without a note of his trademark sarcasm.

"Don't worry about it," she told him. How was she going to improve this kid's demeanor? Anger. She'd encourage him to be less angry, at least in this setting. Not in her job description — she was a pharmacist, not a therapist! But he seemed competent in every other way, so she wasn't going to report him to HR the day she inherited the kid.

"Classmates not like your name?" she gently prodded.

Waylan shook his head, concentrating on his blue-gloved hands, counting out capsules of Keflex.

Managing employees was a bit like parenting. Except that she'd had an unusually confident child, who practically self-parented. How had her daughter developed such a thick skin? While CeCe was serious about everything, she wasn't an angry person. Having such a confident daughter hadn't prepared Bethany for this socially awkward young man. Waylan, nearing thirty Bethany guessed, was her first surly teen.

"My friends, okay *friend,* called me Way."
Waylan turned the plural friends to singular
friend with alarming venom. "So the stupid
sports kids always said, 'No way . . .
Waaaaay,' to each other, back and forth.
Whatever that was supposed to mean. Their
IQs were lower than their dirty gym socks."

Bethany laughed at this last part; she
noticed a smile pull at the corner of Waylan's mouth.

"You know what that's from, right?"

"I could give a shit." Smile gone. Forget
the progress she'd thought they'd made.

She turned to him. "Look at me."

He lifted his gaze from his work to her
eyebrows. Close enough.

"No matter *what,* no swearing. Not my
rule, hospital rules. Not even hospital. Flat-
out OSHA."

Bethany had a headache. She'd not been
feeling her best lately. Everything about the
pharmacy was too-bright white, which had
never bothered her before. The buzzing
lights overhead, the linoleum counters, the
floors — glistening with their mirages of
floor wax. She rubbed her temples.

"Anyway, it's from an old *SNL* skit."

Waylan nodded with disinterest, his orders
filled, leaning back on the counter.

"Saturday Night Live."

97

Waylan rolled his eyes. "Yeah, we *have* a TV at our house," he mumbled.

Bethany stopped filing the filled orders alphabetically, turned, and just raised an eyebrow at him.

"I'm sorry." He looked at his white sneakers.

"Thank you. Well, you are too young to remember the skit 'Wayne's World,' which became a very funny movie. My point is that the two main characters, Wayne and Garth, were the dumbest dudes on the planet." Bethany winced at herself for using the word *dudes.* This was not helping.

But now she had his full attention.

"Okay," she tried to maintain a light tone . . . "my point being that the joke was on those kids, because they were inhabiting two pathologically dumb characters with IQs lower than their dirty gym socks, as someone I once know said. And the point is that they were the dumb kids, and you do know who gets teased in school, right?"

Waylan's sideways look and shoulder scrunch to his ear said *yes.*

"The smart kids. The smartest kids."

Again, the corners of his mouth pulling upward into the littlest bit of a smile. Almost. Maybe by next week this would be a bona fide look of friendliness, or at least not disdain, and Waylan could wait on a few more customers.

If she'd had her daughter's confidence, she probably would have been able to bang this kid into shape his first day. She would somehow have managed to enforce what she considered to be unenforceable — congeniality.

Patients and their families who used the hospital pharmacy, she explained to Waylan, as they set to work filling more orders, were not very likely having a good day. Whether it be chemo, a broken leg set in the ER, or a hospital discharge with pages of instructions, they needed a bit of kindness and compassion. She hoped this didn't sound critical of *him*. Angry people made her overthink everything, when you got right down to it. How grateful she was to be married to a man with equanimity. "Also," she explained to Waylan, "patient family members, while showing no visible signs of injury or illness, might just be the ones hurting most."

"Like on the inside," Waylan said, nodding to himself. Then he turned to Bethany, met her gaze, and nodded more emphatically. For the first time he seemed thoughtful, instead of just smart. There was a big difference, after all. And his full attention on her during this explanation of the importance of customer compassion was a big step forward.

Or so she thought. The next day, Waylan was more courteous to the customers, to be sure, even if he couldn't yet look them in the eye. He was more courteous to Bethany. Yet when she complimented him on his improving skills, or said anything to him for that matter, his face flushed brighter than her red Sharpie pen. Instead of sulking and skulking, he stammered and stuttered. Waylan's new habit of blushing when Bethany spoke to him made her worry that instead of fostering his outgoingness and customer congeniality she'd managed to encourage a crush. She seemed to be the only person he didn't hate. Was that possible? That a twenty-six-year-old would be interested in a woman thirty years his senior? She made a mental note to share this dilemma with her best hospital friend, Bernadette from PT, when they met for lunch at their usual bench in the garden behind the medical library. Their short lunch breaks allowed them just enough time to sun, take in the flowers, and gab. An excellent manager, Bern would know what to do with this Waylan.

It occurred to Bethany now that pharmacy

school should have included some management skills for her and her peers to draw upon. But all the math and science and pharmacology included nothing along those lines. Customers' well-being — even their lives — were at stake. You had to put their minds at ease. Remind them not to take sedatives with antihistamines and drive. Loratadine and lorazepam were not to be confused. Hone a knack for giving flu shots gently. But what if you inherited from HR a surly cashier and tech to work your counter? A somewhat peculiar and seemingly angry young man?

8

Every morning Sasha opened the newspaper half-hoping to find her husband's obituary. She should have known that Gabor couldn't be responsible for a new family and a mortgage. So apparently he'd chosen to disappear, ignoring her calls and refusing to sign the divorce paperwork. Or! Maybe Gabor had perished, and the girlfriend had gone home to Hungary with their baby.

Between the mortgage and Gabor's illegitimate family, Sasha felt an increasing urgency to become legally unlinked from this man, who sparked nothing but trouble. Again, always taking Sasha crashing down with him. Maybe that's why she didn't feel a twinge of jealousy for this new girlfriend. She felt bad for her. This woman's life would *not* be easy.

Sasha was surprised by a welling in her chest for the coming baby, however — a boy, she imagined, perhaps with Stefi's eyes.

A wistfulness to hold him. Maybe she'd buy him an outfit with her store discount.

Sasha could not help but contrast Gabor with Rudy, who was still grief-stricken so many months after his wife's death. He'd shown Sasha a photograph of Bethany at their last wedding anniversary party, her mouth wide open with laughter, a twinkle in her eye. She was pretty, their life clearly happy. Rudy was married to a dead woman, and Sasha had a dead daughter and was married to a deadbeat husband. There was a sort of kinship in that — in both living with ghosts. It was a deep, unspoken thing to have in common. An experience that both defied description and didn't need to be described to understand. Sasha also liked Rudy because he was kind and funny. She always looked forward to seeing him at work now. A store friendship that had grown into a romantic giddiness. But would it be difficult dating a widower who still loved his late wife so?

As Sasha pored over both the San Francisco and San Jose newspaper obituaries, she wished she were a widow. It became easy to nurse a non-gory movie version of Gabor's painless death.

Perhaps she should report him missing. But she didn't want to find him; she wanted to erase him from her life. Stefi was gone, she was losing their home, and she wanted a real divorce. She wasn't crazy about the idea of calling the police, though. In Hungary you didn't call the police so often. She was between the generation who had no trust for the government, police, authorities, and the generation that celebrated democracy. Freedom. Except for the lack of jobs. There was no freedom in being poor.

Two years ago, a neighbor had called the police to their house during an argument when Gabor, drunk, had thrown hot oil at the wall — not at her, but close enough. She'd screamed so loudly she frightened even herself. The shame of that memory made Sasha's skin heat up and tingle. Tears stung the corners of her eyes. She blinked quickly and covered her face with a kerchief from her pocket, pretending to need it for her nose and then her forehead. However, the policeman had been respectful and kind. Adhering to an apparent protocol. His very presence put Gabor in check immediately. Then the officer spoke to Sasha in private, asking her personal questions that oddly did *not* shame her — questions she wished her family back home had asked, questions that telegraphed concern for her safety. She surprised herself as she answered candidly, explaining that Gabor was an (unfaithful) alcoholic prone to flying into rages. It had gotten worse since Stefi had died three years earlier, and he'd recently lost yet another job due to his drinking. The bitterness was back, as unpredictable and unruly as a bad storm. The officer suggested she come down to the station, file a report, and get counseling. See if maybe she needed to obtain a restraining order.

"I want a divorce," she told the officer, buttoning the top button of her cardigan and crossing her arms over her chest. She had recently gotten an outstanding employee review and a small raise at the gymnasium. Her boss at Nordstrom had complimented her on her knowledge of the Swiss Army Watches.

"You can serve him with papers," the policeman offered. "You may not even need a lawyer. Call the county clerk's office." There was empathy in his tone now. "It's in the very front of the white pages." She thanked the officer, and started the divorce in motion. But, in a moment of weakness, the anniversary of Stefi's death, she had given Gabor time to get his life in order before insisting he sign the papers. Then he was gone.

When last she'd spoken to Gabor, he said

he and the then-pregnant girlfriend, Oksana, were moving to San Francisco. (She was so young! So excited by Gabor's promises of city living!) Yet Gabor did not answer his cell phone these days, despite Sasha's increasingly desperate messages. Now she probably really needed a lawyer. The last thing she could afford. She would ask Rudy. She knew this much: Rudy was a true friend.

As she turned from the obituaries to the police report (bar brawl? public disturbance?), a burning in her stomach worked its way up into the back of her throat. She added more milk and sugar to her tea, hoping it would help.

"How do you stay so thin?" the women at the fitness club always asked Sasha with envy. The members ranged in age from their thirties to their late forties, fifties, and even sixties. It seemed that those approaching menopause asked this most often. Sasha didn't have visible paunches or droops. Yet she felt them coming on, gravity and stress from working two jobs tugging at her youth.

The girls in their twenties came to the gym after school or work, with earplugs already in, and got ready so quickly they didn't speak to anyone. The women in their thirties were exhilarated by being away from their children. The middle-aged group, now troubled by teens and cellulite — well, Sasha felt warmth toward them.

"You work too hard," they'd comment, smiling admiringly at Sasha as she moved briskly from one makeup and blow-dry station to the next, wiping, sanitizing, emptying trash baskets, clearing wet towels.

"I'm all the time working." Sasha shrugged and laughed, not wanting to seem unfriendly, hating her English, her accent. "Two jobs," Sasha would add, trying not to sound self-pitying. She was grateful for both jobs; at least at this one there were always people around and she was always moving, so it never got boring. Not like the glass case of watches that mocked how slowly the afternoons ticked by.

"She works at Nordstrom, too," a woman named Marcie told her friend, who wore thong underwear that Sasha tried not to notice. (Still, Sasha was curious about the mechanics of this underwear. After all, she might be properly dating soon. Surely this meant upgrading from her graying married drawers.)

"Oh, I worked there in high school," the woman said conspiratorially. "How 'bout that discount, hunh?"

Sasha smiled. But there was no shopping

for her, except for Stefi's clothes, and a few gifts the one time she and Stefi went back home. The money left over after her living expenses was sent to her parents. Before moving to America, she had been in accounting at a china-packaging company. She could barely live off her salary, let alone help her parents. There was democracy now, freedom. But without a degree, with her uneven English, opportunity did not come too easily. That would take a few generations, it seemed. Certainly there was no thong underwear yet!

Working two jobs wore her out, but it distracted Sasha into thinking she was fine, until she was home alone. At night she sometimes fell into crying jags that filled her with shame the next morning. Her mother had survived many hardships. Yet she was a stalwart woman who rarely cried. Sasha had been like that, too. In America, where she expected to gain strength, she did feel happier in many ways — she had a job, a paycheck, and a nice enough place to live. She had been better able to provide for Stefi. But then Stefi died. Ever since, Sasha had spent all her free time at home, where she could abandon customer service and perfecting her English and curl up like a sow bug in Stefi's bed, pulling the Aladdin quilt over her head.

For Sasha the loneliness was worst in the evenings, which meant it was worst in the winter, when the nights were relentlessly long. But this was California! Compared to Hungary, the summer lasted twice as long. In October and November there were bright warm sunny days, the roses still in bloom. Still, this malaise. She missed her baby. The desire to envelop her girl in her arms. Press her cheek against that impossibly soft corn silk hair, breathe in the sweet baby shampoo smell. Stefi had been built more like her father, like an ox or elk. Sturdy and strong. A ten-pound baby, who became a solid toddler, then a lean little girl, but with the muscular legs of a ballerina. Stefi had white hair like Sasha's had been when she was a baby. It turned golden-white on her arms and legs during the summer. Stefi's only less-than-sturdy characteristic was her poor eyesight. It broke Sasha's heart to send her off to school in thick, cumbersome glasses, reminding each teacher not to let her daughter hide the specs in her schoolbag. Still, Stefi never stumbled clumsily or tripped on carpet edges. And despite her thick glasses and foreign accent she made friends. Friends! "Practically everyone in Silicon Valley is from somewhere else,"

Stefi's second grade teacher explained. "We're all outsiders, whether foreigners or nerds. Your daughter is as bright as a new penny!"

The elementary school teachers were so young, kind, optimistic. Stefi enjoyed two years of doing well in school. At this point, Gabor was still a functioning drunk, at least until after her homework was done. Friends, and playdates. "Playdates" were uniquely American. It was strange to Sasha that these words described the way in which her daughter had died. It had been a terrible accident. Certainly not the other mother's fault. Sasha had made sure the mother knew how she believed this, hoped it might make carrying the burden of a playmate's death a little bit lighter. Whose fault was it? No one's fault. Everyone report to the Department of No One's Fault. The Offices of Grief will open shortly.

The pain of missing Stefi was dulled a bit during the working day. Soothed by listening to Rudy play the piano. His music made Sasha feel suspended in time, as though at a party, or floating in a dream, as though everything might be all right. The warmth of the glass jewelry case against her hips, the tiny electrical shocks it gave off, the din of the department store's ambient noise —

it was all a salve to Sasha. She had a place to be — work — and a time to be there and people who had specific questions, who needed her to unlock the display case, set out the velveteen tray, and spread a watch glimmering in the lights from above. She knew the pros and cons of every watch. The women in Cosmetics were outgoing and playful. Judy, from MAC, always hooked her arm into Sasha's and led her through the handbags to the Men's Department to feign interest in neckties while giggling and flirting with the well-coiffed guys. All the guys' teeth were so white, their shirts so spotless and wrinkle-free, manicured hands, perfect hair. Sasha appreciated their friendliness, but felt a little intimidated by their starched personalities. But Rudy seemed — if not from her country — from her planet.

Recently, the department store had begun to make Sasha feel more optimistic. The piano singing sweetly, the watch case buzzing, spotlights from above making sequined evening dresses sparkle, the whir and click of the endless stream of shopping register tape. This most American place she'd been in America filled her with the hope that she could do this: She could divorce her husband and start over. Not that she knew exactly every step of the way, nor what

111

would follow a divorce. She was afraid to long for happiness. How could she achieve happiness without Stefi? But *peace.* What she yearned for was peace.

That afternoon at work in the gym, Sasha closed her eyes and breathed in the smells of chlorine and melon body wash in the club locker room, repeating the word *peace,* feeling her lips move. Back when she was first married, Sasha had found solace — security and comfort — just in knowing she wasn't alone. Solace in knowing that she was loved by her husband. (Before he became an unpredictable drunk.) That he was there for her. Solace in knowing that he'd come home at night. Knowing that he'd wonder and worry if she wasn't there. That it would occur to him if she was gone for too long or didn't show up for work that something might be wrong. Knowing that he'd come looking for her. When she was first married, it felt necessary to know that she was loved, desired, and needed. But things got simpler as she aged — just knowing someone would worry that she might be in a ditch if they hadn't heard from her was a relief. Just seeing Gabor's boots and Stefi's tiny sneakers by the door brought comfort. This is what people who didn't live alone probably didn't realize: the solace of another person's shoes by the door. Just that.

The simple implications of this presence of others hit Sasha on her first night on her own. She took a taxi to a hotel, to flee from Gabor's drunken rage, but she wanted to call someone to let them know she'd arrived safely and to say good night. She wanted to call *Gabor* — how stupid! This was still what she disliked most about being single.

But as Gabor had turned to drink, his love turned to possessiveness. He wanted her home every night cooking supper. At first she liked this feeling of being needed, even if it was in a more menial than sensual way. Her husband wanted her home, with dinner on the table, the red potatoes peeled in stripes. Never peeled all the way or left with all of the skin. But pared and peeled just so, with the eyes nicked out and the nice skin left on. Sasha hadn't minded these demands, because it was *her* cooking Gabor craved. Gabor was convinced he couldn't do the potatoes himself, that not even his mother had made them so well. That gave her a sense of pride that she would define as a sort of security, albeit simple. Then Gabor's possessiveness morphed into a sort of bossy ownership. At first this possessive behavior seemed like love, Sasha realized, but then she came to her senses, realizing it was unhealthy.

Even though she wanted nothing but to be freed from this alcoholic, the anxiety of his drinking had been replaced with the anxiety of being alone in the world. And then came the physical pain; after their fall on the ice, her back had never been the same. One morning she was simply making her bed, snapping the Ikea comforter up and out like a sail, and the next thing she couldn't move. She walked like a hunch-backed old man, and the MRI revealed bulging disks and a stenosis. The doctor recommended an epidural, which he did admit would be painful, but when she saw the length of the needle and felt the initial sear of pain, she fainted so quickly she didn't experience any other sensation. The shot helped for a long while, until it didn't and the pain came back. It was like a neighbor upstairs playing music, at first not too bad, then the bass thumping relentlessly in her back: *pain, pain, pain.* The pain pills dulled the discomfort, made it seem far-away, in another building . . . several streets over . . . and sometimes it even took it away. Heat, ice, heat, ice, and then the pills: at first one, and then two, with a strong cup of tea and a piece of toast with cinnamon and sugar — the way her mother had made it when she was a girl. The pain dulled, then lifted, and then went away, and with it the worry went, too.

Suddenly she was filled with a sense of security she hadn't known since she and Gabor were newlyweds and he'd pick her up in his arms and rub his thick bristly vegetable-brush mustache against her stomach and carry her to bed and lay her across the comforter and cover her with a blanket and run her a bath. Or was that her mother? It seemed she wanted someone to help her, to take care of her just a little bit. But things weren't as bad as she thought, the pain pills said, as she munched her toast and sipped her tea. *She had a job! She had health insurance!* People knew where she was and what she was doing when she was at work. If she didn't report to work, how long would it be before they came to look for her? She might be out cold under the kitchen table having fallen, her hair in her buttery toast. Honestly, though, she was a young, perfectly fit woman and she had girlfriends. She had a telephone, and in this country they had 911 and 411 and dial zero for operator. And even the Ask-a-Nurse line at her doctor's office. The pain pills say this was enough.

One night at three in the morning — that awful doldrums stretch when it was too late to be up and too early to get up — she had called the nurse to ask her if she could take the extra half tablet, and that's when the nurse suggested warm milk and a plain ibuprofen, talking to her in a kind, soothing voice. The woman had taken down enough of Sasha's information to suggest that she did know where Sasha was and what she was doing — drinking milk! — and not in a ditch. Not taking extra pain pills anymore. Sasha would have liked to call this Ask-a-Nurse every night to say good night.

For that's what she wanted more than a fancy date with a steak dinner. Those little bits of dialogue: *Good morning, good night, I'm going out, I'll be back at four, Hello, I'm home!* Gabor had stopped saying these things for the most part. Stopped telling Sasha that he loved her. He had taken to grunting more than speaking. Of course, now the memory of him caring about his pared, striped potatoes and the recollection of his begging her not to divorce him were a comfort that made no sense.

And now, Sasha suspected that Rudy was beginning to care for her more than just as a work friend. That he would truly be worried if she didn't show up for work and hadn't called in sick. His increasing attentiveness, their chats, made it seem as though he would know in a matter of hours if she were stranded somewhere. He would get to the bottom of things and find her!

Perhaps Rudy would be pleased to learn that Sasha needed so little. *Hello, I'm home! I'm going out for a bit! Good morning, good night.* A hug. A kiss. That's all, really. No diamonds or cars or furs. Maybe a little lovemaking and a big pot of soup on Sundays, with bread baked and rolled in cornmeal with big slabs of real butter. Yet it seemed to her that most men didn't understand this. They made a woman wanting to be with them seem like such a death sentence. They didn't realize there were many women, such as Sasha, who wanted her partner's shoes by the door as much as anything. It was the implicitness of another — that solace in knowing you weren't alone.

Her mother used to say that Sasha had attachment issues. (Her father was the softy.) This from one of her mum's hokey self-help books. No, Sasha thought. If you craved air, food, water, and a blanket, did that mean that you had attachment issues? Because, for Sasha, these longings were as fundamental as oxygen.

She thought back to her mother's words:

"You have a deep need to feel loved," she said, as though this were a medical diagnosis. *To be loved,* Sasha thought. A simple need, really. Shoes by the door. A thing missing in her life that was simple when you got right down to it, yet frustratingly unattainable, especially if you didn't want to go on x Internet coffee dates in y weeks. Sasha seemed alone in thinking this was a ridiculous algebraic approach to romance.

9

Since their food-court lunch, Rudy had not been able to stop thinking about Sasha. It had been a nice date, right? A date! It had felt easy, simple, and yet it filled Rudy with anticipation. He kept having half visions of their future dates. Real restaurants with white tablecloths, the reflections of tea candles in wineglasses. But then Rudy made the mistake of telling CeCe about Sasha, his enthusiasm clearly unnerving his daughter. She declared that it was too soon and sudden for Rudy to start seeing one woman exclusively. Since when was CeCe an expert on dating? In a flash, CeCe was at his laptop at the breakfast bar, building him a profile on Match.com.

"This is great. This means you can start braving *more* coffee dates," his daughter gushed. Rudy couldn't imagine from where she'd gleaned this knowledge of Internet dating sites. Her divorced girlfriends?

"Getting to know Sasha *has not* been sudden," Rudy protested. He pulled a stool up to the breakfast bar, nervously peering over his daughter's hunched shoulders as her fingers flew and clacked over the computer keys, as though she were booking an international flight and seat assignments. "It happened over the course of many months and started as a true friendship —"

"Well, one person, without meeting anyone else . . . I don't know. My friend Sandra told me you really should meet a number of people."

"Why don't I just go on *The Dating Game?*"

"What's that?"

"Exactly."

While entering this world was Rudy's worst nightmare, caving in to his daughter's frenzied idea, letting her continue to tap away, was easier than arguing, and perhaps even letting her down. He was a crap widower. He sighed so heavily, CeCe stopped typing to ask if he needed a few aspirin.

"There's no medicine for dread," Rudy replied, hoping he wasn't exuding self-pity.

"Don't worry. We'll get this set up, and if you don't like it, we'll change it later." CeCe patted his leg.

"What are your passions?"

Sasha, he thought. "Opera," he answered.

CeCe scrunched up her freckled nose. "A little nerdy?"

"Plebe."

She frowned at the computer. "What about hiking?"

Rudy couldn't help notice how his daughter looked like her mother — the heart shape that her face formed with its small, rounded chin, with a tiny dimple.

"Bird-watching!" CeCe exclaimed, as if that were any less nerdy than opera.

"I have a club for that." Rudy imagined the satisfying feeling of ticking off the species on his Audubon card as he crackled through the dry brush — pine siskins and Tweety Bird yellow warblers. "And I hardly want to advertise being a bird-nerd!" Not that anyone would read this, Rudy knew. He would take it down as soon as CeCe left the house.

"Okay, *opera,*" CeCe conceded.

It was "opera" that led Rudy to his first Internet date after all. Before he had a chance to take down the profile, replies flooded in and he found himself, at his daughter's insistence, off to meet a strange woman at a hotel bar near the airport.

121

(Weird choice. Warning sign?) He lamented that he was too embarrassed to tell Sasha about this first-in-his-lifetime event. Certainly they'd have a laugh about it. Even though they'd only had one lunch — a daytime excursion! — Rudy felt like he was betraying Sasha. But he hadn't even told her about the profile.

When he arrived at the bar, Rudy waited a full twelve minutes, then became convinced, with joy, that he'd been stood up. It was the great childhood feeling of a snow day from school or perhaps a prize won on a game show.

This woman, Barbara, was an opera buff three years Rudy's senior, according to her profile (he certainly didn't mind that — but it had creeped him out how young some of these bald old men expected their dates to be). Rudy hadn't exactly been dreading the rendezvous, because their online discussion of opera had made Barbara sound like a potentially good show companion, at least. He had tired of attending the performances alone. Dressing up, driving to the city, eating a little something, taking his seat. And worst of all: watching some couple's bored college son whom Rudy despised for taking Bethany's seat. He was also a bit mortified by going alone. At first he even wore his wedding ring. But perhaps Barbara would change all that. Even if they didn't hit it off romantically, they might become opera partners? He'd rather take Sasha.

Another five minutes. He ordered a club soda, and tasted the metallic soda tap in the bubbles as he looked around the room. Potted palms, brass railings, too-thin flowered carpet, the faint odor of pine cleaner. Another few minutes waiting and Rudy could ditch this joint. He glanced around the bar. The only other person occupying a stool was a woman in her mid to late seventies, with hair that was stacked like bluish-pink cotton candy atop her head.

She had her back to him, laughing and waving a hand at something the bartender had said. She wore a brightly colored suit — with a loud pattern of hot pink, lighter pink, and lime-green flowers — white stockings, and hot pink shoes. The color combination was like that of a petit four.

Suddenly, she turned to face Rudy. "Rudolph?" she said in a tremulous but teasing voice.

Be cheerful, Rudy thought. He had no idea what was going on here, but there was no need for the irritation he felt. He smiled wearily.

Barbara didn't look dressed so much as

upholstered. Something about the fabric of her suit — it *was* a suit as far as he could tell — made her seem like a sofa that should have matching Laura Ashley draperies with a valance. *Well,* he heard Bethany's voice chide him, *who is it that knows the words* Laura Ashley *and* valance? *Hmm?*

"Hullo." Rudy gave the little bow of his head that he gave passersby at the piano at work, then politely shook her delicate onion-skin hand. He took a seat beside her and abandoned his club soda for a gin and tonic with two limes. Maybe the summery drink would do something about his perspiring. And the limes might clear out the pine cleaner and mildew in his nostrils.

"How nice to meet you." Barbara's voice was soft-spoken and playful, but a bit gravelly. An ozone-crippling quantity of hairspray caused her hair and head to move in unison. Rudy had the urge to share this detail with Sasha. Barbara's eyes were somewhat hard to find, nestled as they were between what seemed to be a lot of wrinkles for fifty-seven. A life full of laughter and smiles — Rudy tried to find the bright side. He was terrible at guessing ages, and he hated to be ageist, but upon a close-up look, Barbara had to be over seventy.

"Any trouble finding the place?" she trilled.

"None at all." Rudy tried to brighten his demeanor as he gazed around the hotel bar. He had honored whatever choice a woman would make — probably based on safety and comfort level. Perhaps she lived in the city and this was equidistant. The place certainly was dark and dank compared to Barbara's garden-party getup. Her suit was adorned with big faux pearl buttons circled with gold. She wore a matching double string of pearls, as well as a lime-green scarf that covered her neck right up to her chin. Rudy wondered if her head, so stiff as she turned from side to side, might be sewed on. *Mean!* Bethany chided. *We women hate our necks after forty. After thirty-five!* Everything but Barbara's hands and face were covered, despite the warm temperature outside.

Barbara giggled. "Say, my friends call me Babs. I was named after Ms. Streisand."

Rudy thought Babs was awfully close in age to Ms. Streisand to be named after her. In fact, Babs looked quite a bit younger, at least on-screen. No matter. Barbara was a stocky woman. Not heavy, but solid. Rudy felt shallow for being disappointed in her ankles, nobby and thick, her feet disappearing into low pumps that were surprisingly . . . geriatric. She was festive, Rudy had to give her that. Almost like a float in a parade. Her nails were painted the same hot pink as her shoes.

"You know," she said, placing a bumpy, age-speckled hand over Rudy's on the bar, "you sly dog — you look remarkably young for a man your age. Wanting to date a seventy-seven-year-old woman! I assume it's our shared love for the opera!"

Rudy choked on a bit of the pulp from his lime. It slid sideways down the wrong pipe, burning his throat, sending him into a coughing fit. "Opera!" he agreed, his eyes watering. "Opera!" He nodded his head ferociously, not wanting to hurt Barbara's feelings with the confession that he'd had *no* idea that she was more than twenty years his senior. Something between him and CeCe and the dating site had gone terribly wrong. *Calm down,* he heard Bethany say. *Live in the moment.*

What the hell, they had three drinks each, nibbling at not-very-good club sandwiches, drinking their alcohol more leisurely as the evening progressed, sharing their stories of being widowed when they were younger. They launched into an ebullient, detailed discussion of their favorite operas.

"Oh," Barbara sighed. "None of my friends enjoy the opera. At least, none of my friends who are still alive." She looked woefully at her drink, a sidecar, then excused herself for a trip to *powder her nose.*

When she returned from the restroom, she'd newly applied a streak of bright pink lipstick. Oh! A smudge of the lipstick had found its way outside the lines of her mouth. Her thick foundation creased like rainwater on clay.

The booze loosened Rudy into an open-minded reverie. As much as he wouldn't mind a friendship with an older woman who shared his love of opera and who was kind and outgoing, he wanted to share *everything* he loved with Sasha. Barbara was great, but she deserved a gentleman her own age to escort her on special outings. Still, he didn't have the heart to suggest this. Vexed, he shooed away a fly hovering by his unfinished sandwich. The bartender cleared away their plates.

"This has been nice." Rudy patted his lips with his napkin. "We both have season tickets, perhaps we could work it out so we don't have to go to the opera alone every time."

"Yes," Barbara agreed, fanning herself with a cardboard coaster. "Let's agree to go once, and then I think you need to find a young lady closer to your age."

Rudy did not share the fact that he hadn't known about their age disparity before their meeting.

Barbara finished her drink, chewed the cherry. "I just wander those crazy dating sites — even the seniors' one! — searching for opera lovers. I adore opera. I have no one to go with."

"You can't talk about it on the ride home," Rudy agreed. "And going out to dinner beforehand. Who wants to do that alone?"

Babs nodded enthusiastically.

"Marriage of Figaro?" Rudy asked. "I think I can get us two tickets together." Maybe he could buy the couple's insolent son's ticket. If it worked out, they might be relieved to unload the seat. The tickets were expensive.

Rudy couldn't wait to tell CeCe about this. He'd obeyed her orders, kept up the profile, gone on a date, and would go on another to the opera. With a lovely grandma. So there.

Rudy's sympathy for Barbara softened him. They were both in the same boat, weren't they? Lonesome. Looking for love. Sure, but also *companionship.*

"I can get you a discount at Nordstrom," Rudy was surprised to hear himself say.

Maybe it was the gin.

Barbara's eyes brightened. "Really?"

"Sure." Rudy took out his wallet to pay the tab. *Slow down, cowboy.* Was he going to take Babs square-heeled pumps shopping?

"Well, really I love Talbots best," Barbara confessed with relish. "But I just may take you up on that sometime, dear."

Somehow, Rudy was touched by this term of endearment. It indicated they'd made a platonic bond. Frankly, the date hadn't been nearly as frightening as Rudy had imagined.

People, all people, needed connection, Rudy thought, opening the leatherette bar tab holder.

Rudy shooed away the credit card Babs tried to slip inside the check holder with Rudy's. She allowed for the treat and they exchanged personal email addresses so they could work out the details of attending *Figaro* together.

"Your kindness means so much to me." She said this without a touch of irony, squeezing Rudy's arm. "I'm so sorry for the loss of your wife. Too young," she said. "Too young."

"And your husband," Rudy added.

"You are going to find a nice new wife in no time," Barbara told him.

"I, well . . ."

"It's so much easier for men."

What an unfair truth, if this were the case, he thought.

Then he felt that invisible string again — the commonality of grief and loss a fly-fishing line arcing from one stranger's heart to another's, uniting him with Sasha.

"And I bet that 'senior dating site' is going to provide you with a dashing opera buddy much sharper than me," he assured Barbara.

She blotted her lips, stood, straightened her skirt, and assumed a locked and loaded demeanor. "Okay, then!" she chirped. "As my granddaughter would say, send me the deets!"

With that, Barbara was gone, up the padded stairs of the sunken bar, disappearing through the lobby of the hotel.

At home, the phone rang before Rudy was barely in the door.

"So?" CeCe said, bursting with vicarious excitement.

"*So.* I just had drinks and sandwiches and opera chat with a seventy-seven-year-old woman."

"What! She lied about her age!"

"She did *not* lie. She thought I chose her, knowing her age, thank you very much.

130

Maybe the dark underbelly of dating isn't as dark as the underbelly of dumb dating technology."

"Well, open the site," CeCe insisted, her manager mode setting in. A grieving widowed father wasn't a project to be left unfinished!

"I don't want to open the site, sweetheart. I'll be opening the site tomorrow, when I take down my profile."

Rudy heard the clacking of CeCe's keyboard in the background. He laid his sport coat over the stool at the breakfast bar. He crossed the room to flip on another kitchen light, reached into the fridge for his favorite ginger ale.

"Ohhhhhhh. Oh, Dad."

"Yes, my electronic matchmaker?"

"I made an error. I missed it when I proofed your profile. Oh, Dad."

"Did you enter me as a woman? A seventy-five-year-old woman in need of a bridge group?"

"No," CeCe's seriousness gave way to laughter that burbled with hysteria and ended in a snort. "Dad, I put that you're seventy-four. Not fifty-four. I typed a seven instead of a five. Oh. My. God."

"Well," he took a sip of his ginger ale, "despite wishing for the first time in my life that I were color-blind, I actually had a fine time. And, I have a date, not a *date* date, but a friend, with whom I will attend the opera. At least one show, we decided."

"Oh, noooo. She's *way* too old for you. You have to cancel. You'll get right back on there tomorrow and find someone in your age group."

"Nope, I found my opera date. It's a friendly outing, with a nice older lady who wants both of us to find buddies closer to our age."

"Buddies?"

"Sweetheart, lighten up. I just drove all the way to an airport bar to breathe enough disinfectant and mildew to give me Legionnaires' disease. I'm going upstairs to put my feet up before the respiratory infection sets in."

"Okay, but I'm fixing your profile right —"

"Oh, nooooo," Rudy told his daughter, kicking off his shoes, excited to tell Sasha this whole story. "I have done my due diligence. No more online dating." The only woman he wanted to take on a real bona fide *date* date was Sasha. And with any luck, that spoiled kid he sat next to at the opera would one day be replaced by her.

"But Dad, I just saw in the community

college catalog that there's an adult education class Tuesday nights for online dating. You get all the latest hot tips and then get coached by an expert."

"Oh, for the love of God." Rudy had imagined taking an adult-education course at the college in intermediate or advanced Italian, in order to better enjoy the opera.

"But, it's only two nights. You can do anything once, right? That's what Mom always said."

"And I went on one online date and I love you for helping me and I am going up to bed now. I've got to shower the maraschino cherry vapors out of my hair."

Rudy made a kissing sound for his daughter and hung up the phone.

The next morning Rudy would email Barbara, then take down his dating profile. He knew he enjoyed Sasha's company more than anyone else's. He didn't want to go on ten coffee dates or get ghosted. (CeCe had explained this kooky term to him, which she'd learned from a recently divorced girlfriend.) He was a widower. Permanently ghosted!

As he crept around the house, turning out the last few lights, making sure the front door was locked, he realized that he felt buoyed by his crazy Internet meet-up. By the fact that he'd potentially made a new friend and that he felt ever confident to move forward with getting to know Sasha. More than as a friend, work comrade, and coffee date. As a *date* date.

10

Making dinner for Bee every night after he'd been downsized had become one of Rudy's great pleasures. Now he found himself cooking for Terry Gross on the radio. Although he loved Terry, she wasn't going to tuck into a gourmet shepherd's pie with him. He'd discovered there was no joy in eating by himself. No matter what bottle of wine he opened or what record he put on the stereo, he wanted to fix food for others. CeCe appreciated his Tupperware-packed dinners for three, which she would always say she was going to freeze. "Freeze! Eat it tonight or tomorrow night," Rudy would insist. But his daughter had an obsession with freezing food. Everything in their stuffed freezer was neatly packed and labeled for flavor loss, freezer burn, and a sea of spoiled food in the case of a prolonged power outage.

No, he wanted to make dinner for Sasha.

Two nicely set places, with candles and courses and wine and dessert. They'd dine at the kitchen table, to make the meal cozier and less formal. All he had to do was march over to the watch counter the next day (no skulking, he confidently told himself), and ask her. He would not tell Sasha that he hadn't been on a dinner date since college. As college sweethearts, he and Bethany didn't go on dates as they first got to know each other. They spent hours at the same table of friends in the college cafeteria, drove into town in carloads for tuna melts and french fries, toiled in the same study group. Eventually, Rudy and Bee drifted apart from their group and became a real couple. Yet it was so incremental and organic and without anxiety that Rudy wondered if he'd ever even *been* on a proper date. But he and Bethany had entertained — had had plenty of dinner parties. So this would be that sort of date. Having someone over for supper. In fact, he'd bill it as supper, to make the meal seem less formal and date-like. Call him old-fashioned, but he now hated the word *date.* Dating websites, *Dating the Second Time Around!* — CeCe had forwarded one such audiobook to him to listen to.

"I'm listening to *Madame Bovary* currently," he'd texted her back.

"NOT a happy story, Dad," she'd replied.

In the last month, Rudy and his adult daughter had begun texting like teenagers. He liked the method of communication. It meant brevity and immediacy, without the nagging feeling of needing to call her back and assuage her worries about him.

"Well, I loved listening to *Anna Karenina,*" Rudy texted back. He had. The characters' troubles, the narrator's dulcet reading voice — audiobooks had become a salve since Bee died. Someone in the night. A cast of people in the night. A ballroom dance floor, a Russian winter, a dropped handkerchief.

"!!!" CeCe replied to the mention of *Anna Karenina.* Okay, so both stories ended in suicide. Did she think he hadn't thought of this? Rudy was not going to harm himself. He just craved literature. Heft. Meaning out of the senseless world.

"Well-told stories," he replied. "More importantly, company. That's not depressing."

"Not depressing?!"

"That's right, I find the greatest novels of all time — their beauty and grace and tragedy less depressing than DATING books at MY age. Especially to listen to. Blech."

"I'm just trying to help." Frowny face.

"I know, sweetheart. I love you." Hearts. Kisses. Emojis made expressing emotions by text less treacherous.

Inspired by this thought, Rudy decided to text Sasha. "Feel like having supper at my house this weekend?" He used the emojis for wine and the dinner plate, which he felt added a whimsical and casual touch. Thirty seconds later, she wrote back "Sure!" Smiley face.

Rudy got up early the Saturday Sasha was coming to dinner. She had said yes! He had cut the beef into chunks and soaked it in red wine the night before — prepping for the beef bourguignon. Now he drained the meat, reserving the juices, rolled the pieces in flour with salt and pepper, and fried them quickly, just to sear the outside of each piece. It was best if you didn't cook too many chunks at a time, allowing for more space to turn and brown each and every side. For this he used tongs. Rudy began to hum as he worked — a song from *The Fantasticks,* from his repertoire at work — which always made him think of parenting their unique daughter.

"Plant a carrot! Get a carrot! Not a Brussels sprout . . ." He belted out the rhyme with

Tourette's vigor. ARGH! Would these songs be stuck in his head forever? He had nothing against musicals, but Rudy was pretty sure he'd never attend one again. Unless Sasha had her heart set on them. He'd go with her. Hell, he'd go to an Amway meeting with Sasha. As he plucked the meat from the pan and set it aside for the stew, juices running onto the plate, he knew that this conviction wasn't just a first-blush-of-love feeling. Couples seemed willing to do anything with each other at first. But as the years wore on they became set in their *own* ways, less open to their partner's likes and whims. Bethany always teased Rudy — giggling, yet pleased — because he was a husband who would still go clothes shopping with his wife after all their years of marriage. Not that they'd launch out on trips to the mall for Bee's spring wardrobe, but if they were out and she saw a sale, he'd go into the store with her, sink into one of those armchairs outside the fitting rooms, happy to read the paper, a book, or listen to music on his phone. The thing was, Rudy always told her, he never got bored, only lonesome.

Since living alone, he'd learned that there were actually people who didn't understand the difference. And it turned out that loneliness was an embarrassing thing to speak of. (Why? It was like telling people the intimate bathroom details of food poisoning — the word *lonely* akin to *diarrhea*.) It implied that you personally were deficient. And after you'd gone to all the trouble to work up the courage to mention the pain of living alone, people were often quick to suggest activities. Not even activities with others! Computer solitaire! These fill-in-the-hours ideas were always posed by those in a couple or with family close by or living at home.

Rudy had mentioned lonesomeness to the wife of one couple friend of theirs who laughingly told Rudy a bit later in their conversation, "We've got a *terrible* ant problem. Oh, my word! You would *not* be lonely with all these ants!" She laughed at her own joke, and Rudy was instantly mortified that he'd even divulged his isolation without Bee. But his dinner hosts and people he'd run into at the supermarket constantly asked how he was doing! Maybe people just wanted to hear about your casserole count right after the death, then fast-forward to your dazzling dating life. They didn't want to hear *lonely* quietly confessed near the kale. In fact, Rudy had even imagined that CeCe's setting up his online profile had provided a vicarious rush for her. Was his own daughter harboring dating fantasies? Did people think being single midlife somehow was fun? They certainly didn't want to hear that the king-sized bed had become as big as an aircraft carrier and cold as the sidewalk in winter.

The house phone rang out, startling Rudy. With his hands deep in meal prep, he let it go to voicemail. When he heard the caller ID identify the police station, a flash of panic distracted Rudy from the dinner. He needed to call Detective Jensen back. He needed to deal with the possibility that his wife had been murdered. How could he procrastinate over such a task? The problem was he couldn't *absorb* the wretched possibility.

Rudy snapped on public radio assuring himself he'd return Jensen's call the next morning. He would get to the bottom of everything. Eventually. But his head was a traffic jam this morning.

I'm making dinner for a woman at work, he wanted to tell Bee. He loved his dead wife. He always would. But Sasha was special, too. Even Bee would have liked her. She would have liked her lightheartedness, her ability to laugh at herself — that unpretentiousness — her genuine interest in Bee herself, and her deep, deep, varied love for music. Rudy hoped that Sasha and CeCe would get along. He frankly couldn't imagine anyone not getting along with Sasha. Maybe this traffic jam was good. There simply wasn't a lane open for date anxiety.

"It. Will. Be. Fine." He said these words aloud to the skillet of juices from the meat, turning the flame off underneath, unsure if he meant the date or the murder investigation or the rest of his life. He poured himself another cup of coffee, the last thing he needed.

"All right?" he asked the package of frozen pearl onions he'd set out on the counter.

"Good morning! Using a FROZEN vegetable!" he texted CeCe. He hoped he wouldn't hurt her feelings, teasing her about the freezer business. How he wished his daughter had her mother's sense of humor.

Rudy had tried quartered red onions, but really nothing beat the frozen pearl onions in this dish. He scraped the bottom of the pan, working up the brown bits, flicked the flame back to low, added in the butter, then the flour, making a roux. From there he added the red wine, which he mixed with vermouth — his little secret, it made the dish smoother and sweeter and more robust. As he stirred the gravy until it thickened, he gradually added in beef broth. With his other hand he refilled his coffee again and took a bite of rye toast. The kitchen was warmer now, steam and the savory smell of cooking filling the room.

Good thing he and Sasha had already had coffee and lunch and many talks across the watch counter. They wouldn't be starting from scratch on their first dinner date over Pine-Sol at an airport Ramada Inn. The thing about being in your fifties was that you knew life was short and that this adage was true: On your deathbed you were more likely to regret what you *hadn't* done in life than what you had.

When Sasha arrived, Rudy was relieved to find that she was wearing jeans and little pink flats, with a cream-colored sweater set. Around her neck was a pretty necklace of pearls, which he complimented her on. She blushed, fingered the necklace.

"My grandmother's," she said. "One of the few very fancy things she had back home.

"Ahhhhhh." Sasha tipped back her head, inhaling deeply, and complimented Rudy on the smell of the house. "Delicious!" she exclaimed.

They made their way to the living room, which was off the kitchen. Sasha gave Rudy a gift she'd brought, a box, of some weight. Rudy opened it to discover two tissue-wrapped lumps.

"This is from Hungary," she told him, peering over his hands into the box with some pride in her voice.

Rudy peeled back the wrapping and saw a beautiful matching porcelain trivet and spoon holder, brightly colored with birds in blue and yellow and green.

"Because you cook and I know you enjoy birds." She clapped her hands together happily.

"They're beautiful," Rudy told her. "I just love them." He did. They were so intricately made, yet sturdy and utilitarian. He motioned Sasha into the kitchen, where he brushed off and placed the two pieces prominently on the counter.

"Ah, see, you need," Sasha pointed to Rudy's stirring spoon, coated with juices from the dinner, lying on a simple plate.

"I'll use them soon," Rudy insisted. "First I want to look at them. Enjoy them while they are spotless."

He opened a bottle of Tapestry wine — a bottle of mixed reds that was delicious but not too heavy. She tasted it then gave a smile and a thumbs-up.

"We are so lucky to live in California,"

she added. "So much delicious wine." Sasha looked out the big picture window over the kitchen table. "And beautiful wildlife, birds." She smiled at the feeder.

"Aha! The brown-backed chickadee," Rudy pointed. He feigned seriousness, trying to poke fun at himself. "Easy to confuse with the black-capped chickadee and the house sparrow."

Sasha giggled. "Well, they all seem happy!"

Sasha's cheer, her seeming inability to complain, although her life was clearly difficult, always amazed Rudy. He opened the oven, lifted the lid off the stew, Sasha standing beside him to peek in as he gave it a stir. The dish smelled flavorful, but all Rudy focused on was Sasha's perfume — a clean, springy scent, like verbena and lemons and a little something spicy. He closed the oven and turned down the heat so that the dish could simmer while they chatted over cheese and bread.

Everything on Rudy and Sasha's date went brilliantly, until it became a catastrophe.

As they sat in the living room nibbling on cheeses and paprika pickles Sasha had also brought, Rudy got up to put on his favorite Erroll Garner record. Erroll Garner and Dave Brubeck were his two favorite pianists.

"I know, I know, I know," Sasha began.

Rudy turned to her.

"I know you play the piano all the time at work. But I'd so love it if you'd play something for me now. Something maybe you don't play at the store."

It was as though she'd read his mind. Music that would just be for them.

And so, instead of putting on the record, Rudy rook a seat at the piano bench, relieved not to be in that dang tuxedo, but rather in khakis, a dress shirt, and V-neck cornflower-blue sweater that Bee had always said made him look handsome. He began to play Erroll Garner.

He turned to look at Sasha. She smiled, sighed, and closed her eyes.

But as Rudy hit a high key on the piano, a twangy, dry thump came from under the baby grand's open cover.

"Must be a bit of dust," Rudy said, as he stood and bent over to stick his head under the great lid of the piano. He lifted the damper of the key that had gone awry, and was trying to gently pluck away a bit of dust that had indeed adhered itself to the felt. The next thing he knew, his shirtsleeve was caught in the piano's strings. His shirt was slightly too large, given that he'd lost weight in the past month. He'd gone from emotional overeating to undereating — quick slices of toast over the kitchen sink for supper. His sleeves loose and dangly. And now he was trapped, with one arm tangled in the wires. Somehow his cuff button was part of the mess. It was impossible to move his arm and see the snarl, without potentially damaging the string or damper. He didn't care about his dang cuff.

Sasha was now sitting up, her hands covering her mouth, laughing.

"I know I shouldn't," she said.

Rudy announced, cheerfully. "My arm has just been eaten by this piano. I cannot seem to untangle my shirtsleeve and I do *not* want to force it, in case it breaks the piano string."

Sasha shook her head vigorously, laughing, her blond hair falling across her eyes in the most endearing way. She got up, crossed the room to Rudy, and gave him a sip of wine from his glass.

"Oh, how can I help you out of there?" she asked, her hand on her hip, the picture of beauty and competence.

"My cell phone. Maybe I can call the piano tuner and ask him to come and get me out of this fix."

"What? Is the piano tuner like a doctor-on-call? He will just come over on a Saturday and remove you from your own piano?

Rudy, Rudy, Rudy. We will cut you free and any damage to your shirt I can mend for you."

"Well, he's been with me a long time." Rudy felt ridiculous, but the kick Sasha was getting out of the situation made him feel more like Charlie Chaplin than an idiot. They'd tell this story at their wedding. Right?

"Rudy." Sasha was still trying not to laugh. "Listen to me —"

At that moment the smoke detector went off, and they both leapt, the piercing shriek of the thing taking any rom-com mood out of the situation.

Rudy instinctively moved to turn the smoke detector off, but his arm tugged at the precarious innards of the piano. He told Sasha where the step stool was, tucked beside the refrigerator.

She grabbed and unfolded it, quickly scurrying up the steps, to silence the smoke detector. "There," she said, climbing back down. "Now." She blew a bright stray wisp of hair away from her eyes and raised a finger in the air. "The dinner."

The next thing for her to rescue. Rudy should start a list of all the things she'd rescued him from since he met her. She'd saved him at the store one day from a drunk who wanted to sing with him at the piano. Where had the security guards been? The next thing he had known Sasha was there, taking him by the arm and insisting he was needed in Cosmetics, where they looped through the labyrinth of makeup ladies to hide beside the MAC counter.

"Don't worry," she called out now from the kitchen. "A little juice just bubbled over onto the bottom of the oven. Found the pot holders!"

She returned to the living room just as Rudy's back was beginning to ache from bending over with his upper half in the piano. He held the lid open with one hand, not wanting to end up even more compromised by a guillotine situation, in which case the paramedics might have to be called!

"Now, silly, sweet man," she said, "you do not need to spend the night with your head in the piano."

"I know, I know," Rudy agreed. "What is wrong with my brain!" *You're in love,* the wine told him. While this epiphany might be real and true, Rudy also knew that since his wife had died suddenly, and since he'd learned that she'd potentially been murdered, his brain raced anxiously from both hopeful conclusions to worst-case scenarios. Sasha was two minutes late for work? She'd been in an auto accident. CeCe's husband Spencer seemed aloof? He was likely involved in some sort of malpractice ring. His dangling shirtsleeve got caught in the piano string? He'd spend the night curled inside the baby grand while the dinner burned down the house.

Rudy breathed in through his nose to calm himself, counting to four for each breath. Sasha was in her stocking feet now, with an apron tied around her waist, her beautiful hair pinned up in a clip. Rudy loved how at home she looked in the house.

"We can leave a message for the piano tuner to come Monday and check the strings," she told him. "In the meantime, why don't you take off your shirt and leave it in the piano?"

Of course. Rudy could make a perfect mango soufflé, which was what they'd have for dessert. He could sight read, stuff a pork chop, change the oil in his own car, and frame a picture in a pinch. But this obvious solution had not occurred to him. It was the cataclysmic thinking, but the truth was, Sasha's proximity had the capacity to lower his IQ at times. This didn't seem like a good phenomenon when you wanted to impress a new love interest.

"I'll have to change my shirt!" he yelped,

wishing this hadn't come out with such alarm. None of his fantasies of serving Sasha dinner included *this* scenario.

"I assume you own more than one shirt?"

Rudy felt his breathing and pulse slow. Sasha's humor defused his silly expectation of the evening going off like a Harvey's Brisol Cream commercial.

"Yesssssss," he answered. "Many in my closet upstairs. You can't miss them."

Sasha returned shortly with a fresh Oxford shirt.

Rudy took it from her and began snaking his arm out of his sweater. He was nearly there, about to twist around and pull his head through his sweater and shirt, which he'd unbuttoned from under the sweater, when he was overcome with embarrassment.

"Turn around," he implored Sasha.

She giggled. "Okay."

"I'll go into the bathroom," Rudy told her, stepping toward the small bath in the front hall.

Sasha called after him: "You know, Mr. Rudy, I have seen it all at the gymnasium locker room. Granted, ladies. But I have seen women blow-dry the underneath of their breasts as they rush to get dressed. Imagine!"

Women blow-drying their privates did not make Rudy feel better about this date that had gone off the rails . . . or off the strings, ha ha. He mustered a laugh.

Finally, as they ate, they listened to the Erroll Garner record — a pianist new to Sasha — whom she said was becoming a favorite. The beef bourguignon and salad and bread were all delicious, she declared. She even had enough room for the mango soufflé, which Rudy put in the oven just as they were finishing their meal.

Rudy wanted to leave the dishes for later, but Sasha insisted they clean up together, to get the mess out of the way for morning.

"You never sit down for long, do you?" he asked her, as she rinsed the plates and he loaded them into the dishwasher.

She stopped, wiped her hands on a dish towel. "I find it hard to. It makes me anxious. I feel like if I stop moving something bad might happen."

"Like getting caught inside a piano?" Sasha laughed.

Rudy added, "Maybe that's why you are so thin! Slim, I mean." Thin didn't sound very complimentary, he decided. "I think that's why I wanted to cook for you. This gal, she needs some calories! Some meat on her bones!" He felt silly as he clamored to compliment her, to wear this new identity with class — a widower dating a new woman for the first time in decades.

As Sasha dried the salad bowl, she suddenly slowed her pace, pensive all of a sudden. She set the wooden bowl on the counter next to the drainer. She turned to Rudy, wincing a little, as though trying to choose her words carefully.

"You know, I'm not an animal at the pound who needs rescuing." Her typical light tone had lapsed into seriousness. "Not a project for anyone."

"Of course!" Rudy said. "You are brighter and more capable than just about anyone I know, for starters." He was talking too fast, hating himself for making such a cliché comment about fattening someone up. He meant what he'd said about Sasha being so sharp and funny. But the truth was, Rudy did want to rescue her. Not in a naive, damsel-in-distress fairy-tale way, but in reality. He wanted to help her because he had feelings for her, and because — as a financially established citizen who'd lived here all his life — he was at an advantage to do so. And life simply *was* easier with two people. To wit: Rudy was being rescued in little ways by Sasha all the time. She had rescued the dinner out of the oven, retrieved fresh clothes for him, and now the kitchen was nearly spotless. Maybe Sasha needed someone to take care of, too. He knew Sasha had had a daughter. He didn't want to pry, but maybe Sasha missed taking care of her.

The truth was that cooking for Sasha, chatting over the meal with wine, listening to records, learning more about Hungary and her youth there, finding out more about her daughter if an appropriate moment allowed for the question — having Sasha's *company* — was about the most romantic thing Rudy could think of. It wasn't that he was a prude. He'd just been married so many years that he wanted meaningful companionship for a night, more than sex. No ripping off each other's clothing and swinging from chandeliers.

"Don't worry." Sasha kneeled before Rudy, who sat in a kitchen chair now, kneading his hands, looking down, ashamed by his inarticulateness. "I know you didn't mean it that way." She squeezed each of Rudy's shoulders, her hands warm from the dishes through the fabric of his shirt. "I am sensitive."

She leaned forward as she balanced on her haunches before Rudy and kissed each of his cheeks, then his mouth. Her lips were soft and just a little damp and sticky from the wine and then they were gone. Rudy stopped trying to explain his feelings, trying to explain anything. He just watched her eyes. He couldn't remember ever knowing anyone with gray eyes before. *They* rescued him. Whisked him away from everything that hurt.

Sasha furrowed her brow, perhaps taking Rudy's silence as hurt feelings instead of tongue-tied self-reproach.

He took her hand and led her to the piano. Then he patted the bench. "Madam." Sasha sat.

"How about . . . instead of Chopin, a corny show tune, an octave lower to avoid my poor shirt sleeve in the strings?"

"It would be a cutting-edge jazz performance piece to play with a shirt sleeve in piano strings, no?" Sasha poked Rudy in the ribs, bumped his shoulder with hers.

Rudy began playing, a store staple he hadn't resorted to in a while. It was a song he sang to CeCe when she was a baby. He sang it all the way up until her twelfth birthday. Their before-bed ritual had been Rudy reading two stories and singing one song. This had always been her number one request. Even long after his daughter had outgrown this ritual, Rudy still sang the song to her, amazed by the fact that it always made her buttoned-up face break into a smile. After-dinner bourbon gave him the courage to croon it for Sasha now.

Rudy rolled out the first notes on the piano with a dramatic flourish — "Tea for Two" from the musical *No, No, Nanette.*

He wiggled his eyebrows with silliness as he reached the chorus, then sped up the melody, ". . . Just me for you, And you for me alone!"

Sasha laughed and sang along, pretending to sip tea from a cup.

"Lyrics by Irving Caesar and music by Vincent Youmans," Rudy told her as she continued.

"I know this show tune," Sasha said, tickling him below the ribs. "This couple, they want to live in nice place, afford rent. Play this for me next time at the store, would you?"

Rudy gave a final lounge player roll of the keys all the way up to the dry-sounding plunk of the shirt-tangled string, made a little stage bow over the keyboard, and closed its cover. "But of course, madam. It will always be my pleasure!"

"You, my friend," Sasha proclaimed, "are a good man."

11

Rudolph Knowles, Rudolph Knowles. As the department store whirled and chimed around him, Rudy was lost in playing a jazz piece from his favorite Charlie Haden album. He alternated between feelings of euphoria recalling his evening with Sasha, and exhaustion and worry, from a restless night's sleep, dreaming of Bee and the murder investigation. He dreamed that Bee was in their driveway the morning the ambulance took her away, only she wasn't in the ambulance, she was standing in her bathrobe, asking what had happened to her. And where had Rudy been, she wanted to know. Had they been in an accident? He was telling her he didn't know yet when he awoke, drenched in sweat, freezing and sticky at the same time.

Rudolph Knowl— Rudy realized that the department store PA lady was paging *him.* He continued to hit the keys, but more quietly now. Maybe he was imagining this — *Rudolph Knowles, Rudolph Knowles.* But there it was again — the voice as smooth as butterscotch pudding. What to do? Where to go? There were probably instructions in that thick human resources packet Rudy had never cracked. He never considered himself a true department store employee. He was a musician. A father, a downsized husband.

How to make this sexy automaton stop? Everyone in the store went about his or her business. Sasha wasn't working that day, so he couldn't ask her. He looked across the tables of gloves and past the Coach pocketbooks for a familiar face in Cosmetics, but didn't recognize anyone. He could go up to that office by the gift wrap and customer service window and inquire. But first he'd finish this song. Three more bars of "Send in the Clowns" and he'd be on the escalator.

Bethany's Shoe. Bethany's Shoe. At his wife's name, Rudy pounded the keys, and stopped playing abruptly. The PA woman spoke these two words with the same even tone. It sounded as though she were paging a woman: Bethany Shew. Or maybe there was a Bethany Shew who needed to report to men's sleepwear or some such.

Rudolph Knowles, Rudolph Knowles. Bethany's Shoe, Bethany's Shoe.

For crying out loud! This was *not* the midlife crisis Rudy had envisioned. He hadn't envisioned *any* midlife crisis, frankly, but certainly this must be something akin to that, or perhaps a stroke. Bethany would have known what to do. In a situation such as this he would turn directly to her. Call and describe his symptoms. Having a pharmacist wife, he found that he rarely had to go to the doctor except for his annual checkup. Perhaps the PA voice calling his name was a hysterical reaction to the fact his wife had been murdered, he thought, with an odd sense of calm. It was as though he were outside his body looking down upon himself. *Bethany's Shoe! Bethany's Shoe!* A pain shot through his temple. Murdered! Plus, there was the not-so-brilliant epiphany in the shower this morning that he'd wasted a chunk of his life in the "temporary" trade of playing show tunes while gazing mindlessly across a sea of Manolo Blahniks and Cole Haans five days a week. Maybe he'd been breathing the crisp, expensive smell of new leather for so long that footwear had invaded his consciousness. He tried hitting the song's final high C with a flourish, but it looked more like a spasm.

Rudolph Knowles, Bethany's Shoe. As he closed the lid over the piano keys, his hands trembled visibly. Perspiration drizzled down his back. His skin felt slick, trapped inside the tuxedo. He arose, dizzy, clasped and unclasped his fluttering fingers then grabbed his satchel of sheet music from inside the piano bench. As he fled the store, he tried not to appear to be running.

Was this a clue? He was going to return the detective's phone calls again that afternoon. Jensen hadn't been in that morning. By the time Rudy had gotten a call back, he was on his way to work. And then he'd gotten distracted by music, his lifelong first aid, and the slightly hung-over fuzzy-headed warmth of post-date memories. After Rudy had gone back to sleep the night before, he'd succumbed to a recurring dream — of Bee on her back in her white nightgown as she had been that last morning — and it had taken a nightmarish turn, with the blare of a phone ringing that he could not find in their room until he realized she was gone. He could not get back to sleep afterward, despite warm milk and Count Vronsky.

Leaving the store, Rudy jogged through the mall's corridors, past the too-sweet smell of the soft pretzel shop. Words continued to ring in his ears, two at a time, in the precise tone of the PA woman's omniscient buttery voice. *Get out. Go home. Help Bethany. Help* her? How? You could not *help* a dead person. There were many other things you could do for them. Mourn them, miss them, curse them for dying, toss their ashes into the sea, light yahrzeit candles on anniversaries, somehow summon the strength to look through photo albums. Press articles of their last-worn clothing to your face and breathe, your brain groping for their scent, your heart resenting the fact that the cotton of the white eyelet nightgown was beginning to smell almost generic now, just another fusty piece of laundry. If anything, the dead should help *us*! The living were the ones who needed help. Why couldn't the PA lady — with her ungodly amount of self-confidence — page Bethany to come down the escalator from Housewares and sit beside Rudy to turn the pages of his sheet music and console and catch up with him?

Rudy crashed through the double glass doors and out of the mall. The bright sun seared his eyes. He grabbed the warm, smooth railing of a pedestrian overpass to the garage and panted, catching his breath. His head dropped to his chest. He needed to collect himself. Separate reality from hallucination. The PA — real or recorded — had paged him at the store. But they had not paged his dead wife. He was just woozy. People's names were repeated through the ceiling's speakers all day, every day. With great relief, Rudy now heard these statements in Bethany's common-sense voice, rather than the bossy coo of the PA woman. Bethany always made him feel better about unsettling events, shooing away his worries with a simple explanation, warm squeeze of her hand, an understanding smile.

He breathed in deeply and continued toward his car, a breeze cooling his forehead. His wife's practicality seemed to follow beside him now, and his fist loosened around the satchel filled with sheet music. This morning, he'd woken late after his poor night's sleep. He'd showered, donned the tuxedo, which always made him too warm, grabbed his coffee out of the coffee-maker without stopping for his usual rye toast spread with cottage cheese. No wonder he was light-headed and off-kilter.

Now there was work to be done. The detective needed his help. All-business Jensen. Rudy dug into his suit jacket pocket for the card the detective had coolly handed him. It was made of thick, stiff paper, with simple Helvetica type — masculine, savvy, in the know. Before reaching his Volvo, Rudy turned back toward the mall. What if it was Jensen who had paged him? Perhaps there'd been an important development in the murder case. It was no time to flee like a child! What was the matter with Rudy! Well, what wasn't? And what did he care at this point? He opened the car door, tossed his music into the back seat, took off his jacket, saw sweat stains creeping toward his waist, slid back into the hateful top layer, and re-locked the car.

People stepped out of his way as Rudy jogged back through the mall, this time grabbing a doughy pretzel and Coke, not even caring that he was a sweaty, middle-aged man in a tuxedo scarfing mall junk food and running red-faced past Victoria's Secret. Escalator, that fancy tea shop where the tea tasted like air freshener, the circle of leather chairs where people collapsed as though they'd been shot. He took long strides into the department store, brushing crumbs from his lips and straightening his posture. Just past the restrooms on the second floor he found customer service and then the tall counter where the employee relations woman stood watch outside the company offices.

"Pardon me." Rudy drew air through his nose to catch his breath. "I am Rudolph Knowles, one of the store's pianists, and my name was called . . ." He pressed his palm to the countertop, grateful that his hands had stopped wobbling. "I've been paged, it seems. What shall I do?"

"One moment." The woman pointed a long eggplant-colored fingernail through her coiffed hair to scratch at her scalp. Her hair was alarmingly red, with an amber stripe through it — one long highlight that made a dramatic swoop across her forehead. She was dressed in a crisp white blouse and black pencil skirt. She picked up a telephone and punched in two numbers. "Mr. Rudolph Coal is here? He's been paged?"

"Knowles," Rudy corrected her.

The woman nodded, covering the receiver with her long white fingers. "Sorry," she mouthed to him. "Rudolph Knowles? He's our pianist!" She said this last word with a reverence that touched Rudy. "Yes. Knowles. *Rudolph Knowles.* No? Hunh. Okay. Perhaps he misheard. Thank you."

"Gosh, Mr. Knowles," the woman said apologetically, replacing the receiver and throwing up her hands. "They say they didn't page you." She smiled, and Rudy thought of all the effort it took for a person just to arrive to work at a place like this — the unwelcome alarm clock, finding a white shirt without a splotch, tights or stockings without runs, the coiffing and caffeinating and the this-won't-be-forever pep talk as you trudged along at twenty miles an hour merging in a funnel onto the freeway.

"Ah, well thank you so much." The fluorescent lights buzzed like cicadas in Rudy's head. He tried to smile at the woman, realizing she was probably barely thirty.

"You know, I wish I'd never quit my piano lessons," she mused. "You play so beautifully."

"Everyone always wishes they'd stuck with it," Rudy said a bit bashfully. "But it's hard to imagine people notice the piano that much here," he added, his eyes wandering up to the industrial fluorescent lighting above.

"Oh, people love it," the woman cooed. "It kind of makes you feel like you're at a party, you know. Like maybe you'll pick up something special and fun."

"That seems to be the idea," Rudy agreed. "Well then. Good day, I must be running." He wanted to ask the woman everything about the paging system. But he forced himself to make Jensen his top priority.

He waved to her as he headed toward the

elevators. They were hidden beyond gift wrap and returns and lord knew what else. He jogged toward the escalator instead.

Then on the way back down the escalator he almost did a double take when he heard it again, *"Rudolph Knowles, Rudolph Knowles. Keep moving."* Well yes! Obviously! But where to? Or just in general? Time for a change? Or speed it up to solve the mystery of his wife's . . . he could not even *think* the word. He forced himself, pressing his lips together to form an *em* sound. "Murder," he whispered to himself. He did not want to know.

"Rudy Knowles . . ." Rudy reached the bottom floor, turned, and broke into a run past the Lancôme counter and out the store. He would have liked to throttle the PA system woman and her velvet, amber-honey voice. It was smoother than the automated telephone ladies, than the bossy GPS ladies, than any person he had ever known in his life. And yet, with so little to say!

"Rudolph . . ." He covered an ear with one hand, and as he tried to bring his other hand to his head, he hit a sign on a stand announcing some kind of store sale and kept running as it slapped the floor behind him. He passed the coffee cart near the store's entrance, the usually pleasant smell

of coffee making him gag now. As he burst out the door of the damn store leading to the proper outside of the mall, back into the heat of the day, the bright sun scorched an immediate headache into his forehead. He saw a garbage can ahead and had the overwhelming and unsavory urge to bury his head inside it, escaping from the sights and sounds of this awful day.

He would drive straight to the detective's office and tell him about being paged by the phantom PA lady. He'd tell him every single detail. He didn't care if Jensen thought he was crazy. Maybe this was a clue of some kind! The voice was as clear and calm as every single one of the pages Rudy had heard before. There continued to be an undeniable certainty to it. Maybe he was losing his mind. Who cared? That was the thing about losing the person you loved most. There wasn't much to lose after that.

12

Detective Jensen's office was in a low, concrete building beside the main police station. Inside, the air was chalk-dry and smelled of photocopier ink, burned coffee, and stale take-out food. The brown-and-tan checked floor felt gritty beneath Rudy's loafers. Suddenly the industrial, outdated feel of this place made him appreciate the department store's glamour — even if it was fabricated.

A woman at a desk in the appointed "ROOM 353" slid open part of the Plexiglas window surrounding her to greet Rudy. Jensen was ready for him. Rudy was perspiring already, even though he'd showered after shedding his work tux and changed into a cool cotton dress shirt and khakis. He was relieved when the receptionist led him into Jensen's normal-looking office and not some sort of interrogation room from a TV detective show. Rudy had been to a number of places he didn't want to be since Bee left him — the funeral parlor, a cheesy hotel bar on an Internet date — but this had to top them all.

Jensen stood, shook Rudy's hand across the desk.

"Thank you for coming in." His hand was warm but dry, his handshake firm.

"Did I have a choice?" Rudy thought of Jensen's stacked-up phone messages. How just the sight of the business card the detective had presented at the store gave him heartburn. *Murder.* He took one of the two chairs before the big faux wooden desk.

"Your cooperation is helpful." To be fair, Jensen seemed gentler in his own surroundings. Maybe it was the mortification of having a detective show up at your place of work that had made him seem more severe upon their first meeting. In front of Sasha, the Prada ladies, and a sea of strangers and well-dressed mannequins.

Jensen's office had thin, worn, pine-green carpet and cinder-block walls that had been painted an institutional Silly Putty color. The one window in his office looked like it hadn't been cleaned in a year. Through it lay a view of a driveway, a chain-link fence, then a park.

"Nice place ya got here." Rudy was not a

sardonic person by nature. But it was all he knew to say in this outrageous situation.

At that moment the woman from reception came in to offer them coffee or Cokes.

"The two staples of our diet." Jensen smiled. "I'd recommend the Coke at this hour."

The receptionist agreed to get them two Cokes. She quickly returned with cans and straws, and Rudy had to admit the cold beverage soothed his nerves. He realized now that his agitation had made him clench his jaw to the point of a headache. He massaged his temples with one hand, while the other gripped the cold Coke.

"I'd just like to ask you a few questions about your wife, about her work." Jensen leaned forward, elbows and arms on his desk, hands clasped.

Rudy nodded. *How about I ask* you *a question or two?* he thought, the dialogue from random cop shows replaying in his mind.

"Did your wife like her job?"

"Loved it. Was great at it. Was beloved in return by everyone in the hospital." Rudy felt irked by the fact that Jensen didn't know this.

"Of course," Jensen agreed mechanically. "Did she ever say anything about a fellow coworker who seemed troublesome?"

170

Rudy shook his head. "I don't believe so, no. She was funny, you know." He felt his voice speed up with defensiveness, defending Bee's stalwart honor. "We always traded stories about our days at dinner. Bethany's stories were often funny. But her humor . . . it was never at the expense of others."

"Sure," Jensen said, seemingly disinterested. His concern was a little too cool, too robotic. Had his line of work just numbed him into placidness as bland as the slightly lumpy, oatmeal-colored cinder-block walls surrounding him? "But did she ever express concern? Maybe if you think back, you'll remember something you didn't take seriously at the time."

Are you a human being, god damn it? Rudy wanted to shout. Rudy could not help the anger that coursed through him, slamming his Coke on the edge of Jensen's blotter before him. He hadn't meant to do this, the arm and hand just flailed and pounded on its own, causing Jensen to jump back in his seat a little.

"You asked me a question," Rudy said through gritted teeth, "and I answered it. I don't recall her being worried about any particular employee. She was head pharmacist; she trained many pharmacy techs and cashiers. It's a very difficult and detailed job. Some of the kids were surly, sure. But she was not a person anyone, *anyone,* would want to harm."

"I get that perfectly," Jensen assured Rudy. "But we are talking about a sociopath or a psychopath here. You must understand that I am not implying that your wife was in any way a target due to a flaw of hers. Or that either of you missed any warning signs that would have changed the outcome. Ironically, an admirable, lovable person may be a target in a situation like this. And we don't even know if that is the case."

"Great. It pays to be an asshole." Rudy gulped from his soda, anger making it feel as though his blood were bubbling in his head.

"Was there any troublesome employee in particular? In the last year she worked there?" Jensen looked a little desperate the more he leaned over his desk. "I'm not interrogating you. Please. I'm asking for your help, with anything you can remember. Anything that sticks out."

Now Rudy did remember. "Some kid with a cowboy name and an attitude. He was a good worker but a handful. You know, she shared that on one particular bad day that she had."

"Bad day?"

"Bad day," Rudy snapped. "Ever had one?" *Help,* he tried to tell himself.

Jensen rubbed his face. Rudy imagined this was a grueling day for the detective, too. The guy looked tired. Circles under his eyes, puffy and brownish and droopy all at the same time. There was a Texas-shaped stain of something on his tie. Lunch at his desk, probably. One of those deals where you try to blot it out and it just gets bigger. Rudy wasn't sure why, but it was the thought of Jensen trying to get his lunch off his tie that made him feel for the guy. And the photos — turned at an angle so that Rudy could see — of a wife and kids. Three kids, all under the age of teenagers, it looked like.

Rudy picked up the photo closest to him, of the whole gang and looked at it. Tears pricked the corners of his eyes. Jesus, was it possible to be any more emotional? Wanting to flip this guy's desk over one minute and crying at a family of kids with dubious haircuts the next?

"These yours?" he asked Jensen, his voice lowering.

"Yep. My wife, oldest boy, and the Irish twins."

"Just imagine . . ." Rudy tried to keep his voice even and calm. "Just imagine that your wife didn't wake up one morning. She seemed fine, then you couldn't rouse her, then paramedics are busting into the joint. Then she's dead."

Jensen nodded slowly.

"You get through that. Through the nightmare daymare eerily unreal days. The funeral, casseroles, condolence cards, flowers, and then, then —" Rudy's hand involuntarily smashed the desk again, the side of his pinky finger feeling bruised and broken — a pain that shot to his heart, equally bruised and broken. "*Then* come the platitudes. AT LEAST SHE DIDN'T FEEL ANY PAIN! AT LEAST SHE DIED PEACEFULLY! HAVE YOU EVER SEEN A DEAD PERSON?"

Jensen nodded, of course he had. The receptionist peeked in. Jensen gave her a nod to say everything was okay.

"THEY DO NOT LOOK PEACEFUL!"

"I know," Jensen agreed. "I know. Even a death causing zero exterior trauma to the body. I know. I'm sorry. Your wife seems like she was really, really lovely."

"She was." Rudy massaged his fist-pounding hand, unable to look up at Jensen, not wanting him to see the tears — tears, always betraying him! — creeping down his face, catching in the stubble on his chin.

"I didn't realize she managed the entire pharmacy."

"What are you *doing* then if you're not gathering that kind of info?" Rudy looked up, quickly wiping the tears away with his fingertips.

"We are looking into every aspect of this suspect's life — place of residence, family, work history . . ."

Rudy nodded. Outside, a whistle rang out, and there was the cheer and chatter of children in the park beyond the fence. Rudy had finished his Coke. With his good hand he crunched the can.

"Listen, I know this isn't easy." Jensen rocked back in his chair, a tilting thing on wheels.

Rudy wanted to tell Jensen that he *did not* know, *could* not — but somehow he sensed now that the man across the desk had seen enough to know death all too well. And he was not a platitude guy.

"Especially given that it's a week away from the anniversary of your wife's death. Of Bethany's death."

It *was*? A year? Rudy was flustered. He studied the big calendar tucked into the blotter on the desk. He wanted to see the whole year, but there it was in big squares — the month of June, when Bee died. The cheerful California poppies blooming again, as though nothing had ever happened. The neighborhood kids with towels slung around their shoulders heading for the community pool swim-team practice as though nothing had ever happened.

"It is?" Rudy stared at the calendar as though imploring it to speak to him.

Jensen nodded.

It was. Eight days until June 6. One year. Bee wasn't out of town at a pharmacists' convention. She wasn't at her sister's in the Midwest. She wasn't at work that afternoon, wouldn't be home for dinner.

"Oh." Rudy's rage gave way to heaviness upon him. A leaden blanket over his shoulders, quicksand around his legs, his arms as heavy as logs, his hands burning and aching from hitting the desk. A fog rolled into the office, making the beige walls blurry. Beyond the window the kids had been herded in from the park, dark clouds and asphalt taking their place.

Jensen bent his head to meet Rudy's eye. "Listen, I'll have more questions about this one fellow your wife found difficult, but not today. I have a lead into what he's been up to that might help, and I want to explore that first. The fact that you made that connection to him was very, very helpful. I think you are speaking of the same fellow."

"What's the kid's name?" Rudy's urge to kill this employee, murder him right back, had been reconstituted as sheer despair.

"I can't divulge that, but we have him in custody, so there's no need for you to worry."

Worry. Rudy wasn't worried. He was sick. He had the flu. He wanted to crawl under the desk, under the 1950s-style tile floor, and sleep until forever.

Jensen reached his hand across the desk. As Rudy rose to shake it, he held on for too long, using it as leverage to get up out of the soul-sucking chair. They exchanged goodbyes, Jensen repeating sorry and thank you and promises to get to the bottom of all this.

Rudy nodded in response to each of these statements, the magnet under the floor too strong to allow for speech. One year. Bee gone. He had raged into the place like a lion and was going out like a lamb. Like an ox. He plodded out of the detective's offices and slowly down the grim hallway, the double doors at the other end too far away, too far away from his bed, which was all Rudy could think of now. His side, Bee's side, all of their pillows and the duvet. He missed being married. The living with your best friend part of it. The finishing each other's sentences one moment and angrily zinging Scrabble tiles perilously close to your partner's eye the next. Sharing the secretly winging-it fear of parenting with whispers in bed at night.

"She got her period today," Bee had informed Rudy late one evening.

"She what? She's twelve!"

"Girls are starting a little younger now, they say. Hormones in the milk, improved prenatal care, who knows." They were watching a terrible comedy on television, talking during the commercials.

"Should I say something to her?" Rudy had asked.

Bee bit her lower lip, thinking. "Don't *congratulate* her."

Rudy decided to spare his daughter the mortification of old Dad chiming in on this life event and just gave her an extra tight hug that night. Oh, but how he'd wept openly when he gave CeCe away at her wedding. Everything about their daughter had been a funny, frustrating, maddening, delightful surprise.

Right now, Rudy was going to drive home, skip dinner, skip turning on the lights, skip the record player and cabernet, and head straight upstairs and under the covers, cocooning into the gentle center of his marital bed.

13

"Papa?" Something was wrong. CeCe hadn't called Rudy "Papa" since she was a little girl. She must be in danger. He hadn't saved Bethany. Now he must rescue his daughter! Where *was* she?

"Papa?" She was playing in the white water of the surf, which only came up to her waist. Every tenth wave or so, a big swell rolled in that could knock a child tumbling. It wasn't enough to watch from his towel. Rudy had better wade into the water with her. Breakers always came in a series, increasing in size, the largest startling the swimmers. But then there were rogue waves — anomaly monsters that could sweep a person from the shore to their death. (Or maybe CeCe was trapped between the steps of the ladder on the slide in their backyard?)

Something — the surf! — shook Rudy's shoulder. He tugged away from its grip, trying to wade through a strong undertow. Why had he let her swim alone? What was *wrong* with him?

"DAD!" A statement this time. The signature tinge of disdain.

Rudy was in trouble.

He opened his eyes. He'd been sleeping. In bed! During the day.

Cecilia had her back to him now, opening the curtains. Sharp shoulder blades, expert creases ironed into the sleeves of her brown cardigan. The afternoon pierced Rudy's head. He sat up, combing his fingers through his hair, smiling, hoping he looked alert.

"It's two o'clock." Cecilia winced at this unfortunate fact, as though it were a bad grade on his report card.

In the days following his chat with Detective Jensen, Rudy had gone from catnaps in the afternoons — something hailed by Bethany as healthy — to sleeping in later and later. Getting up to make toast, which he ate back in bed. By Friday, he was sleeping whenever he didn't have to work, and had stopped changing out of his pajama bottoms and T-shirt. A few days he called in sick.

At work, Rudy could tell that Sasha was clearly concerned. They had only had one *real* date. But it seemed to hold such promise. It felt like a lifetime ago, when it had only been a week — and now she met him at the stairs every day during her break, shyly asking what she could do to help shake him out of his doldrums. A movie? She was a wonder to Rudy, but those brief moments of contact brought him a big lift then plunged him into shame and despair for being so disheveled, so suddenly incoherent. He found himself ducking out of their typically lively chats sooner than he wanted to. It was like he was lost on the freeway now, and couldn't find the exit back to his old self.

Hell, he couldn't even read anymore. Concentration had become so fleeting. Where once there had been concentration, now there were moths and flies, flittering, fluttering, landing too briefly on the words in the pages of his books. The same page over and over and over each night before turning out the light. The inability to focus, the forgetting to buy milk. He feared the worst — dementia, Alzheimer's — then decided it would be a relief to not remember that he'd ever even known his exquisite wife. Once the light was out, he lay there, his thoughts the only moths now, just hanging there limply, shedding that weird mushroomy dust. Sometimes he'd give up on drifting off, flick the light back on and just stare at the wall. He hated the wall. He loved the wall, the color Bethany chose to paint their bedroom — the very palest celery. Over the weekend, he went from sleeping all the time to not being able to sleep at all. He'd always been a heavy sleeper. (Someone who might snooze through a person's death, say. *Jackass.*) Now he slept lightly, watchfully.

On Monday, he dragged himself to Dr. Martin, his physician, (not Bee's quack!) who prescribed Ambien as a temporary measure. Rudy only took it one night — just before turning out the light, as instructed — and fell asleep soon after. He awoke the next morning in that only-moments-later way as if emerging from surgery. Only there was no grogginess. There was nothing. It had been a dreamless sleep. He had the uneasy feeling of not knowing where the sleep had *gone.* There was always a little twinkling of something left in your brain when you first woke up. He knew he hadn't gotten up and ordered a llama on the Internet or fixed and eaten raw pancake batter. But still the feeling spooked him. The pills hardly felt like a grief remedy. Ambien was probably a good medication to have on a trip, when you had jetlag. On your retirement to Italy with your lifelong partner who knew all about art history, Rudy thought bitterly.

"I won't be bitter," he said aloud to the room. It was a promise to Bethany. He was not one of those people who would go to her grave and speak to her. He'd never been religious. But now he envied these people. It was a ritual, after all. And just as good, he imagined, and far cheaper, than talking to any shrink. He once saw a family picnicking at a gravesite on Memorial Day and thought how purely un-morose this was. He'd had the urge to wave to them, which would have been ridiculous, of course, but he'd felt such admiration for their outing.

"I'm just really worried about you." CeCe, sitting on the bed beside him now. She had been talking for a number of minutes. Rudy didn't want to let on that he'd missed whatever else she'd said. She gently rubbed his shin through the covers. She scooted closer to him. It concerned him that her tone was void of any impatience or irritation now — that it was so empathetic. Empathy wasn't a Girl Scout badge CeCe had earned.

Rudy sipped water from the glass by his nightstand. Again, he was ashamed of how unkempt he was, *unbathed.* Surely he had bad breath, maybe even smelled badly in general. But the sadness, and the magnet in the center of the bed, conspired to make the shower seem miles away. His mouth felt mossy. Again he tried to pat his hair into place, but there wasn't any patting to be done really, because it was greasy and stuck to his head. His hand brushed the sharp stubble on his chin. He saw himself through his daughter's eyes, and frankly was surprised she didn't look more horrified.

"I'm fine," he insisted. "Become a bit of a night owl." He sat up further on the pillows, tried to make his voice jolly.

"The store said you called in sick."

"Stomach bug," he fibbed.

CeCe nodded. The long silence was like a dripping faucet in Rudy's head.

"I can't sleep," he finally confessed. "Then, during the day, I can't stay awake."

"I understand." CeCe spoke as though addressing a good but off-kilter employee. "Which is why Dr. Martin would just like to admit you to the hospital long enough to get some rest, have some tests done, rule a few things out. Perhaps try some medications? Mainly get some rest."

"What? Who gets rest in a hospital?"

"Well, as I was explaining, he and I were talking and he's very concerned and would like to admit you today."

Admit? Today? Were those the words Rudy had missed while struggling to wake up?

"To the . . . hospital?"

CeCe stood, crossed her arms over her slender belly, nodded. "It won't be for long. And I'll come every day." She paused, added, "Dad. Missing work, daytime sleeping? And I see your refrigerator and cupboards . . ." She trailed off.

"CeCe, darling. I love you. However, you are not my parole officer."

As he set his feet on the floor — socks mismatched — Rudy could see that his stalwart daughter's eyes were filling with tears. One escaped onto her cheek and she quickly brushed it away. Her hands were small and red and chapped. He wanted to rub them between his to warm them. The last time he'd seen CeCe cry was at her mother's funeral, and before that — well, he couldn't remember.

He stood and gave her a light hug, worried again about not having showered.

"Honestly, sweetheart. I promise you I'm all right." Bethany hadn't even been admitted to the hospital, and she'd *died!* Why did Rudy need to go? What tests couldn't be done in a lab or with an MRI? "Oh! And I've just *had* a bunch of tests," he pointed

186

out. He remembered now that he'd had the checkup that CeCe and Spencer had insisted upon after Bee's frighteningly sudden death. Aside from low sodium indicating perhaps an electrolyte imbalance, low magnesium, and a slightly elevated pulse, Rudy was in pretty good shape.

His pajama bottoms were sweatpants, the top a long-sleeved cotton Jingle Bell Fun Run tee from a Goodwill bag when Bethany had last cleaned out their closet. She'd died before having a chance to take the bags in, and instead of doing laundry, Rudy "shopped" from them, reaching in and putting on whatever was his. Now he donned his moccasin slippers, and headed for the bathroom, where he peed, brushed his teeth, took a long hot shower with a shave, and changed into the jeans and polo shirt he was grateful to find his daughter had hung from the back of the bathroom door. He emerged feeling refreshed, and made a pep rally–like pitch for brunch.

"C'mon!" he declared too loudly. "I'll make you eggs Benedict!"

"Pretty soon it'll be suppertime," CeCe said softly.

"Good thing this establishment serves breakfast all day." He clapped his hands together. When you got right down to it, being mentally fit was something you could pull off in bursts — like acting in the school play.

His daughter smiled weakly and left the room ahead of him. As he started down the stairs, she made her usual tour of the house to look at and cradle and touch all of the pictures of her mother — on walls and end tables, the refrigerator, tucked between the glass and frames of mirrors. Rudy had sprinkled more photos of Bee all around the house since her death, but at CeCe's place she'd only hung two additional photos — black-and-white portraits of her mother in college — as though she were on a grief diet. Rudy wondered if there was anything his daughter wasn't disciplined about. It was a funny feeling as a parent — being proud, filled with loving admiration, and also a little afraid of this perfect child.

The eggs in the refrigerator were expired, but not too expired, Rudy was pretty sure. There wasn't any milk, but by some miracle there were English muffins and a stick of butter. A package of bacon in the meat drawer! He got out two frying pans. He put on an apron, turned on the radio, and set some coffee brewing.

"Smells good." CeCe nodded at the pan

on the stove as Rudy layered in strips of bacon.

"Well, I had lunch," she said, her tone suddenly a bit nervous. "But I'll join you." She took out placemats and silverware and started setting the kitchen table. "Napkins?"

"Bachelor," Rudy sighed, pointing at the paper towels. Bee had a system where everyone had his or her own napkin ring, so you could tell which was your linen napkin. But the rings lay empty in the basket on the side table now, the napkins all dirty somewhere. Rudy loved, yet somehow didn't have the heart to keep up with, Bee's day-to-day household customs.

"It's not like the booby hatch," CeCe explained, her voice serious, apologetic. "It's the medical-psych floor."

Rudy held a strip of bacon dangling from his fingertips. "The *what*?"

Since Bethany's death, Rudy had become a connoisseur of worst-case scenarios. He worried about all the terrible things that could go wrong or happen to a person — ran these scenarios over and over in his head during the insomnia. Car accidents, hiking tragedies. He'd convinced himself it wasn't safe to take a shower while living alone. He'd remembered a story about a shaving cream can exploding and killing a woman.

189

"As I was saying." CeCe took ChapStick from her purse, dabbed it on her lips a bit excessively. "At Stanford. The medical-psych ward — well, people go for all kinds of things."

The bacon popped and snapped, and a spray of fat burned Rudy's wrist. "Dammit!" he shouted at the pan. The heat was too high. *I can't even cook goddamned bacon and eggs for my daughter on a Sunday afternoon.* Rudy felt a wave of self-hatred like nausea. Then it was interrupted by another thought. Was it even Sunday?

"Well, Dr. Martin will admit you ahead of time and you can go straight up to the unit — it's very private. He and I have been talking, and he's let me know that there's a bed available this afternoon. They're holding it." She folded sheets of paper towels into triangles, creased and creased them again. Arranged forks and knives over them. "You'll get back on a regular schedule. Depression is very common after the loss of a loved one, Dad, especially a spouse."

Rudy thought CeCe sounded like one of those TV ads on late at night — the plaid lady blending into the plaid couch, suddenly getting up and smiling after taking the advertised pills. Rudy did not feel like a plaid sofa, as depressing a piece of furniture as that might be. And Dr. Martin was *his* doctor. CeCe wasn't even his patient! This was certainly a violation of privacy, his daughter always thinking everyone needed to rise to her standards or the earth would crash into the sun.

"What about HIPPA?" he asked. "And *what* is *rest* a euphemism for? Because we all know that *rest* is the last thing you get in the hospital. Besides, it was your mother who clearly needed medically ordered rest. But we all missed that one, didn't we? Let her work so many hours, always standing, never complaining. We missed that one, and we lost her, and now you want to commit *me*?"

"What, Dad, *no.*" Cecilia's eyes filled with tears again, and she rushed toward the stove, trying to hug him.

He took a step away from her, holding out the bacon tongs as though he were ready to joust.

She didn't know it, but Rudy harbored more criticisms of himself than his daughter could dish out in a lifetime, because there was no one who hated Rudy more than Rudy when it came to the loss of his beautiful wife's life.

"Let's look at reality: I *lost* my real job, and your mother went on working herself to death so she could get her hospital pension while I worked at my kooky part-time idiot job."

Women adore him at Nordstrom, Bethany had always bragged at parties or when they ran into friends, exaggerating the regard in which he was held at the department store. He felt silly now for having appreciated that praise after his humiliating layoff.

"You want to commit me to the nuthouse? Fine." He turned off the heat under the eggs, the yolks of which were becoming a little too solid.

CeCe gripped the back of a kitchen chair as though it were a towel she was trying to wring out. "It's not the nuthouse," she said in an almost-whisper. "Not the cuckoo's nest."

"I'll go, but I am *not* losing my mind." Who was he kidding? He had already lost his mind. It was as though he'd left it in the car trunk or piano bench. He felt that absentminded, that blank and lonely. His mind had become a haunted house. Sleeping all day unbathed in sour old Goodwill bag clothes? Christ, he didn't even know what day it was now.

Rudy had always been absentminded — a trait Bee compensated for. What was Cecilia's definition of losing it, anyway? Laundering your ChapStick? Putting the milk away in the cereal cupboard? Rudy was guilty on two counts there. He'd accidentally laundered a large load of nothing but water and soap. During the worst draught in one hundred years — before he lost Bee. He remembered her chiding him sweetly. "Composing a sonata in that bright mind of yours, no doubt," she'd insisted, kissing his cheek, forehead, and hair in a signature display of affection he'd appreciated and taken for granted at the same time. Isn't that what marriage was? For better and for granted . . . *Sweetheart, not right now, let me finish this one page, episode, email.* Sure, Rudy had once put the Dustbuster away in the refrigerator. CeCe could write that into her little report to Dr. Martin. It was as though his daughter had come out of the womb clutching a clipboard. But, honestly, was there a more useless appliance on the planet than a Dustbuster? Refrigeration could only improve upon its feeble performance. Why was Rudy so irritated — no, *angry* — with his daughter?

Okay, sure, every day by at least noon he was certain he was, indeed, collapsing into insanity, but this was not for his compulsively flawless daughter to determine.

"Nobody says you're losing your mind,"

CeCe said softly. "Thank you for going in, going in and just, just, just getting checked." For a brief time as a child CeCe had stuttered. Every so often it came out — always shocking Rudy, because he couldn't ever remember her being anything but perfect. "They have a bed available tonight. We just go to the ER, but they take us right back and admit you. It's completely private."

Rudy served up the plates, watching his daughter's face as he did so. He could see she was genuinely worried, her eyes red around the rims from crying, the circles beneath them as purple and delicate as plum skin.

He thought of one word: *burden.* He had become a burden to his child. He sighed. Certainly he wouldn't trouble her with the Detective Jensen situation now. This was hardly the time.

"Don't worry, sweetie, I'll go. Thank you for all the work you've done."

He gathered himself, breathed in calm. It was easier to think of this trip to the hospital if it was for CeCe. What had he done for his daughter since her mother died, anyway? He hated himself for just moments ago wanting to shake her by her slender shoulders — the familiar knobs at the top like finials. For wanting to shout, "GRIEVE MY WAY!"

"I got a list from the doc of what to pack," she added more cheerfully. "You can bring your laptop and everything."

They sat down together and ate, both of them clearly hungry by now. No eggs Benedict. Just eggs and toasted muffins and bacon and thankfully juice from an unopened carton.

Rudy covered the top of the carton with his hand.

"Guess the sell-by date."

"1974," CeCe said through a mouthful of eggs, a bit of her lopsided smile even showing.

"No, smarty pants, next week. So there."

"I probably bought it." CeCe slathered half a muffin with jam.

"You've got me there," Rudy agreed. The sun was setting and they were eating breakfast and then they were going to the hospital. To the nuthouse, booby hatch, medical-psych whatever.

Afterward they loaded the dishwasher, Rudy hugged his daughter and kissed the top of her head. Then he wordlessly climbed the stairs back up to his bedroom. She followed along, to help pack his bag. He planned on wearing a dress shirt and V-neck sweater. He wasn't sure what lay in store for him, but he was certainly going to dress properly today (no freaking tuxedo!). Even if he was going to the psych ward.

■ ■ ■ ■

II

■ ■ ■ ■

14

"Why don't you take the place by the window, Dad?" CeCe suggested.

Just hours into his stay at Stanford, Rudy had to admit, the hospital's psych floor, though not fancy, was . . . nice enough. Not the bleak snake pit he'd imagined. His fairly large room had two neatly made beds separated by a curtain. The signature light blue waffled blankets matched the pale blue walls. The psych ward seemed like any other hospital setting. Except there wasn't any life-or-death paraphernalia hanging from the ceiling or walls, no needles or crash carts or even the smell of rubbing alcohol, unless you counted the hand sanitizer on the wall beside the door to the room.

"Gel in gel out!" a cheerful sign by the door reminded entrants. Rudy and CeCe obeyed on their way in.

"Sure." Rudy agreed to the space by the window, wanting to seem agreeable —

compliant. The window was expansive, the entire length of the wall at the far end of the room, so that the person in that bed had a view of trees, sky, clouds, and the busy parking lot below. Ambulances and cars dashed up to the ER.

The nurse stood between the two beds, biting the corner of her lip with a hesitation that perplexed Rudy.

"Do you feel safe by the window, Rudy?" The nurse was young, with a long black braid and purple scrubs dotted with daisies. She was serious, but kind. Rudy realized that the staff must know from his admittance papers that he was a fairly recent widower, with "unspecified" depression, according to his family doctor. (A year was recent, how dare the platitudes imply otherwise!) Okay, he had been having difficulty with self-care lately. Apparently sleeping all day on Sunday and eating toast for dinner every night indicated this. In recent days his desire to cook had been downgraded to toast. Yet, honestly, was there a more perfect food than toast?

When they'd gotten to the hospital, they met with an admitting psychiatrist in the ER. CeCe added details to Rudy's answers to the doctor's questions, stating that her dad couldn't get out of bed sometimes.

"Well, I *can* get up," Rudy argued. He didn't want the doctor to think he was physically incapacitated, even though the long Sunday sleeps were more restful than his nighttime tossing and turning, when he couldn't stop picturing Bee, dead, in her nightgown. About how she hadn't looked peaceful. Peaceful was falling asleep with a good book spread across your chest. Closing your eyes and tilting your face up to the sun for a warming moment. Dead, gone forever, was different.

When CeCe stepped out to go to the restroom, Rudy had tried to explain to the admitting psychiatrist what he'd experienced with the PA system where he worked, and that it wasn't a hallucination. The paging system — always calling out people's names — now wanted him to do something about his wife's shoes.

"I sound certifiably insane." He shook his head, rubbing the fine cuffs of his old wool pullover sweater. At home, ashamed, he'd dressed as though he were going to a neighborhood cocktail party — a crease-free dress shirt and sweater straight from the dry-cleaning bags. As soon as he'd stepped onto the ward, he imagined the crisply attired Men's Department headless mannequin quipping at his outfit: *For the nuthouse?*

Honestly!

"Your wife's shoes?" the psychiatrist asked, not at all judgmentally.

Rudy nodded. "I thought perhaps she had to special order some at the store and now they needed picking up. But I checked the Shoe Department, and the woman at the HR office upstairs said that no one had really paged me. But those monotonous pagers, you know? Please tell me you've noticed them."

The kind doctor said that he himself couldn't recall hearing the store's pages, but they must have been disconcerting. "Department stores and the whole dang mall are simply overwhelming," the doc added. "And grief does weird things to us."

Rudy liked the unclinical word *weird,* and the inclusive *us.* The doctor didn't hide his clipboard from Rudy — they both could see all the notes made. With his clean-smelling hands, under "DIAGNOSIS:" the shrink wrote *major depressive disorder — complicated by grief.* He showed this to Rudy and explained that it was common, as well as natural, let alone just plain understandable after such a traumatic, life-altering event. The words *common* and *natural* were heartening.

Now, upstairs on the unit, Rudy set his

bag on the chair next to the window-side bed.

"You feel safe . . . by the window?" the nurse repeated, sliding a tray with a sandwich and a little carton of cranberry juice onto the revolving hospital tray table. Later, Rudy would discover that this was the best feature of the room. It was like a good airplane seat, with its extensions and compartments and ability to go up and down.

Oh, *safe.* Right. It dawned on him that this window worry meant *suicide risk.* He peered out the metal-framed window, which he couldn't even imagine how to open. Plus, they were only on the second floor.

"Yes," he smiled. "Safe. Thank you. Even if I were to muster opening that window and jumping out, I'd probably only break an arm and then have to crawl right back into the hospital via the emergency room." He nodded out to the ambulances.

It was clear CeCe did not find this one bit funny. In fact, Rudy could see his daughter's eyes well with tears. She sniffled, looked away.

The nurse's lips turned up at the corners just a little. "That's about the long and short of it, but we don't like to take any chances. We want you to be safe."

"The window is nice," he replied. "Thank

you." He followed this with an apology to CeCe.

"It's okay," she said, as the nurse hustled out of the room again. "I'm just scared, Dad."

Rudy couldn't recall ever hearing these words from his daughter. Not even during childhood. Not while watching *The Wizard of Oz,* or when their house back east shook with the crackling boom of giant thunderstorms in the summer. During these storms she would bring her sleepover cotton sleeping bag and place it on the floor beside her parents' bed, but it was always with that dignified, balletic posture and lower lip protruding slightly, not in a pout, but in a show of brave defiance.

He hugged his daughter to his chest now, and she let him. Really let him. Her faint perfume smelled of coriander and dryer sheets; suddenly Rudy wanted to weep. But for once — *you dumb sod,* he thought — he needed to hold it together, for his daughter.

"Your old man's going to be just fine," he insisted, feeling a bit helpless. CeCe's eyes welled with tears again. What if all the crying she hadn't done in her entire lifetime came right now? Of course she'd cried at her mother's funeral. Cried with more abandon when the last guest had left after the gathering that followed at the house. Spencer had held her tightly, the smell of the medical disinfectant soap on his hands always apparent even to Rudy. He was slim, but sturdy. A rock. An inflexible rock — not the medical student who had given CeCe piggybacks through the quad, the two of them tumbling into the leaves, laughing and kissing. Back then, he'd loosened her up. Now he seemed uptight around her.

Rudy wanted to make a joke to lighten the mood, but his first attempt at humor over being admitted to the psych ward had bombed. He wished Bee were there.

Bethany's shoes. Bethany's shoes. The words shot into Rudy's head as intrusively as a smoke alarm. He felt the overwhelming urge to shout them out. It was a sort of humor hysteria that had come over him in the past forty-eight hours.

"I'm fine." He shook CeCe gently as he hugged her. "What about you, hunh? Hospital not the easiest place in the world to hang out, is it?"

"Spencer should be here," she said bitterly. Then she wiped her cheeks with the backs of her hands, forced a smile. "You're in good hands," she confirmed, digging into her immaculate green leather bag — it was as big as a briefcase almost, but surprisingly empty. She pulled out a packet of tissues and blew her nose and wiped her eyes. "I'm silly," she snuffled.

"You need to be *more* silly." Rudy kissed her on the forehead.

"This I know," she said. "From Spencer." She raised her eyebrows, her freckled forehead bearing weary wrinkles. "*And* my daughter. How can a four-year-old know that you have no sense of humor?"

"Oh, honey." Rudy had always hated himself for worrying that Spencer would tire of his daughter's hyperefficient, control-freak ways. But she did such a good job at work, at home, with Keira. Rudy was so proud of CeCe. Had he not conveyed how proud he was of her? *BEE!* he wanted to shout. *Family meeting!* They'd never had a family meeting, but it seemed time for one now. With his wife, who was the best of both Rudy and CeCe — she would straighten them both out.

CeCe looked around the room, giving the not-half-bad nod of approval.

"Honey, you are *the best* mother."

To Rudy's surprise, CeCe kicked off her shoes, plopped on the bed, and took a big bite of his sandwich. He nestled beside her, scooping up the other half of the turkey-on-wheat lunch. The small bag of potato chips

206

cracked with a loud pop as he opened it, making CeCe jump.

"Yeah, not really," she mumbled. "I'm not fun. It's true. You should see what some of these other mothers come up with. Ha," she laughed through a mouthful of sandwich. "Maybe I should check in and be your roommate."

"For the record," Rudy said, pointing the open chip bag to her, "that was a joke. Sense of humor confirmed." Bee, no doubt, would have giggled with them.

"Would you like another juice?" the nurse asked, bustling back in with a contraption on wheels that had a computer atop it, and a tray that stretched beyond a small keyboard to include room for little medication cups and a pink plastic pitcher. Alongside this traveling station were a blood pressure cuff and some other nonthreatening-looking gear on one side, with a little basket on the other.

CeCe pointed to a bottle of water in her efficient bag. "No thanks. And I've got to go." She leaned back on the pillows.

"Since you're eating," the nurse said, "I'm going to take your bags and go through them just to make sure you don't have any scissors or clippers or razors. It's fine to have them; we just keep them at the nurse's station for you. You may sign them out any time after your first twenty-four hours." Rudy imagined clipping himself to death with nail clippers. Where would one begin? Oddly enough, he'd felt better in these first surreal two hours at the nuthouse than he had since Bee died. Humor. He saw humor in things for the first time in a year. Granted, it was a hysterical, nervous humor, and it was killing him that he couldn't share every bit of this experience with Sasha over dinner, but he wanted to laugh. Yet he wasn't sure that this was a good thing. It might not only upset his daughter, but also alarm the doctors, and frighten the other patients. What if he burst into hysterical, maniacal laughter once he ventured out of his room — like those lunatic characters you see in the movies?

"Your computer bag and phone and books you are welcome to keep. We want you to come to all the groups, but you're welcome to use your computer. We prefer that you minimize work emails, however. It's better if patients watch something on it at night or listen to an audiobook on your phone. We want you to socialize a bit, too. Eat meals in the dayroom with everyone else, and don't isolate yourself. Okay?"

"He's a professional concert pianist,"

CeCe said.

"Hardly concert," he told the nurse. "Department store."

"Okay, Dad, I'm going." CeCe stood and resumed her typical briskness, brushing crumbs from her slacks, pulling her top taut. She slipped her shoes back on, grabbed her designer bag, and kissed her father's forehead and both cheeks. For once, he was relieved to see his daughter's signature businesslike nature return. She patted his leg before disappearing out the door, chirping "Gel out!" as she went.

"I love you!" he called after her green bag. He wished she didn't have to leave.

When the nurse returned, she had even more information — so that Rudy would be prepared for the next day. Rounds were made by the doctors in the mornings, before, during, and after breakfast, which was from seven-thirty to eight-thirty. The first group didn't start until ten, giving patients plenty of time to take their meds, have their vitals taken, meet briefly with their docs, eat, and wash up. Although, she pointed out, it was perfectly fine to attend meetings in sweats, even pajamas the first day.

No stiff rented tuxedo. "Thank you.

Thank you for all the information, it's helpful."

"I always say the scariest thing is the unknown," the nurse said matter-of-factly. "I hate to inundate people with too much information, but you can always ask me anything again tomorrow. We want you to feel reassured and focus on getting well."

"My wife died," he told her. Rearranging the crumpled napkins on his meal tray. The sound of his own voice saying this startled him. The fact of Bethany's death was still surreal.

The nurse nodded. "Sometimes we're just crushed by our own grief," she said, returning his bag and Dopp kit and rolling up the computerized gadget tray for taking his vitals. As she squeezed the blood pressure cuff, she continued, "It isn't something that ever really goes away necessarily. It *changes,* gets better and worse, but it might always be with you."

"Well, it was *almost a year ago already,*" Rudy said, a little chagrined, as though he should have manned up by now.

The nurse wagged her finger. "I'm telling you. The first anniversary is the worst. You're in shock, you want a refund, and you walk around like a zombie. It feels like your loved one might be on a trip, Bali, business

— who knows. Then *bam* that first anniversary descends and some of us just fall
apart."

"You understand," Rudy said.

"Lost a brother," she replied. "*And* I'm a
psych nurse." With this, she tapped her
temple and smiled.

15

Bee was upstairs still sleeping and Rudy was downstairs playing the radio quietly, a bit irritated by the morning guy and his sanctimonious announcing — as though only *he* knew a nocturne from a mazurka. Rudy smelled oatmeal, but he wasn't making oatmeal.

Weekdays he cooked the breakfast she liked most, but rarely had time to finish before setting off to work. Two soft-boiled eggs with buttered whole-wheat toast. First he put the eggs on, and then popped down the toast. He buttered and cut one slice into strips, then squares, placing them beneath the eggs (that way you got a bite of toast with each bite of egg); the other he cut in half and arranged on the edges of the plate. His mother had always done this for him and he considered it an act of love. Rudy's menu varied on weekends. Blueberry or apple pancakes. Real bacon. *Heart attack.*

212

He'd tried fixing made-to-order eggs for CeCe starting in junior high, but that girl was a picky eater — the opposite of low-maintenance Bee. Sometimes Rudy even wished his wife were a tougher customer, but boy, did she always appreciate the detail that went into preparing a meal, or even a snack!

Look at this! she'd exclaim when Rudy laid a plate before her. *It's lovely. Yum,* she'd muster as she ate, and *ohhh.*

CeCe viewed food as utilitarian. Meals were calculations of protein and calories that would keep her going through field hockey or a calculus exam without putting on weight. They were not to be enjoyed. Bee and Rudy's friends dealt with teens who would not buckle down and get serious about their studies or curfews or chores, and so the couple shied away from worrying aloud over their frighteningly diligent daughter. How unkind it would be to share with friends that they didn't think their daughter was a fun babysitter, or light-hearted party guest. (Those kids would *not* do their homework; CeCe would come home complaining about her babysitting charges: They'd wanted to make sundaes!) At this particular description of a Saturday night with the Wilson kids, Bee had had to hide behind the hall closet door, stuffing the corner of a mitten in her mouth to stop from laughing.

"I'm so sorry," Bee confessed, lamenting her parenting skills. "I think I gave birth to a forty-year-old and I'm terrible at this." Rudy hugged his wife until she promised that she believed she was a good, kind mother.

"It's not enough to get a 4.0," CeCe said, scoffing at her father's praise of her report card. Apparently you needed to get better than that these days, because so many kids were acing their AP classes — with A *pluses*.

"Darling, I promise you, you will be happy wherever you go to school, and you are going to have some great schools to choose from," Rudy insisted encouragingly, trying not to show his blooming concern that CeCe might collapse into a breakdown before she even got to write her first college application essay. What with her field hockey, ski club, French club, organized beach cleanups. (Could a child with a clipboard and whistle make friends?) Then their daughter met with her first failure: She did not make the swim team. Rudy had started swimming with her weekends to practice. By work on Monday his eyes were rimmed red and his nose stung from the chlorine. But she didn't make the team, and it was clear that as soon as this news had been delivered to her parents, it was not to be discussed further.

Rudy listened for the creak of the stairs as his wife started down, the pause she always took on the landing. The quiet clearing of her throat, something she did often in the spring when allergy season hit. That's how Rudy could always find her in a store. The syncopated clearing of her throat. "You've been coughing for two years," he told her once, slightly annoyed. Annoyed! Now he wished she were hacking in his ear.

Bee still hadn't come downstairs and that wasn't like her. Rudy worried she wasn't feeling well. Maybe she'd had *another* heart attack. Hopefully a milder one. Like an aftershock after an earthquake. Rudy started up the stairs two at a time to check on Bee, but he couldn't seem to reach the landing at the top. There were too many steps. Floors and floors of carpeted stairs, as though he were in a hotel. He called out Bethany's name. Where *was* she?

Rudy was back in bed now. He felt the warm, moist small of Bee's back, which had become padded with more flesh now that they were in their fifties. Both of them were thicker around the middle. In their thirties they'd spread out and sprawled around in their king-sized bed — a luxurious, grown-up purchase. In their forties they lumped in the middle, giving in to the trough that had slowly formed from their weight. Legs entwined. He liked to watch her back or side rising and falling under her worn pink nightgown.

He thought he might start swimming again to trim down and shape up. Then, when Bee retired, they could swim together. Turkey bacon and fresh fruit after morning laps.

For now he focused on his own rhythm, kicking off from the deep end of the pool. His arms sliced through the water, his mind floating away from the worry of how to pack up Bee's clothes and where to take them, instead picturing his elbows marking out a neat crawl stroke.

"Good morning, Rudy. Rudy? Can you try sitting up for me?"

That damn department store PA woman! Sucking the serenity out of a perfect moment. Although she was right: You did have to get out of bed before you could swim laps. Rudy swam to the surface, up through the blue-green water of the Y's pool, and clutched the pool's dry, porous cement edge. Rudy tipped back his head to see white, pockmarked square ceiling tiles above.

In a chair beside the pool — no, his bed? — sat a young man. A very young man, indeed, dressed in tan corduroys and a V-neck sweater, wearing a badge and holding a clipboard. He probably had one of those petitions to sign. Something earth-shattering when your arms were full of groceries in the parking lot outside the Whole Foods.

"Good morning, Rudy, I'm Quinn," the fellow said cheerfully. He held a Styrofoam cup with a straw in it. "Your assigned medical student. I'll be checking in with you once a day. Hey, and I'm a musician, too. I play the clarinet. You'll also meet with a resident once a day, and an attending psychiatrist. That's your treatment team."

This was a lot of information for anyone who hadn't even brushed his teeth yet. A tan table was pulled up beside the bed at eye level, its items coming into focus: a pink plastic pitcher, another Styrofoam cup with a straw, and a tiny plastic cup of pills. Rudy managed to sit up on one elbow, looking across the room to a whiteboard on the wall. Someone had written neatly in marker the date, a doctor's name, a nurse's name, a letter, and a number. Unit and floor? Right.

Rudy was in the hospital. The curtains were open, but only a little way, like a suggestion. Maybe sunshine would be okay now.

Quinn handed Rudy the cup with the straw. The ice water was heavenly inside his dry, sticky mouth. He closed his eyes. Hospital. Rudy was in the hospital. Psych ward. *Teaching hospital,* he remembered, knowing the drill from Bee. *Her* hospital. Rudy felt shy and exposed. He'd been to holiday parties with Bee's coworkers from these buildings.

Sleep, Rudy thought. *Sleep.* It seemed all of Quinn's information and the cup of pills and juice were enough for the day.

"How's your depression today?" Quinn asked.

Rudy pushed himself up onto the other arm, too. "Heavy? It's making it a little hard to tread water here in the deep end of the pool, Quinn," Rudy said.

Quinn scratched out a few notes. "And your anxiety?"

"It's making me want to go home and scream."

"Why do you want to scream?" Quinn asked.

"I don't know." Rudy sat all the way up, ran a hand over his lumpy hair, struggled for the right words. "It's like an itch. It's

218

not too bad. Don't worry. I won't scream."

"Well, if you need to, I'm sure we can work something out," Quinn said, finishing up his notes. Rudy imagined he might be one of those kids who followed one band around the country attending all their concerts — a kid who didn't want to grow up.

Rudy recognized his two antidepressants in the little clear plastic cup. Suddenly the capsules filled him with sadness and shame as he thought of Bee, at work downstairs on the first floor in the pharmacy. But she wasn't there and Rudy was up here. On the *psych* ward. He wasn't doing a very good job of being a widower. What a nuisance he must be for CeCe. He began to sniffle, as he pointed at the little vial of pills.

"Pharmacy," Rudy told Quinn. He could not express how the sight of the pills made him want to pull the waffled blue blanket up over his head and stuff it into his mouth to silence the scream that he felt like an itch, a sob, percolating in his chest.

"Your wife. She worked in the pharmacy." Quinn nodded.

It was funny, at the hospital the staff knew basic personal information that some might find intrusive. But Rudy found it a relief not having to explain everything. Not having to explain finally falling apart, falling into bed, as heavy and bloated as sandbags swelling to block floodwaters.

Quinn pointed at the cup of pills. "I understand. Trigger. That's a trigger. So we can get rid of it."

Rudy nodded, opening a little carton of cranberry juice that was also on his table, and swallowing all the pills at once with a refreshing tart swig of juice. The nurse had returned, watching to be sure Rudy got his medication, then handing him a graham cracker.

"It's good not to have an empty stomach," she told him.

Maybe what people needed to get well was this simple, Rudy mused. The words *I understand,* followed by a graham cracker. He thought that in the afternoon, during their free time, he might try out the piano in the dayroom. He might noodle around and work on a quiet tune called "Fuck Platitudes."

After Quinn left, the nurse came to take Rudy's vitals, then he met his assigned shrink. This left him little time to wash up. He did so quickly, pulling on a sweatshirt and black track pants from the top of his bag, brushing his teeth and splashing water on his face at the shared sink and mirror near the door to the room, then combing his hair, a hopeless spongy mess. He was careful to hang his hand towel and wash-cloth on a hook on one side of the mirror, should a roomie materialize for the other bed in the room.

Frankly, he didn't mind this pared-down version of his life. Not exactly freedom from his dead wife's belongings, but a tone of non-judgmental low pressure the unit conveyed.

As Quinn escorted Rudy to the dayroom, he felt embarrassed by his day-old beard and his cobbled together outfit — his navy sweatshirt from the science museum, worn over his pajama top, didn't even match his black track pants. He hadn't had time to change his white gym socks and was ashamed for some reason by his scuffed brown corduroy slippers, which CeCe had chosen for their hard soles. They should be at home, in his closet!

"I assure you," Quinn told him, pushing his thin, gold wire-rimmed glasses up on his nose, "many people are in their pajamas. Plus, I guarantee you'll wake up a little earlier each day, with more time to get ready if you want it. It's not the army, I promise."

Rudy had seen the community room the

evening before, only now the long table was populated with sleepy comrades quietly eating. His outfit anxiety dissipated as he saw that everyone was disheveled to some degree. They pushed their chairs about to make room for Rudy. As he sat down, a few of them introduced themselves and others just said good morning. These didn't look like whack-job *Cuckoo's Nest* droolers. These looked like everyone from Nordstrom shoppers, to overworked working stiffs, overwrought students, and people who were just, well, *tired.*

Clearly, everyone on the floor had been trying for some time to merely hold it together; now that they were in the nuthouse, they could let go a little — stop trying to pretend they were *okay!* Still, Rudy believed himself and his cohorts to be a fair sampling of the general population — citizens who'd just been T-boned by life. Broken by a family death or illness. Crushed by stress. Wrought with a predisposition for depression, anxiety, and serotonin run amok. Rudy now took umbrage at the descriptor "he looked like he just escaped a mental institution!"

Quinn explained that the kitchen had sent Rudy a generic breakfast for this first morning, but on his tray there was a form of choices to fill out for his coming meals. The table was scattered with sections from the *San Francisco Chronicle.* Sports pages and film reviews and crosswords that normalized the breakfast scene.

It was funny: The patients who clearly lived with others at home — who bore wedding rings or spoke of parents or family — complained that the eggs were lukewarm or the oatmeal was runny. Those who lived alone, were visibly depressed, and had no one to cook for them lifted the silver coverings over their plates and declared: "Eggs!" Rudy was in the latter group. He knew that the hospital kitchen workers must have gotten out of bed very early for the breakfast shift. It was nice that his tray had both scrambled eggs and oatmeal. It wasn't perfect, but it was hot, thanks to an insulated thermos bowl, and came with a little packet of raisins, brown sugar, and a carton of fresh milk. Not sour milk lingering at the back of the refrigerator stinking up the remaining bits of good food. Not withering apples from the crisper. No bread with corners of mold. No little cups of yogurt that had been your wife's and peered out at you daily, whispering: *expired, lonely.*

After breakfast, Rudy followed his cohorts

as they shuffled through the dayroom to a set of double locked doors leading to the lockdown side of the ward. They waited for an attendant to buzz them over. Rudy's side of the ward was medical-psych. He and his fellow unit mates weren't allowed to go beyond the end of the floor on either side of the U-shape from the nurse's station unless they were checking out against medical advice — patients on the lockdown side were in the hospital for a mandatory stay.

The mixed group of patients filed into a dayroom on the other unit. It was certainly nice enough, given its locked status. Tables that could seat four, potted palms, big windows. On the other side of the room was a large circle of armchairs, couches, and dining room chairs that could double for a group therapy or TV room. There were coffee tables and a tall cupboard filled with board games, cards, and old VHS movies. Here it was clear that anything went in the wardrobe department. After all, those in this group had clearly come in on the fly, against their will, or after an accident of some kind, self-inflicted mishaps included. People certainly hadn't packed their cruise attire.

Patients shuffled and stumbled in late, apologizing to the leader, who had introduced herself as Candace. She was soft-spoken but enunciated well, introducing herself again, pointing to the badge clipped to her sky-blue sweater, adding that she was a PhD therapist who specialized in cognitive behavioral therapy. A few more latecomers arrived, looking as though they'd been unwillingly rounded up.

"Thank you just for being here," she told them. Rudy was comforted by this statement. So what if you were in a cobbled together outfit of clothes and hospital pajamas and slippers and bed head? You showed up. Maybe it was Rudy's imagination, but suddenly the grumpier latecomers didn't look so unhappy to be in the room. He felt the weight of the air in the room clear, saw shoulders lift a little. If this was an accomplishment, who knew what you could do next?

While they were a motley-looking sleepy group — sweaters with pills and petrified smudges of food, and a few patients even dozed off — this didn't seem to bother Candace. In fact, she explained that some medications — especially when recently started — made it difficult to get up in the morning, but that just rising, eating a little something, and getting into the routine of coming to group was a big step. Rudy noticed one woman who lay on the floor, on a yoga mat, with an ice pack on her head, because she had a migraine.

Candace, who was reassuringly calm, rather than chipper, asked everyone to go around the room and tell the others his or her name and briefly how he or she was doing today. "It can be something very small, like 'I slept well.' "

Some patients were so shy they just mumbled their names while studying the floor and mechanically replied, "okay," in response to how they were feeling. Others launched into paragraph-long lists of worries and imprecations that Candace had a diplomatic, seamless way of kindly wrapping up so that they could move on.

When the woman next to Rudy reported, "The doctor said I shouldn't smoke crack with my asthma inhaler," a slumped man came to life with a bark of laughter, then covered his mouth.

The man shook his head, wagging his matted brown hair. "I'm not laughing at you," he told the woman. "I'm laughing with you. Or else I have to cry. I hope you feel better." He wore a huge cast on one of his arms that caused it to remain upright from the elbow on, dirty fingers emerging from where the cast ended just shy of his first knuckle.

Candace smiled as everyone chuckled. "Thank you, Kevin. That's right, we don't want to laugh at anyone," she said more seriously. "We don't want to laugh or make judgmental comments — or even give advice — just a few words of support go a long way." She thanked the smoking-with-asthma woman, who clutched a worn paper-back from the dayroom shelves, pushing it between her knees, looking shy, but un-offended.

When it came Rudy's turn to speak, his voice was husky and dry from his medica-tion. "I killed my wife," he blurted.

Suddenly all the fidgeting in the room stopped.

"Oh, I know that's not true," Candace said. "Tell us your name."

"Rudy. My wife died. She died of a heart attack and I could not save her. The para-medics came and they couldn't save her. She was already dead. She was dead when I woke up. I should have woken up when she got sick in the night. When whatever hap-pened . . . I should have woken up. I *talked* to her. I told her there were buds on the cherry tree outside our window, when she was *dead.* Buds! Who gives a shit!" Rudy felt his voice escalating to a near holler. Then he saw the kindness in Candace's green eyes and the sea of people, nodding or blinking, none of them alarmed or afraid or disapproving. Some of the nods even came knowingly.

Candace spoke of grief and sudden death and survivor's guilt and PTSD and survivor's guilt again. The murmurs among Rudy's cohorts were a soft, warm blanket around his shoulders.

A few days after Rudy met Kevin in group therapy on the lockdown side of the unit, he was moved to the medical-psych side, and became Rudy's roommate. As Kevin made his way down the hall with his arm bent and big cast raised in the air, he looked like the Statue of Liberty approaching. Rudy wondered if he'd put his fist through a wall or a window, or been in some sort of manly fight. Later, during a quiet lunch, he and Rudy got to talking. Kevin hadn't punched anything at all, but had tried to kill himself by cutting his wrists. He'd carved out a brutal vertical gash down the inside of his forearm with a buck knife. Before he could get to the second arm, he'd passed out. His poor sister discovered him and called the ambulance. He had surgery to repair his tendons then was released to the lockdown unit. His biggest concern was how he'd frightened his baby sister. The tenderness with which Kevin spoke about her touched Rudy. The group tried to make him feel less guilty about that fateful night. One thing the population seemed to have in common was self-loathing, which Candace said could be replaced with more positive thoughts. Not kittens and bunnies and bows, she promised, but the simple replacement thinking that was at the core of CBT. Rudy took notes, and hoped against hope that Candace was right.

A few days later, after lunch (which came awfully soon after breakfast when you considered that all they'd really done in between was sit and shuffle short distances), there was a message for Rudy on his cell phone. It was from Sasha, who was very worried about his sudden absence from work.

Rudy hadn't planned to tell her about his stay at the hospital. He'd called her after he was admitted, saying he was home with the flu. He could hear the concern in her voice when he said he wasn't well. "I can come over with soup," she said. "Don't be embarrassed about how you look — I've seen it all! My ex Gabor had many health problems."

"No, no," Rudy reassured her, "it's nothing like that." He sighed. The truth was, he didn't want to burden her. It was probably more burdensome to disappear on a person, though, to "ghost" her as CeCe had described. If they were ever to have a real relationship, Rudy should be honest.

During their free time after lunch and before occupational therapy, he returned Sasha's call. After they went over the details of how he was feeling — all of which were legitimate, he gave her the more precise picture — he was in the hospital. "I . . . I . . . had trouble getting out of bed." Grrr. This wasn't a diagnosis. "It's the first anniversary of Bethany's death and, well, CeCe came over and suggested that I recuperate with some help from doctors, and, well, the doctors thought I ought to do so, you know, be in the hospital." Rudy held his breath during the silence that followed.

"Oh, Rudy, are you okay?"

"Fine. It's only the psych ward." He realized how ridiculous this sounded and broke into nervous laughter, then sucked in his breath.

"Oh, Rudy, I *completely* understand. After Stefi's death, if I could have gone to the hospital, I'm sure it would have helped. I think I would have crawled to such a place."

The compassion in Sasha's voice was something Rudy knew, he *knew* was unique. Certainly you couldn't call up just any friend, especially one you just happened to be falling in love with, and tell them you were in the nuthouse and they'd get it. And her description of the other department store pianist had Rudy in stitches.

"He plays like Muzak . . . I don't know some seventies songs about sailing and he SANG. Terrible!"

This made Rudy go from pacing beside his nightstand as far as the phone cord would allow, to collapsing on his bed, laughing and trying to picture this. The store pianists weren't supposed to sing!

After giving Sasha the information about the hospital and answering her questions, they agreed to talk the next day.

After signing off with Sasha, Rudy considered whom else he should let know of his whereabouts. He thought of all the casseroles Bee's many friends had dropped off after her death. The frozen lasagnas. The bagels, cream cheese, lox, and OJ. Ready-made meals. One woman from Bethany's book group, Glenda — who was tall and always wore spotless white pantsuits and stylish shirts with big collars and big necklaces and heels that clicked intimidatingly fast along the floors of the house — came over and did Rudy's laundry, much to his chagrin. His boxers! She had a take-charge attitude and alarming speed, which made it impossible for Rudy to refuse her help.

"I know I'm barging in," she'd chirped, insisting Rudy show her the way to the hampers. There were piles, too. Unsorted piles of dirty clothes that had resulted in Rudy delving into those goodwill bags. Combined with the weight loss, he knew this wasn't a good look and imagined Glenda on the phone to CeCe as soon as she pulled out of the driveway in her mini Mercedes.

"Oh, this isn't anything to be ashamed of," Glenda insisted. "It's called grief. When my sister died at thirty-seven of ovarian cancer, I wouldn't ring hospice in to the apartment building to declare her dead so that the coroner could come and retrieve her body."

She turned to Rudy, who stood there speechless in sweats and a long-sleeved grad-school tee, thanking *God* he had showered that day — the first in many.

"Top that one." She smiled at Rudy, pointing a red fingernail at him. "Locking hospice out of the house."

"I'm so. I'm so." Rudy sat on the toilet

seat and covered his face with his hands so Glenda couldn't see that he was crying. "I'm so grateful."

But now Glenda wasn't someone who needed to know he was in the hospital. Rudy imagined her motoring in and mopping the ward's floors — which, frankly, you didn't want to look at too closely. There were splotches of pee in the bathroom, and smudges of spinach on the dayroom floor, withered dry daffodils on the piano. Stanford was a first-rate hospital, yet it was so clear that psych patients got the last dribs and drabs of sheets, towels, housekeeping. Still, the doctors and the smart PhDs who led the groups were what really mattered. Egyptian cotton bath towels and five-hundred-thread-count sheets weren't going to cure mental illness. There, he'd said it: *mental illness.* To himself, at least.

Rudy looked at the light-blue wall peppered with essential information — a calendar of events, his chart and medications. It was a good thing to roll over and open your eyes to: Here's what time it is, here's what day it is, here's where you are, here's your phone number, here are your doctors. The whiteboard left room for activities specific to you. Rudy's first day, the gentle male nurse had asked what his goal was for the day. He could not think of anything other than showering and maybe going home.

"Shower?" Rudy had assumed this didn't count.

Beside "GOAL" the nurse wrote, "SHOWER." "Great. Later on I'll show you where the shower room is and everything you need."

"SHOWER" was a legitimate goal after all.

After dinner that night Rudy absentmindedly tinkered at the keys on the out-of-tune upright piano in the dayroom. Kevin sidled up with a Styrofoam cup of cocoa, which he set on the top of the piano.

"Do you know anything from *Man of La Mancha*?"

Rudy pulled out the bench, sat, and started plunking out "The Impossible Dream." He was beginning to hum the vocals when Kevin broke out into the most beautiful tenor.

Other patients gathered around to listen. There were two who were out of it on account of medication; they sat slumped in two of the dayroom chairs dozing, but perked up when they heard the music. A nurse passed by and smiled at the scene.

When Rudy and Kevin finished the song,

Rudy shyly cupped his hands in his lap.

"You sing beautifully."

"You play beautifully."

"Nah, hobbyist, really. Department store pianist."

"Laid off San Jose City Opera singer."

"I'll be damned."

"Here's to windmills."

"Here's to windmills," Rudy agreed, holding up his own Styrofoam cup of cranberry juice and ice.

As an orderly quietly approached Rudy, Kevin bowed and backed away.

"Oh, hi," the orderly said, whispering conspiratorially now. "You have a guest."

Rudy assumed it was his daughter. He wished it were Sasha.

"A Detective Jensen," the orderly added, speaking softly. "You can meet in the conference room for privacy."

"I thought this was supposed to be a *retreat* from stress," Rudy griped.

"You checked that visitors and phone calls were okay," the orderly said apologetically. "Would you like me to tell him you don't want to see him?"

"No, no, that's okay." Suddenly it occurred to Rudy that the orderly might think he'd done something criminal. "My wife died suddenly," he said. "They're looking into it." The orderly nodded, unfazed. Each day it became more apparent: The staff here *had* seen it all. And they were perhaps the least judgmental people on the planet. A planet where "SHOWER" was a fine goal for the day.

16

The conference room where Rudy met with Detective Jensen was behind a closed door along the same hallway as the patients' rooms. It was surprisingly like any other corporate meeting room: One large and long fake wood-grained table, surrounded by black chairs on wheels, a flip chart with colored pens at one end and a spaceship phone in the center of the table for conference calls. All pre-layoff reminders to Rudy. *Downsized.* (Honestly, these terms couldn't be any more dehumanizing. Downsized into a smaller version of himself? A little man, a husk that might blow away down the driveway in the wind.) But a room like this, carpet the color and texture of Teflon — like his rented tuxedo — was a reminder that he didn't long for the corporate world.

Jensen peered out the tiny window at the back of the room where the red lights of ambulances and the unloading of gurneys could be seen. He seemed to be one for dramatic entrances, and if arriving first robbed him of that chance he would keep his back to Rudy and remain silent, until turning around and taking off that ridiculous fedora and raincoat. *So, it's raining out, Humphrey Bogart?*

"Please have a seat," Jensen said, as though he were running the dang joint.

"Okay, Detective Jensen." Why did Rudy hate this man? There was just the tiniest bit of smarminess: *I know more than you know, and I'll decide when you need to know more, and I'll always know more than you know, and your wife isn't just dead, but maybe murdered, maybe went on a cruise with your neighbor who has the ride-on mower you've been coveting. Do not covet thy neighbor's ride-on mower!*

But he didn't hate Jensen. He hated having to see the guy again. The prospect of some act of violence against Bee.

"Listen," Jensen said, lowering his voice, perhaps in deference to the hospital. "We have good news. Well, it's conclusive news, and in our world of unsolved crimes, conclusive news is good news."

"My wife is alive?" Rudy asked.

"Err. No. Of course not." Jensen looked nervous, which tickled Rudy for a moment.

"Detective Jensen. I'm joking. I may be in the nuthouse, but," he said, knocking on his head, "this coconut isn't totally cracked."

Jensen's relief was palpable. "Of course, Mr. Knowles. We have some resolution. This young man who confessed to murdering Mrs. Knowles, Bethany, fits every element of the profile of a false confessor. He is a troubled fella, but we have no reason to believe that he harmed your wife, nor that he even had a grudge against her. This was confirmed by both our full investigation and another review of the autopsy report."

Rudy's anger against this false confessor, okay, this detective, this entire business, made him feel he was choking with tears and bile. He wasn't sure why the anger boiled over so vigorously now. Surely, the fact that his wife wasn't murdered was good news. But *good* was not an appropriate word. Was he supposed to celebrate?

Detective Jensen plowed forward. "These attention-seekers are criminals of their own kind — you can press charges for his claims — but we know he did not hurt your wife. There is simply no evidence other than his confession. I thought this development might put your mind at ease."

Rudy squinted grimly at the detective.

Jensen bit his lip and rolled the brim of

his fedora, which he cradled in his hands in a way that was not improving its shape.

"You think it's a joke," Rudy continued. "Like *ha-ha, you'd never end up in the booby hatch and it's only your noir life that has brought you to the psych ward.* Well, guess who the patients are on this floor?"

Jensen raised his eyebrows, opened his mouth to say something, but nothing came out. For the second time, he seemed rattled. Speechless. "No, I, not at all —"

"An opera singer with the San Jose Opera, an ER nurse from the Valley Med Trauma Center who saw a few too many people burned over ninety percent of their bodies and has panic attacks. A college kid who works at a yogurt shop, and if you heard this kid describe the number of toppings available I'd swear that's what put him in here. A young doctor who works *here,* a student who hadn't slept in three nights, a lovely mother and wife who is bipolar and needs a lithium adjustment, which is too dangerous to do outside the hospital. Did you know that small amounts of lithium can be very helpful to people? It doesn't mean they're not fit for society. A man who ran a restaurant with his wife and when she died he could not go on. He hadn't been able to get up and shower for three weeks, and self-care is a big part of grief and depression and trauma, it turns out, Detective Jensen. Write that down in your little notebook," Rudy spat as he pointed at Jensen's notebook, one of those long flip jobs, like a reporter's. He was crying now, mucous and spit and tears a globby stew on his face, but he didn't care. He reached for the box of rough tissues at the center of the table, pulled out a wad, and cleaned up his face.

Jensen opened his mouth again to speak, but Rudy continued.

"May *I* make a confession?" He leaned across the table at Jensen.

"Of course."

"I can't handle talking about my wife's autopsy right now. And I think that's okay." He slammed his forefinger into the table to make the point, then drew it away, massaging the aching knuckle.

"The patients here are not that different from you or me. They are people who stepped off the curb and got run over by life. You should hear their stories. They broke down. But they're not nuts. The *world* is nuts. I awoke one morning and my wife was dead and some dingus in a fedora and trench coat came to tell me at work — at *work* — that my wife might have been murdered. And now," Rudy said this last part with arsenic and sarcasm, "he tells me it was all a *false alarm.* And now all variables point to the joyous fact that my wife died in her sleep — *my original nightmare!*"

Rudy did realize that this last fact was not Jensen's fault.

Jensen massaged his temples. "I'm sorry. Your wife died of cardiac arrest in her sleep and there wasn't any foul play."

Rudy stood up. He felt as though he were floating above himself now. His brain told him: *Stop, calm down.* But he slammed his hands on the tabletop.

"Fuck you and your fedora! I want *my wife back.* I WANT MY WIFE BACK!"

The orderly and Rudy's nurse had slipped into the room.

Rudy lowered his voice. "And if you wanted to deliver this good news, Christ on a bike, you could have called *ahead* and given me notice. What kind of entitled bullshit do you cops think you can get away with by just showing up unannounced and throwing around the discussion of autopsies when someone is at the hospital for rest? And how am I supposed to explain this mess to my daughter?"

Jensen said, "It's not a mess. It's over. You don't have to tell her. Or tell her some day

in the future. Or I'd be happy to talk to her
—"

"NO. I will not worry her with this now." Rudy thought of CeCe's marriage, her grief, her having to take care of him.

"Okay. And I'm sorry, I did phone your doctor for permission to visit, and of course he discussed none of your information with me — he just okayed my coming. I should have let you know in advance." Jensen rubbed his cheeks, which were blue with a shadow of stubble. Frankly, he'd looked much more composed when he arrived that day at the store, suddenly emerging from the mannequin population.

Rudy's nurse gently held his forearms, urging him to look into her green eyes, and asking him to please breathe with her.

"I know 'breathe' sounds *so* annoying right now," she said, "but please, just a few breaths. In through the nose for four, hold for four, out through the mouth for four."

Rudy clutched her forearms, holding the soft purple cotton of her scrubs as though he were in water over his head at the edge of a dock and she was his only help up. She breathed with him. It wasn't exaggerated or goofy. It helped to hang on to her, look at her, and breathe simultaneously. This breathing thing wasn't BS.

The orderly lowered the lights by flipping off half of the overhead fluorescents.

Jensen sighed heavily.

Rudy sat down. It occurred to him that maybe Jensen hated his job as much as Rudy had loathed the corporate environment on some days. Having to deliver bad news and good news that wasn't even good. Jensen had handled his hat to the point where it was squashed into a lump of felt. These cracks in the detective's demeanor made him seem more human. The tension began to leave Rudy's body, and he started to feel badly for taking his depression out on a man who was probably just doing his job. However badly.

"You want some lemon pudding?" Rudy asked him.

"Er, no thanks."

"Really? Because my neighbor at lunch is a diabetic and got this one by mistake so I got two. It's actually great. I may try to emulate it at home." Rudy looked at the taut plastic wrap around the plastic dish of pudding. He couldn't imagine not being able to get out of bed and look up lemon pudding in his cookbooks and on the Internet — a task he'd enjoyed before he fell apart.

"You know, if you're ever in here, never check the pork or the beef on your menu," he advised Jensen. "Always go with the chicken or fish."

"I'll keep those menu choices in mind." Jensen laughed lightly. He looked tired. Two gray semicircles matching the fedora hung under his eyes. He stood up, straightened his hat with his fist, making a soft pop. He came around the table to Rudy and shook his hand.

"I'll be in touch," he told Rudy. "After you get home. In case you want to take any measures against this guy when you've had time to think about it. But it'll be brief. Tell you what, I'll email ahead to let you choose a time we can meet."

"Sure," Rudy agreed, pulling a deep breath in through his nose again. One, two, three, four.

"You know what?" Jensen added. "That pudding looks good. And I haven't had any lunch. Maybe I will take it."

"It'll help coat what hurts on the inside," Rudy told him, holding out the dish, which included a plastic spoon on top.

Jensen put on his coat and hat, took the pudding, thanked everyone, and was out the door.

A little while after Rudy was back in his room, sitting in the chair by the window, his friend the nurse with the purple scrubs poked her head in. She wore a cautious look — a tiny wince, brown eyebrows raised.

"You have another visitor," she announced. She steepled her hands under her chin. "But she seems lovely. Very sweet."

Oh, how Rudy loved his dear flawed daughter. *But not tonight. Not tonight responsible, dutiful CeCe.*

"A Sasha?" The nurse smiled.

"Oh. *Oh!*"

"Someone special?" the nurse asked.

"Yes. I just wish . . . I *looked* better." Rudy patted the top of his head. He was fortunate in that, as a middle-aged man, he was not lacking hair. Yet the salt-and-pepper curls became unkempt if they weren't regularly trimmed and groomed with a dab of the curling cream Bethany had brought home for him from her salon. Without that special salad dressing for after the shower, his hair grew out, instead of down, and he *looked* like a mad symphony conductor. "I feel like a disheveled badger," he told the nurse, panicking.

"You look nice. I wouldn't tell you if you didn't. Your color is great and you've had your shower today and you're dressed. I'll give you a few minutes to look in the mirror and do anything that'll make you feel better. She can't see you from the nurse's station."

Rudy did have on old khakis and a frayed but brightly hued oxford shirt, which was above and beyond what he'd worn on previous days. "Color," he laughed. "The color this season: anger, tinged with despair."

"You're smiling," the nurse observed with a note of hope.

You look fine, he heard Bethany's voice say softly. Bee's voice still popped into his head all the time. Intrusive thoughts were normal with PTSD, the doctor had explained. But Bee's voice didn't butt in rudely, like the PA lady at the store. It was a part of Rudy's own inner monologue — had been for he didn't know how long.

"I'm okay, I think," he assured the nurse, comforted that they were in cahoots over his nerves and presentability.

She turned back into the hall and soon Sasha stood outside Rudy's room. He saw her from his position perched on the edge of his bed before she saw him. As she turned to thank the nurse at the doorway, Rudy saw that Sasha's wispy blond hair was woven into its typical French braid with pieces that escaped at her neck and temples so beautifully that he wanted to cry now, instead of screaming. What was *wrong* with him today? *I'm on the psych ward,* he reminded himself, trying to think of this as a reassuring fact.

Sasha's delicate face broke into a broad grin. In one hand she held a grocery bag, and her other arm was folded around a pile of books and magazines. A smaller paper bag and a basket sat on the floor beside her. Rudy hadn't noticed that she'd also brought those. And she got past the guards with all of these treats, none of which must have been sharp.

"Comrade!" she said cheerfully. They weren't fellow employees; they were comrades. "I would have come sooner, but I worried to intrude." She blushed a little, nodding at the bags at her feet.

Rudy hoped Sasha hadn't noticed the dumbfounded amount of time he'd spent admiring how pretty she was. He quickly stood and held out his arms to help her with everything she'd brought, to take her jacket.

He returned her greeting, "Comrade!" And delight tingled all the way up his neck and across his scalp.

17

Sasha felt a little guilty as Rudy leapt toward his hospital room door to unburden her of all the bags and packages she'd brought. He was the patient! But Rudy quickly arranged everything atop the long, narrow counter that covered the radiator under the room's big window.

He peeked down his front, brushing and picking at his clothes, seemingly checking for smudges of food and brushing away imaginary crumbs.

"The other day I had oatmeal on my sweater!" he said brightly, clearly trying to compensate for embarrassment.

Sasha shrugged. "You look nice." The truth was, she liked seeing Rudy in casual attire — he looked like a regular guy, home with the flu or cleaning out the garage.

"Please, sit." Rudy gestured to the one chair for guests. He had positioned it at an angle in the corner between the bed and the radiator, so his visitors could look both around the room and down at the busy emergency room. Sasha was impressed that he'd even put a stack of magazines on the radiator top, next to a bouquet of daffodils that he said CeCe had brought, with space for a cup of tea or juice that Rudy could apparently fetch from the little kitchen by the nurse's station anytime. She had the feeling Rudy could make any place homey.

"Okay: Here's the question I've been mulling over since the first day I got here," Rudy told Sasha, as he seemed to be pulling taut a minor wrinkle in his shirt. "Can you *see* crazy? Can you see *unresolved grief?* I feel like they must have been eyesores I was carrying around for a long time, like stuffing bulging out of a tattered old sofa."

"No. I would tell you. I promise." Sasha laughed. She didn't add that, either way, it didn't matter when she was with Rudy. She felt comfortable with him in a rental tuxedo or hospital clothes, if he were grieving for his wife or playing a bawdy Broadway show tune.

"I just need an ottoman," Rudy lamented, gesturing at the area before Sasha's chair. "I wish there were a way you could put up your feet after your long hours at two jobs. *Feet above the heart!* my wife always said."

Rudy smacked his forehead. "God, talking about my dead wife."

He wrung his hands as he perched on the edge of his bed. Then he got up and slid his small, hard suitcase out from under the bed, placed it at the foot of Sasha's chair, lifted her feet, and rested them atop it.

"Thank you," Sasha told him. "And I do want to hear more about Bee, you know."

Silence. The ticking of the big plastic clock on the wall.

"Did you eat dinner yet?" Sasha clapped her hands on her thighs.

Rudy said, "Nope! I'd actually be relieved by escaping the five-thirty booby hatch dinner for a night."

Rudy pulled the rolling hospital tray table between him and Sasha, and lowered it a bit as a sort of dining room table. "Voilà," he said.

The supper she'd brought him smelled great. Sasha set the table with plastic cutlery and napkins from the bags. She unpacked and opened Styrofoam cartons onto their shared place settings: hot latkes with sour cream and applesauce.

"Wow, terrific." Rudy rubbed his palms together. "Telepathic, actually. Among my favorite suppers. How'd you know?"

Sasha shrugged. "Comfort food. I love, too."

Rudy looked apprehensively around the room, rubbing his palms together nervously. "It's a bit like my college dorm room."

"But what a nice view," Sasha replied, pointing to the window. "What is this tree?" She nodded at magenta flowers on a tree against the darkening sky.

"Er, crape myrtle." Rudy sat back down on the bed. "The only other seat in the joint," he said nervously. "What could be more intimate, yet creepy, than sitting on a bed for a chat?" He added, laughing, "Even when the doctor comes in, I feel weird sitting on a bed.

"And the weirdest part about the beds on the unit is that they're air mattresses that move with you, even if you sit gingerly. It's a feature to alleviate bedsores. Granted, no one in the psych ward is faced with this risk, but the beds are out-of-commission toss-offs from the ICU. It's sadly clear the psych ward doesn't get the best amenities. Look," Rudy showed Sasha how the bedsheets were imprinted with a San Francisco Hospital insignia — cast-offs. The unit, with many patients on Medicare, simply wasn't competing for business, like the flowery maternity ward, which was even advertised on local TV.

As they ate, Sasha pointed to the playing cards and books she'd brought. "I thought we could play gin rummy and I could read to you. You said you loved audiobooks. I can be your stereo."

"Sasha." For a moment she thought she'd done something wrong, as Rudy took her hand. "I'm so grateful. You've thought of everything."

"The nurses up front went *through* everything," Sasha added, laughing about her bags.

Sasha recalled entering the unit. Through the double doors of the psychiatric ward, the first thing she'd reached was a high-countered, imposing nurse's station, where she had to sign in as a guest. After that, the staff behind the desk looked through her packages for Rudy, making sure there was nothing off-limits or dangerous. Sasha wasn't sure why, but she felt a little embarrassed by this procedure, perhaps because of the quantity of things she'd brought Rudy: dinner, drinks and snacks for later, games, magazines, books. It was a little like airport security, where suddenly you brimmed with anxiety, fearing maybe someone had snuck a knife into your belongings.

They asked her to show them what foods were for Rudy to have later, and they took them away, saying they'd mark them and put them in the refrigerator. The nurses and administrators — Sasha wasn't sure which, frankly — were kind, so she decided that they really would give Rudy his drinks and snacks later. Then she'd proceeded on down the long corridor, the floors as shiny as ice on a skating rink, the pale blue walls hung with fine art prints, and knocked lightly on Rudy's door.

Now, Rudy's face dropped, as though he wished Sasha hadn't had to go through the front-desk search.

Sasha reached over and patted his arm. "The staff was *very* nice. They wrote your name on the perishables and stored them in the refrigerator for you. You can have anytime you like."

Rudy asked Sasha if he could get her a tea, coffee, cocoa, or juice.

"Oh!" She jumped up and grabbed a thermos out of a canvas tote bag, from which she also produced a pack of playing cards, books, a backgammon set, and *New Yorker* magazines. She thoughtfully arranged them on the radiator, nightstand, and hospital tray table. "I brought thermos of tea. Silly?"

"I'm so touched," Rudy told her. "Not just by your thoughtfulness but also by your uncanny intuition that these very activities are great. The truth is, it's been hard for me to read. For some other patients, too! It's like: *Word, word, word, punctuation, proper noun, page turn . . .* I have to read even simple newspaper paragraphs over and over. It's like nothing permeates my brain. And reading was always a great escape for me, since I was a child." Rudy's eyes closed, seeming to remember the books he'd enjoyed most.

"The admitting doctor said that depression could do this. He said that his younger brother had died in a car accident while he was in medical school, and for months he could barely study. So it's common." Rudy spoke quickly and breathlessly, as though he wanted to tell Sasha everything at once.

"Common," Sasha nodded in agreement. She wanted to reassure and comfort Rudy, without frightening him with the knowledge that she knew the blinding blare that grief gave you. That feeling like you were choking on dirt.

They continued to eat in silence, the food a comfort. During their meal a nurse came in and encouraged them to eat in the conference room next time. Family members who brought patients food often gathered there to dine.

Sasha's heart soared at the words *family members*. As special as an agate found and pocketed from the beach. A treasure to be saved and polished.

Rudy's night nurse was Jessie, who, he whispered to Sasha, was among his favorites. As she clamped the clothespin-like monitor on his finger to take his pulse, he introduced her.

"All your vitals are great. Your pulse is way down," Jessie reported, her wide, smooth face beaming at Sasha.

"I'm officially relaxing," Rudy replied. "I guess sleeping around the clock before I got here was hardly taxing. Although, more like a paralysis, rather than a peaceful rest."

"That level of depression *is* stressful," Jessie told him. "The cognitive behavioral therapy taught in group is meant to help — to be applied to both our outer and inner worlds." As she bumped her cart toward the door, Jessie told them, "But don't let the CBT handouts feel like too much homework. My motto is think, but not until it hurts!"

"I love that," Sasha told Jessie. "I'm going to try to remember when I can't sleep." She stood to clear away their Styrofoam boxes and napkins, but Rudy wouldn't let her. He bussed the table and wiped it off.

"I may feel hopeless, but I am *not* helpless," Rudy proclaimed. "That's *my* motto." After the nurse left, he confided quietly that he'd shared this motto with the physicians, too; having no idea until later that hopeless was a red-flag word for deep depression and perhaps even suicidal ideation or tendencies.

"Yes," Sasha agreed. "Let's ditch . . . ditch?"

Rudy nodded.

Sasha continued, "Let's ditch *hopeless.*"

"And let's read this." Rudy chose *The Idiot.*

"Have you ever read?" Sasha asked.

Rudy shook his head. "I'm a little light on the Russian literature."

"It's actually funny," Sasha said. "And look," she opened the book and smoothed her lovely long white fingers over the pages — "the chapters are short." As Sasha told Rudy about this favorite book of hers, her voice sped up and her cheeks flushed, her gray eyes brightening. "The funny thing is. Well, this isn't a spoiler. The protagonist, the *idiot,* is merely an epileptic. He's been away from Russia during his formative years to a sanatorium in Switzerland. He's a prince, but not high up on the prince scale, or whatever you call it. But the sad and sadly funny thing is that they put epileptics in among the mentally ill then, seriously mentally deranged, perhaps people with brain tumors. It's awful! They had no real treatment for epileptic fits. And when he returns to Russia, he still carries this nickname 'the idiot'! Sometimes when people refer to him as such, he tries to explain, 'You know, I'm not really an idiot, I have epilepsy. And it's much improved now.' But no one listens to him."

Sasha covered her mouth, laughing, her eyes welling up with tears. "It is painful humor. Am I terrible for thinking this? I love Dostoevsky for his ironic touch. Some irony is funny, no?"

"Yes!" Rudy agreed. "I can already relate to this idiot, this prince without a family, without a kingdom." And so this would be their shared book for now.

The next night, Rudy awoke, already sitting up, his room lit by the dim night-light and a wide pie shape of hall light shining in on the glossy bare floor. He had to tell someone he was choking to death. Two long, black shadows loomed in the doorway. Then blue figures moved toward his bed. When he recognized that these were the night nurses

— the lovely reassuring one with the short curly hair, and a male nurse from the other side of the ward whom Rudy hadn't seen before — he sighed and fell back against the pillows. His heart thumped in his chest, wanting to get out. The thickening of his pulse in his neck made it feel as though his throat were closing up.

"Breathe," he said. As in CANNOT.

Brenda, that was her name, the woman with the short brown curly hair. How welcoming her familiar face was now — the spray of light brown freckles across her olive complexion. She encouraged him to sit up and sip water. She turned on the low light beside his bed. "We were worried because you screamed. Nightmare?"

The young, burly night nurse ducked out of the room. It looked as though his specialty was restraining especially troubled patients. Rudy had noticed a few large, particularly buff staff members on the lockdown side — like bouncers.

Rudy nodded. Yes, nightmare. The water tasted extraordinarily sweet and good. In his dream, the faceless serial murderers who had abducted him would not allow him water. He was in a cement closet, like a warehouse room or janitor's closet. His arms and legs were duct-taped together.

There was a board with exposed nails, and they were going to hurt him with that next. Something dripped somewhere. They were serial murderers because well, his dream logic told him so. There was no motive. Just arbitrary psychopaths.

Until Jensen showed up in his life, Rudy's bad dreams had been that Bethany was still alive, but dying. Rudy would be pounding her chest, then he'd be sitting up in bed awake, discovering that reality was worse than his nightmare. Bethany wasn't dying, she was dead. And his heart felt as heavy as a suitcase. Now, thanks to Jensen, he dreamed that he was going to be murdered. In a bad TV creepy killer kind of murder. He and Bee used to marvel at how people could watch these "trouble shows," as Bethany called them. Shows where there is "always such big awful grim, terrifying trouble, and *violence.*" And so many of them — nearly all of them — with violence against women. *"Special Victims,"* Bee would say and shudder. Always such violence against women.

Rudy described the dream. How, between Jensen visiting and a few patients watching *Special Victims* that evening before bed, he had gone to bed haunted about his wife's potential murder, even though he had just learned that this hadn't even been the case.

"You know, I try to turn off that show," Brenda told him, "try and encourage another show or activity. Cooking and sports. I swear those are the best for most people. And the singing and dancing competition shows. Everybody loves those." She sat in the chair beside Rudy's bed, turning on the low light behind him. "I'm going to put in a request that we not allow that show to be on."

"There are victims of violent crime here with PTSD." The victims of violent crime counselor had visited him briefly a few days prior to Jensen's appearance, saying that when Rudy was released they would be there for him if he needed support. The volunteer did not give him any of her pamphlets, thankfully. She just wanted him to know about the resource. Good GOD was he weighed down with literature — for widowers, depressives, PTSD sufferers, partners of those with heart disease, cognitive behavioral therapy, living in the present, yoga . . .

"Plan in place!" the social worker had chirped to the group therapy session one morning. "We want resources lined up for you upon your release. You don't have to read up on services immediately, but you'll meet with a social worker before your discharge to sketch out a plan."

Rudy sat on the side of the bed now, his feet dangling over, awake, and nearing anger. "There's *Monk!*" He felt his voice rising in pitch and volume. "A perfectly fine murder mystery!" Who cared if liking that show made him a fuddy-duddy?

Brenda nodded. *"Exactly."* She patted his shoulder. "Can I bring you some cereal?"

Steadying himself, Rudy declined.

"Okay, then, here's what I recommend. Get up and use the bathroom, splash warm water on your face, and look at a magazine for ten minutes max, then turn off your light. I'm pretty sure you'll go right back to sleep. I'll be back in twenty minutes to check on you."

Rudy's heart felt less like a rapidly descending plane about to crash, and his breathing gradually slowed. The sensation of choking was now just a small lump in his throat. Every day in the hospital made him more grateful for psychiatric nurses. Unsung heroes, for sure. He would send them flowers when he got home.

He flipped through *The Idiot,* having already loved what Sasha had read to him earlier. This would be their shared book. Rudy had selfishly chosen it because it was the longest of the tomes Sasha had brought. Certainly, even after his release from the hospital, she would not leave him until they finished the story. For, since Bethany's death, people leaving him — people whom he loved — had become his biggest fear.

Once a week dogs visited the unit — the world's most subdued German shepherds, wide-eyed and blinking and calm. They were brought by animal therapy specialists — and politely sat or stood in the sitting area of the dayroom, allowing patients in the surrounding chairs to pet and scratch and coo to them. Rudy found it uncanny that not one of the dogs ever barked or so much as drooled or even shed. While the unit may not have had the fanciest beds, sheets, or showers, where else could you borrow a German shepherd like a library book?

"Isn't this something?" he asked the animal therapist, scratching a gentle pup behind his enormous ears.

"I missssssssss my daaaaaaaawwwwg," a newly admitted twenty-something boy moaned, rolling on the floor in his makeshift outfit of sweats and hospital pajamas, hugging a pup.

Sasha visited Rudy every evening now,

something he looked forward to all day. Rudy couldn't remember looking forward to anything since before Bee died. Twice a week there was art therapy. Hell, he looked forward to art therapy. Gathering materials, gathering ideas, becoming engrossed as they delved in. Once a week a lovely gentleman who was a painter himself, and who visited the women on bed rest in the maternity ward, and the really laid-up kids in pediatrics, brought a rolling a cart of his own supplies. He unobtrusively helped people with their projects, many of which included the use of his fine colored pencils. Frustrated by trying to sketch out a piano, Rudy asked the teacher how Monet's *The Duck Pond* achieved such depth — how it looked like the ducks were really swimming away from the foreground and deeper between the trees, growing smaller. Ah, perspective! The artist sketched it out in simple circles and shapes, magically making three dimensions appear on the paper — a demonstration that soothed Rudy's nerves.

Patients were allowed to take projects back to their rooms to let them dry, or show to family members, since the OT room was locked once the sessions ended. But Rudy didn't want Sasha to see the decoupage box he was making for her, the carefully thin streams of colored tissue paper he'd been shown how to layer and glue with the watery library paste. At first Rudy had been frustrated by the leaky paste, but as it ran over the colors it bled them together in a pleasing effect — like stained glass.

Rudy made Sasha's gift starting with a simple tan-colored wood box that the leader had provided. He used sapphire-blue; bright, cheerful lime-green; orange; and pale pink tissue paper. The orange reminded him of Matisse's goldfish. He noticed that some people were cutting out magazine photos and incorporating them into their decoupage as focal points. He flipped through a magazine, but couldn't find anything special enough for Sasha. Certainly not a wristwatch from a fancy ad! He would ask the leader for an idea. He knew Sasha liked Matisse. Chopin. He would explain to the leader that his gift was for a special friend. He'd already used this phrase in group therapy, and no one laughed at him, even though he thought it sounded silly. But that's what Sasha was. He was a widower, and she was a special friend. Someone who was dear to him. Was that okay? Yes. Almost everything at the hospital was okay, except for sharp objects and lack of civility.

18

Rudy's psychiatrist, Dr. Ring, reminded Rudy that the antidepressant they were trying could have minor side effects at first, such as nausea, a bit of daytime spaciness, and perhaps even bad dreams. Rudy was titrating onto the medication gradually, to allow his brain and body to acclimate until the proper blood level was attained. "We used to hit patients with these drugs at a maximum dose — POW — then wonder why they felt so poorly. Or more like *not listen* carefully enough to why they felt so poorly. We'd thumb through the PDR, and if the side effects weren't listed, then we attributed the complaints to anything other than the medication." Dr. Ring shook his head, sipped his tea. "Our profession has come a long way but still has a long way to go."

"Just like the rest of medicine," Rudy said. "Cancer, heart disease . . ." He felt a pang of guilt at the latter, because it seemed heart disease was perhaps the most detectable, preventable. He should have called and scheduled a stress test for Bee.

"Men compartmentalize," CeCe had remarked, more sadly to herself than critically of her father. During her last visit they'd had a discussion about CeCe feeling somewhat abandoned by an absentee husband. They lived in Silicon Valley, after all, and she had girlfriends whose husbands worked every night until midnight at some start-up or other. This didn't make it easier for any of them. There were women engineers, too, and same-sex partners, but once children entered the equation, one parent — always the non-engineer — took to working at home. Some ate dinner alone *until* there were children. They were each of them alone, making supper in their partner-less kitchens. Once with children, managing homework, dinner, baths, story- and bedtime alone. Managing their wonder at why every goddamned technology product needed a new version as soon as the last had been released to the world. Bugs. There were bugs! The engineers were as melodramatic as the neonatologists, frankly, standing around the barbecues on weekends over some dumb artisanal sausages and beer that would give you a stomachache later, seriously discussing their importance as though they were preparing to seize Helen from Paris and capture Troy.

"Keira barely knows her father. It's like I'm a single parent," CeCe had confided in her father. "I'm sorry I know that's an awful com-, complaint, considering what you're going through." That slight stutter broke Rudy's heart. She'd wept as though it were she who never came home for dinner with her daughter.

"Now, heart disease among women," Dr. Ring's voice grew stern now. He assumed a more doctorly tone, perhaps trying to reel Rudy in from his obvious daydream. "This is *very* often a silent killer." Rudy wanted to cover his ears. He remembered the literature the social worker at the ER had given him. The heart disease brochure had fallen out from among the social worker's folder of paperwork, "Silent Killer" staring up at him from the floor.

The problem had been that Rudy had hated himself every day for not nursing Bee. *Silent killer. Few to no symptoms.* Still, you could take care of a person. Protect them. He would protect Sasha, even though she'd told him more than once that she wasn't a fairy princess or scruffy pound animal who needed saving.

"I know," Rudy had laughed, deeming himself silly, commending Sasha's obvious strength and bravado. Meanwhile he planned on rescuing her every day. Carrying her over the threshold of a romantic cabin, shooing away creepy watch shoppers, bringing her brioche French toast in bed. He didn't care if he was old-fashioned. If his fantasies were more *Reader's Digest* than *Penthouse* Forum. Didn't everyone need a little rescuing?

He had picked up the pamphlet in the ER and said, "THANKS," as it trembled in his fist. "Warning signs!" he added. "Now that SHE IS DEAD." The word *dead* had coated his tongue with a gluey gunk, and he'd realized he hadn't even brushed his teeth yet.

Fuckyoufuckyoufuckyou. Rudy rarely cursed. But now the words spattered in his brain like hot oil in a skillet. He gulped them down, *breathe, breathe, breathe* "I know," he replied, hoping he didn't sound too angry to Dr. Ring.

Dr. Ring reached over and patted the top of Rudy's hand. He had obviously seen Rudy cringe at the information about heart disease.

"You do know why people keep telling you this — about women being the most under-diagnosed heart disease patients?"

Rudy shook his head.

"There was nothing, *nothing,* you could have done to prevent Bethany's death. Not a single thing. I'm guessing she was even in good health otherwise."

Rudy nodded. "Thank you for saying her name."

"Of course," Dr. Ring answered, sipping his tea. Rudy was flattered that Dr. Ring brought in his herbal tea and sat in the chair that Rudy had set in the corner, angled to look partly out on the ER and parking lot morning bustle. Rudy had tried to make the area appealing for CeCe, then even more so for Sasha. He'd put the big pot of ferns and primrose and miniature daffodils on the radiator, along with paper napkins for coasters, and the few *New Yorker* magazines. In the crook of the back chair, CeCe had brought a little pillow from home, and an afghan, which Rudy ritualistically folded neatly over the back of the chair, always straightening that area before bed. It seemed Dr. Ring was taking a moment's refuge by visiting Rudy first in his rounds, before heading out to the inevitable daily calamities and complaints on the unit.

"Now, as for your antidepressant," Dr. Ring continued. "The brain is just so subjective, and this subjectivity means not only that each drug might affect a patient differently — in terms of both side effects and efficacy — but that the normal criteria for dosing, such as weight and age, have little to do with the dosing of SSRIs, because our brains have little to do with body mass and such. Well, so . . . I just hope you'll be patient. It is slow-going because we only want to change one variable at a time."

"Science," Rudy said, wiping the tears from his cheekbones with the heels of his palms. "It's comforting. Just like music."

After Dr. Ring asked how Rudy was doing and took a few notes, they inevitably spoke about jazz for a few minutes — Dr. Ring taking a genuine interest in Rudy's taste. His daughter was a student at the Berklee College of Music in Boston. She had called home to her dad complaining that they were jazz Nazis.

"I've encouraged her to stick it out through sophomore year, then she can transfer if she wishes, broaden her horizons." Dr. Ring shook his head. "Kid doesn't like one of the best music schools in the country."

Daughters, they agreed. Dr. Ring said he did not know what he would do without his wife's help in raising their children. That if *he* lost his wife he would be so lost he wasn't sure how he'd manage. As they talked, Rudy realized just how much help CeCe had been since Bee died. For a moment, he felt remorseful, taking up so much of her time, worrying her like this, even as she was having marriage problems.

"Why do you feel you have to be strong for your daughter?" Dr. Ring asked. Rudy shook his head, embarrassed that he couldn't explain.

"Your daughter is okay and very concerned about you. This is in no way critical; I just want you to know you don't have to be strong for anyone right now. Not anymore."

Well, then, maybe that was why the seashell air had given way to a hurricane of tree-bending wind, and a storm-surge of surf with an undertow that pulled Rudy under the covers — under the surface of the world — and pinned him there.

He nodded at the doctor appreciatively. He would try to let go of being strong — clearly this was the place to do it. Even if he wanted to be strong for CeCe, and for Sasha.

"Okay." The doctor patted Rudy's leg. "We'll try and get you some outside help so that you truly *believe* that."

This had been a conversation deeper than therapy. Words so devoid of cliché that they made Rudy feel human. Not crazy for being crazy. That was probably the number-one takeaway from the med-psych ward: You're not crazy for feeling crazy. It's okay. Let's see what we can do. Of course, before they entered the ward, the "let's see what we can do here!" drill had already been enforced upon patients by themselves, their family, and their therapists. They knew what they were supposed to do: exercise, eat right, sleep normal hours, regularly take the medication that wasn't working, get out and see people. But was it meant to feel like a life sentence of drudgery?

19

At the health club, Sasha wished she'd forgone the meditation class and just headed straight to visit Rudy at the hospital. (One class per week was complimentary to staff, although Sasha felt uncomfortable when she saw the ladies she knew from cleaning the locker room.)

"Imagine a beach," the hippie girl cooed dreamily, after ringing a small gong and closing her eyes.

No, Sasha would *not* imagine a beach. Or a pond, river, stream, or swimming pool. At times, she barely tolerated the water from the shower when she washed her hair. Why was every guided meditation on a beach? Okay, so Sasha had only been to two guided meditation classes and listened to one CD, but they were all on a beach that wasn't very well described. "The sand is cool between your toes." No, it's warm, or hot. And dusty.

Sasha, Gabor, and Stefi had once spent a

beautiful weekend at the beach. They had filled Stefi's new bucket with dense, wet sand, tipping it over to create tower after tower. Gabor, who could have a penchant for silliness, made the figures into sand-bucket people, with seaweed for hair and sticks, shells, and rocks for noses, eyes, and mouths. He stuck a cigarette butt in the mouth of one, topped another with a stray rubber bathing cap. Passersby stopped to laugh, admire, and take photos. The three of them were a family, at the beach.

Stefi was in constant motion, running through the shallowest part of the surf all day, screaming with irrepressible joy.

At the end of the day, she'd needed a shower back at the motel, Sasha gently scrubbing the sand from her hair, and a fresh set of clothes. After their picnic supper, they had built a bonfire. Stefi had been so happy about toasting marshmallows that Sasha thought her daughter might actually explode. The man at the convenience store had demonstrated how to make 'smores, stacked up the three sugary ingredients for them, and suggested napkins, all of which Gabor complemented with vodka. Their hair had smelled of smoke, and an additional hot bath was needed to wash off the marshmallow goo, salt, and more sand.

So much sand! They fell into bed so exhausted that Gabor's snoring didn't even keep Sasha and Stefi awake.

Sasha had cradled her little girl's warm body under the crisp motel sheets. The room was so simple, but clean, and the beach so perfect — within walking distance — that Sasha thought maybe it had been the best weekend of her life.

When would Sasha tell Rudy what had happened to Stefania? Her daughter had drowned. Not on that beautiful day at the beach. But another day, a terrible afternoon — the screen door slapping behind Stefi as she ran outside, her little feet in red sneakers, a sundress pulled over her bathing suit. So excited to go swimming with her American friend and her mum. The mother appearing to be perfectly competent. Sasha not even worrying. It wasn't like her not to worry! Now, she didn't want to pull down the recovering Rudy — finally emerging from his own grief, it seemed — with the story of her daughter. Stefi. Her whole life. Gone in an afternoon.

A few months after Stefi died, Sasha allowed herself to research drowning. Did it hurt? Had her daughter suffered? She wanted to know even if she was afraid to find out at first. She didn't have the words to ask the policeman who came to their house. She didn't have the words to ask the social worker who visited later. What was it like to drown?

When she finally worked up the courage to look, she discovered that drowning wasn't anything like in the movies. People didn't flail or scream for help. They looked like they were treading water. *Not waving but drowning.* So often bathers on the beach or pool deck — other than lifeguards — were slow to respond. There wasn't even a whole lot of splashing, because the victims were suffocating. Once submerged, they climbed an invisible ladder. The invisible ladder stuck in Sasha's mind — she couldn't un-imagine it now. Her daughter had been eight. She'd taken swimming lessons. She'd climbed up the ladder of a pool. She must have seen the invisible ladder. Sasha should have been at the top, with open arms!

After her research, Sasha wished she'd never read this description — never looked up what her daughter had likely experienced. Ladders and the choking sense of suffocation catalyzed Sasha's nightmares every night that following year. Sasha felt herself suffocating in her sleep because it should have been *her.* She wished that *she* had been the ladder! Isn't that what a good mother was? A ladder, a gate, a cushion, a net. Sasha should have *been there,* holding Stefi by her arms, allowing her to only venture up to her waist in the pool. Waist-high, the rule they had applied for the cold foamy surf at Capitola Beach. In the ocean, Stefi's feet had kicked playfully at Sasha's thighs. Her surprisingly strong grip pinched Sasha's arms, little fingernails digging into her mother's flesh.

The afternoon that Stefi drowned in her little friend's swimming pool, Sasha's other neighbor came running up the walk in her bare feet — two pink lumps of flesh and toes pattering through the muddy grass between the flagstones. Sasha watched the woman approach from the window over the sink, where she had started fixing supper. The neighbor did not knock but rather swung through the screen, tearing off the hook lock in the process.

Daughter drowned pool ambulance swimming day man resuscitate breathe breathe stop breathe. The provenance of the news — this neighbor, her apron, her awful orange hair. Her steep nose, her lumpy bosom. *Away! Shoo, away!*

A pot boiled over, milky white potato water flecked with starch splashing onto the burner, making the blue flame sputter.

Sasha turned to the potatoes. The cabbage rolled with ground beef and onions. She should have been with the girls at the pool. The other child was probably a more advanced swimmer. What was wrong with these Americans, having to do everything from such a young age? Dancing lessons and swimming and birthday party ponies!

"It's impossible!" Sasha had sputtered at the neighbor. "My daughter may not swim in the deep end! Only to her waist!"

Spongy, strawberry-freckled arms folded Sasha into the blue-and-white bosom of the woman's checkered apron. The yeasty sour smell of something cooked yesterday and lilac powder. The soft down of a cheek. The warmth of pudgy arms.

"I'll drive you," the woman said, turning off the burners. The sound of wails rang out over the ring of the telephone and the chime of the oven timer. Why was the neighbor screaming and crying? It was *Sasha's* child. *Oh.* It was she who screamed. And then she could not. Her throat was clogged with something custardy. Water. Over her head! The potato water filled her lungs, thick white starch clogging her throat. The kitchen darkened to burnt orange. The ceiling fan overhead spun faster, like a helicopter taking off and lifting the house from the earth.

And then darkness.

When Sasha awoke, she was on the sofa. Gabor was there, with a glass of whiskey. The neighbor lady held out a glass of water and a tiny yellow pill. Sasha took the water, gulped it.

"Stop drinking." She smacked Gabor with the backside of her hand. The whiskey flew out of his grasp, the glass flying in an arc, Gabor's eyes saucering at her.

The neighbor woman reintroduced herself: Kim. Sasha followed her outside and into her car, parked in the street, all the while marveling at how Kim wore Gabor's ill-fitting shoes. Sasha would never forget this, and later was touched by it. The main thing was that they just got to the hospital — found Stefi. They didn't know yet that Stefi was dead. Maybe Kim knew. Sasha never asked her. The confusion of that day.

After she got home, after the funeral, the kitchen faucet broke and dripped relentlessly. Just a tiny drip. *Pip, pip, pip.* All night long as Sasha buried her head under a pillow, the dripping faucet gave way to the relentless sound of the ocean.

Gabor had gotten so drunk at the funeral that Sasha would not let him come home. She asked his former coworker to please look after her husband for the night, then pocketed Gabor's keys. As the dripping faucet frayed what was left of her nerves, Sasha wanted to call Gabor to come home and fix it. She was hardly more logical than a drunk. She had to remind herself that Gabor wasn't very good at fixing things. That he always broke things a little bit more before making any progress, often abandoning projects midway through — a drape of plastic sheeting a hole in the wall.

The soft gong of the meditation leader's bell brought Sasha back to the darkened room at the club, the waffled sticky mat beneath her, the dull ache in her back, the ubiquitous smell of lavender. She'd made it through the forty-five-minute guided meditation — if you didn't count the guided part. She'd wandered straight from the imaginary beach to Stefi underwater, her two white-blond braids suspended straight up in the crystal-bright, swimming-pool-blue water, two bursts of healthy bubbles of air and then nothing. Then tears itching Sasha's cheeks so that she'd had to wipe her nose with the back of her sleeve.

Sasha hated to be negative or judgmental, but this type of meditation was not for her. She'd stick with the yoga next time. And tonight, during her visit with Rudy, she would tell Rudy about Stefi. Stefania, who didn't like dolls, but loved animals. Stuffed animals, animal books, animal documentaries; *The Jungle Book, The Wind in the Willows, Winnie the Pooh, Stuart Little.* Stefi, whose favorite birthday cake was burnt almond, and who fancied being a sports announcer, like the brilliantly tall and beautiful girl on the NBA channel. Stefi, who always told her mother to try not to worry so much, and had already learned how to make potato pancakes and French toast. Like Rudy, Stefi loved to cook!

Sasha wanted to tell Rudy everything about her daughter, show him each of her school photos. But what if Sasha pulled *Rudy* underwater?

20

It thrilled Rudy that Sasha visited nearly every night now. Sometimes she brought dinner — takeout, or something she cooked that she wanted Rudy to try. Or she came after Rudy's hospital dinner and they played gin rummy. They made their way through *The Idiot,* taking turns reading. Rudy liked reading aloud to Sasha. She was a wonderful listener — smiling, laughing, closing her eyes to imagine.

"Your English is terrific," he had insisted. "But is it more relaxing for you to sit back and listen? After all, you worked a long day. I just ate institutional oatmeal, and practiced my mindfulness." Sasha agreed, and they started trading off.

One evening, Rudy suggested that Sasha should not feel obliged to visit nearly every night, as she had been.

Her face fell, her brow furrowed, her gray eyes widened, as though she'd just realized something: He didn't want her here all the time.

"I mean I love it when you do. I wish you'd visit every night. But I don't want you to feel obligated."

"Question." Sasha raised a slim, pale forefinger in the air.

"You have the floor."

"Do you like eating dinner alone? I mean, not here, but at home."

"It is *the* worst part of the day."

Sasha nodded. Rudy had already eaten his supper of stuffed manicotti and something called tricolored chard. Sasha unpacked some cookies. Rudy set out *The Idiot,* backgammon, and the playing cards. "What'll it be?" he asked. Companionship. He didn't care if they read the dang phone book aloud to each other.

"Tonight, something different." Sasha pulled two photo albums out of a shopping bag and set them on the radiator. "I want to show you some pictures of my life before." She placed her hands over her nose and mouth, her fingertips meeting at the bridge of her nose, just under her eyes. With her elbows on her knees, she sighed heavily, looked at the floor for several minutes.

"I know for a fact, there is nothing interesting in those floor tiles."

Sasha's eyes filled, and she pressed on her cheekbones as though willing herself not to cry.

"There's something I haven't told you."

Rudy climbed off the bed and stepped around their hospital tray–makeshift coffee table. "Hey, hey." He rubbed her back gently, just above her shoulder blades. Her hair smelled faintly of the lilacs and lemons of the first floor of the department store.

She dipped her head lower, wiping her eyes on the sleeves of her blue-and-white striped cotton sweater. Rudy put the box of Kleenex in her lap and took his hand away, just patting her shoulder, not wanting to seem forward or presumptuous.

"You don't have to tell me everything. We've just become close friends. I mean, even if you're a bank robber, I don't care." What he meant was: *You're perfect.*

And so Sasha told Rudy everything about Stefi. She wanted to start with how cute she'd been as a baby — hair almost white! But she started with that day: *playdate.* A distinctly American expression. In Hungary, sure, you asked neighbors and family to babysit. But you didn't plan your kids' calendars like they were little CEOs. Back home the kids played in the house or yard. Still, there, anything could happen. "Stefi

285

drowning — not the mother's fault. Not her fault." Over and over Sasha said this, as though trying to convince herself again, these years later. "Not the mother's fault. And Stefi, she could swim!" Sasha told Rudy. "Stefi could swim." Sasha's voice rose with desperation, making her case. "She'd had lessons. We went to the town pool in Hungary, indoor lessons, every Saturday morning. She would always say, 'Mommy, watch me!' "

Rudy leaped across the room to close the door, grateful for their privacy.

"I know, I know," Rudy said, drawing her to his chest. He knew the shock and disbelief, the anger and self-blame. He knew the relentless replaying of the day, the hours, the minutes, how you lay awake at night going back so you could enact the preceding time differently. He knew the permanent chip in your heart that never went away. You almost wanted a permanent scar on the outside of your body to show the internal pain. People would look and just think, *Oh, okay.* You didn't get over it. Everything was different from that day on. You got better. You healed. You backtracked. But nothing was ever the same.

"She could swim, she could swim, she could!"

Rudy rocked Sasha in his arms, breathing in the clean citrus scent of her light perfume, feeling the warmth of her slim arms, kissing the top of her downy head. "Stefi could swim," Rudy agreed. "Kids learn fast, swimming lessons at an early age are great. She could swim."

He continued to repeat these words to Sasha as he held her, close, but not too tightly, not invasively. Tenderly. As tenderly as he could while trying to exude that he would never let her go. Never let her suffer if he could help it.

Together they repeated the mantra, "Stefi could swim."

"Thank you for sharing the pictures of her," Rudy said, when Sasha's hiccups finally died down. They sat beside each other on the bed now, Sasha still clinging to Rudy's forearms. "She was a beautiful, strong, good little girl," he reassured her. "You were a *wonderful* mother. You have so much to be proud of, Sasha."

Sasha untangled herself from Rudy a bit, bowing her head with sudden shyness, but still clasping his hands in hers. Her fingers were long and delicate and her nails trimmed and polished with a varnish like opals. They were so lovely as she showed off the watches to customers. Rudy always wanted to compliment her on this, but hadn't yet. It was weird, but he never wanted to seem like an unctuous lech. She was a coworker, after all. And he a gentleman, he hoped. Now it felt like they were in something together.

"Uh! I'm so stupid, so sorry." Sasha scooted away from him a bit on the bed, still holding his hands. "Hospital is for you! You need rest, not a hysterical work friend."

An orderly knocked, peeked in the door, then pulled it closed again, giving Rudy a nod. The young man had a ruddy face, bright red hair, and thick forearms. The staff checked on the patients every hour. A rule that touched, rather than annoyed, Rudy.

"Please don't apologize," Rudy said to Sasha, smoothing his padded fingertips over hers. "Do you know that every time we get to talk together, and I learn more about you, that I feel better?" He tapped his chest gently with one fist. "Here, in my heart."

She cocked her head, smiled wanly, and Rudy could see Stefi in her flawless skin, pinkish rosy cheeks, and gray eyes. In her nearly white silken blond hair.

"You help me," he insisted. And he wanted to do everything he could to help Sasha for as long as she would allow him.

It seemed to Rudy as though his hospitalization had softened CeCe. In fact, for the first time in as long as he could remember, he was bolstering her, assuring her everything would be all right.

Tonight she had brought Rudy's granddaughter, along with takeout macaroni and cheese for her and a Pudding Pop she'd stashed in the freezer on the way in. Kiki sat on her grandpa's lap when she first arrived, peppering him with questions.

"There's a man out there with a T-shirt on his head like Aladdin's turban and no shirt and he's singing and playing the guitar while this other man plays the piano and then there are ladies watching TV and other ladies making some beaded bracelets on the big table," she reported, not missing a single detail of the after-dinner action in the dayroom.

"I know," Rudy said, "my little reporter. And you know what? That man is actually a young man, a student from Stanford, and he's very smart and talented at the guitar and a good singer. I think he wrapped his shirt around his head because he's a bundle of energy, who's actually quite funny. And he's studying physics *and* music."

"What's wrong with him? Why's he in the hospital?" Kiki furrowed her brow and sucked at her Pudding Pop.

"Well, he stayed up too many nights in a row studying and got so tired that he couldn't sleep very well. He needed to come in and rest and reset his clock and then get some medicine."

They could hear the music through the closed door of the room. But it sounded good, and only went on for half an hour before meds.

"Oh, I gotcha." Kiki was satisfied with this answer. That was her signature line, which she'd picked up from her father. Only, Kiki used it after listening carefully and thoughtfully to someone, processing an explanation, while Spencer was more likely to use the phrase to cut off a person from a lengthy description. Young doctors. Smarter than their patients. Especially specialists. Cardiologists? *Grrrrrrr.*

Rudy brushed away these thoughts, grateful for how remarkable the staff on the ward had been. In fact, they'd diagnosed the T-shirt-bundled physics musician with bipolar disorder, explaining that it often presented among young men in college and that the demands of a full academic load could lead to spells of mania in trying to stay caught up, the lack of sleep ultimately making you crash. They weren't supposed to discuss their diagnoses or medications at the meal table, but patients did anyway, mostly sharing what they were in for, what they were frustrated by. What they'd do when they busted out of the joint. The hyperactive student musician said he was going to smoke a carton of cigarettes and drive to *LA*.

As they munched cookies after Rudy's hospital dinner, CeCe set up Kiki with a movie to watch on her iPad in the proper visitor's chair, which CeCe had pulled across to the other side of the long window and radiator, so she and her dad could hear their own conversation, without talking over any of *The Little Mermaid.* Rudy told his daughter about Sasha's visits.

"Oh, my lord," CeCe said. "You are *smitten.*"

"No." But Rudy giggled as he wiped crumbs from his chin. He felt as though he'd laughed in church or a meeting.

"You hardly *know* this woman."

"That is not true. We've worked together for nearly four years." Rudy resented the words *this woman,* which sounded generic, illicit even.

"A work romance." CeCe sighed heavily, then tightened her thin lips, as though rubbing in lip balm or lipstick. But her lips were colorless and chapped. Rudy poured her a cup of water.

"Thanks," she said softly.

"No," Rudy said, "someone I *met* at work. There hasn't been any romance yet, for your information. Playing a coworker's favorite waltz is hardly a tryst in the janitor's closet."

"They say . . ."

"Honestly, Cecilia, often your rules of thumb, criteria for conduct, and lists of no-nos aren't so much a moral code by which to live as a broken compass for not living at all." Rudy immediately felt sorry for this loss of temper, his harsh words.

"I don't mean that. I'm sorry," he added. "I value your input." This was not totally true. Not right now at least.

"They say go on fifty coffee dates in three months," CeCe mumbled into her Kleenex. "I sure as hell couldn't do it. Plus, that's a lot of coffee. You must stay up all night worrying about the next nightmare Frappuccino mate.

"Oh, who cares!" CeCe added, "What is wrong with me?"

"It's not you, sweetheart. The world is a big mess. Complete chaos. You're just trying to make order out of the chaos." Rudy was winging it now. It felt as though the therapy he'd been receiving had taught him to help others put life in perspective. This rickety new skill made him feel slightly less useless.

"I don't mean who cares. I care. I will look forward to meeting her." CeCe rolled up her sleeves to reveal pale skin and golden freckles. "Okay, I'm nervous."

"I'm so excited for you to meet her."

"I'm not judgmental. My book group says I'm judgmental." She took a sip from her cup of water. "Ha. Aside from hating them, I don't think I'm judgmental at all!"

"You know, your mother wasn't crazy about her book club, either, honey. And she was the nicest woman. But funny. I mean would never utter a cruel word to someone's face, and not a backstabber. But just . . . funny. You're more like her than you realize. In the best ways." CeCe leaned her head against Rudy's shoulder and together they fell back against the pillows and watched Kiki, mesmerized by her movie. Rudy wished he could be that distracted from the world.

During CeCe's visit the next afternoon — it was after lunch, not technically visiting hours, but she had stopped by on her way to the Stanford Mall to pick up a wedding gift — she said she had thought all night about what he'd said.

"You are my little girl," Rudy told her, stealing the tip of her nose with his thumb pinched between his fingers.

"Order out of chaos." CeCe stared at the ceiling tiles above. "There was never chaos at home growing up. Everything was fine. There was always —"

"We certainly never had to ground you." Rudy chuckled.

"Will we still be able to talk about her? About mom?"

"Are you kidding me? Oh, sweetheart." The nurse kindly popped in with Rudy's lunch tray. "Occupational therapy in twenty minutes," she reminded him.

"I have to finish my decoupage," Rudy told CeCe, tearing open a petite bag of potato chips. They shared them.

"Do you know I think about your mother every day?" he told her. "I imagine I will for the rest of my life."

"Really? Even though you love Sasha?"

"I didn't say I loved Sasha."

"But you do!"

"We'll see."

"Ha. You'll see." CeCe's face clouded over. "I think Spencer wants a divorce."

"Then we'll check him in here. He's out of his mind."

But CeCe didn't laugh at her father's joke. She swallowed her chip with some apparent difficulty, turned toward her father, and pulled at the Kleenex on his night tray until there were none left and the small cardboard box floated to the floor.

She laughed and cried at the same time, which resulted in a snort, which produced more laughing and crying, mucus and tears, and finally the release of her shoulders and the tipping back of her head, a surrender that made Rudy leap to his feet and collect her in his arms.

He wanted to pick her up and tuck her into the hospital bed, like when she was little and fell asleep watching *Face the Nation,* which she insisted she liked.

Instead, Rudy continued hugging his daughter, laughing as he thought about his one Internet date, with whom he *did* plan on going to the opera. He'd tell Sasha. No, he'd ask her. But he wasn't sure he'd tell CeCe.

"Maybe you won't split up," Rudy suggested to CeCe, who had pressed an entire bouquet of tissue to her face. "If you do, to hell with Spencer. We have each other. You know that, right?"

CeCe shook her bowed head.

"You're supposed to *nod*!" Rudy squeezed her in his arms. He kissed the top of her head, remembering the soothing smells of baby shampoo and baby powder when she was a child. Now her coarse, red-blond hair had a grown-up clean, yet slightly musky, fragrance. Like Bethany's deep red roses in their yard.

"Dad, he's having an affair."

"He *what*?" Rudy felt his fists tighten, his heart skip a beat. "Oh, angel." He tipped back his daughter's chin to look at her. But she collapsed against him, more forcefully than he could remember her doing in a long, long time, maybe all the way back to the time her 4-H club goat died. "That is awful and has nothing, absolutely *nothing* to do with you. Look at me, look at me."

CeCe's face was screwed up and red as she cried. "All this time I never —"

"Numero uno," he said firmly, shaking his daughter slightly, bowing his head to catch her gaze. "This has nothing whatsoever to do with *you.*" Earlier, CeCe had skirted around a very euphemistic explanation of her and her husband having no, er, romance, and Rudy had equally skirted around a hopefully helpful reply — *It's so common.* A counselor? He'd needed Bethany, god damn it!

Now CeCe sobbed into the shoulder of Rudy's too-big Golden State Warriors sweatshirt, the thick fabric something for her to grab on to.

"All this time I thought, you know, he's a neonatologist. And I was pissed off because other people's kids would always be his priority. This sounds really, really, really bitchy, but I even said it to him: There would always be some child — some March of Dimes *other couple's* child — who would be more important than his being home for dinner with our daughter. Every single night. Then we made a deal. He would always be home to read her a bedtime story. Then that got pushed out by emergencies. The helipad, the transfers." Stanford did boast one of the best children's hospitals in the state, and newborns with serious ailments were often transferred there.

Rudy rested his chin on his daughter's thin shoulder. It fit just right there. His mind drifted for only an instant, in which he remarked at how he had become a sort of therapist in his psych-ward room. It was weird, but he found himself able to be optimistic and confident for everyone but himself. It was some combination of the CBT therapy and workbooks, and the groups, and ratcheted-up understanding for his comrades on the floor, along with that invisible strand of grief that flew out from his heart to others, like a fly-fishing cast of empathy for others from his planet. Suddenly he'd become an armchair therapist to his daughter and his, dare he say, *girlfriend.*

"So that's the kicker," CeCe said into her father's thick sweatshirt hood. "Mr. I'm-coming-to-the-rescue-to-save-the-day, Mr. I'm-*God*-now-and-I-get-to-tell-you-your-kid-isn't-going-to-make-it — well he managed to fit in screwing a floor nurse as his third holier than thou reason for not coming home to his family."

"Oh, honey. Oh, CeCe." He went on to tell her everything he was thinking, which was that that God-like demeanor of life-and-death specialists perhaps led to a sense of entitlement that made him feel justified in the affair.

"Yeah, well he sure had disdain for our love life. Not that I didn't try."

Rudy continued, telling her that seeing death, working in a hospital, in a trauma setting, constantly jumping into fight-or-flight mode with coworkers gave them a sense of connection that falsely seemed like it should be acted on romantically.

"Your mother was around this for thirty

years, and she swore that it was not that far off from *General Hospital.*

"There's therapy. Marriage counseling. Your mom and I even went once, after her miscarriage. We were like one of those floats in the Macy's Thanksgiving Day parade that's gone all off-kilter, bumping along down the street at half-mast." Rudy felt like he was nearing the end of his psychological explanations and was wandering into a territory of terrible mixed metaphors.

"Do you think our family is keeping the Kleenex company in business?" CeCe laughed through her sniffles, wiping her nose with her wad of tissue that was now nearly as big as an airplane pillow.

Rudy laughed. It seemed his daughter had somehow managed to channel her mother's sense of humor in these recent weeks. It was the closest he'd ever felt to CeCe.

"Counseling?" he repeated.

CeCe buried her face in the entire wad of Kleenex. "He wants a divorce."

Rudy hugged his daughter again, the only thing he could do at the moment, singing in her ear "Itsy Bitsy Spider," which she'd loved as a girl.

21

Rudy had been in the hospital for two weeks and two days. During this time, he'd only been off the ward to wind down the cement stairwell (caged in on the sides by floor-to-ceiling chain-link fencing) to the garden. A few times Sasha accompanied him.

They strolled, identifying the flowers without plaques as best they could. "Lark-spurs, not delphinium," Sasha had mused, bending her willowy body to inspect the deep-blue blooms between her fingertips. It seemed that her Nordstrom work clothes — typically a skirt, billowy blouse, and cardigan — camouflaged how thin she was. Rudy looked forward to cooking for her again in his own kitchen.

And so Rudy was feeling ready to go the morning Dr. Ring came bearing the good news that he would soon be released. Just the weekend and a few days beyond that, to ensure that the medication and dosage they had mutually agreed upon was a well-tolerated best choice: an SSRI anti-depressant, plus a medication to augment that, as well as an antianxiety med to be used as needed.

Dr. Ring sipped from his herbal tea, settling into the chair in the corner by Rudy's, and for a moment peered down on the busy morning activity below.

Bee wouldn't be there when he got home. It wouldn't be as though one of them had merely gone on a business trip and now they each brimmed with stories to share. Bee was never coming back. Rudy was a widower. He wasn't sure what other definitions applied to him now.

He turned to Dr. Ring. "What is my diagnosis?"

Dr. Ring sat up straighter in his chair. "You've got depression. Or what we specifically call major depressive disorder — which is unipolar depression, as opposed to bipolar. You've also got generalized anxiety disorder and trauma from your wife's sudden, shocking death, and your efforts to try to revive her." Rudy nodded, appreciating the fact that this would be easily explainable to both CeCe and Sasha.

Dr. Ring looked into his empty cup with a twinge of disappointment, perhaps wishing there were more of his tea. "Some of us are born with a predisposition for depression, and it is triggered by life events." He paused, looked at Rudy to catch his eye. "Would you say that Bethany was your best friend?"

Rudy nodded, his eyes welling up. Quite frankly, he was getting sick of all this crying. He didn't want to live in a Hallmark movie for the rest of his life.

"Just think of the gravity of that," Dr. Ring said. "The latitude you would allow anyone close to you, had they experienced such a loss."

A nurse bumped through the door with the vitals cart, smiled when she saw Dr. Ring, and said she'd come back.

"It is my belief," Dr. Ring said, looking down at the gingko trees lining the strip of grass at the small parking area, "that grief is like asthma or arthritis."

Rudy nodded, but he had no idea what Dr. Ring meant.

"It is a chronic condition."

"That's encouraging," Rudy laughed.

"Stay with me," Dr. Ring said, holding out a hand. "It actually is encouraging. Because if you accept grief as something you will likely always carry with you, it is less shocking when it rears its head."

"Okay." Rudy uncovered the cup of hot

water on a tray he'd been given for tea, selected an herbal tea bag from a sugar and tea container, mixed it up, and handed it to Dr. Ring.

"Let's say," Dr. Ring hypothesized, taking the cup from Rudy, "let's suppose that someone told you that it was never going to rain again. Ever. Rain was over, done with. There was closure on rain. How would you feel if one day you awoke to a cold, gray morning with rain beating against the window?"

"Despair," Rudy answered. "But I feel despair no matter what when the grief comes."

"Yes," Dr. Ring agreed. "But you've been encouraged to believe you should avoid experiencing despair. But if you know that it will always rain off and on, you recognize it. You may drop to your hands and knees, and pound your fists on the floor, but you know this rain. And sometimes it might come for a short interval. Like a song on the radio. Or the smell of roast chicken at the grocery. And you know it. There it is again. The grief. It is a part of you and you will get help from others to address it and manage it. I'm encouraging you to recognize and accept this new part of you. And this doesn't mean you don't move on. You *can* move on and honor your dead wife at the same time. When my brother died, I will never forget our neighbor's words to me. He said, 'Things will never be the same. They'll get better, they'll be different, but they'll never be the same.' Those words stayed with me forever. Because that is exactly how I felt."

"In some ways, I feel that I'm already moving on, and that does scare me," Rudy said.

Dr. Ring took off his glasses. "In what way?"

Rudy thought Dr. Ring would tell him all of the predictable warnings when he heard about Sasha: *You're in a vulnerable position right now. Don't make life-altering decisions, big plans, other than decisions that will reduce your stress.* And he did. Rudy knew he was right. In the abstract. Just as a medevac landed on the hospital roof above the emergency room, Dr. Ring said, "Life is short. Love heals us. Sounds corny, but it's mostly true."

This adage was better than any pill. Rudy had lived for a crippling year with lonesomeness, and he had the opportunity to be with a person he was starting to have strong feelings for, and he figured the worst that could happen was that it wouldn't work out.

"But what about Hercules's hydra?" Rudy asked Dr. Ring.

Hercules's hydra was a concept and actual illustration Dr. Ring had drawn for Rudy during one of their first talks. Sometimes, rather than attacking one snake at a time rearing from the head of the hydra, you had to cut off the whole shebang from the neck. Grief from the death of a spouse disabling him, job changes, the decision to give away his wife's things — you had to cut the whole thing off at the neck. Not live in limbo, fighting one snake at a time.

Dr. Ring sipped from his tea. Instead of gazing out Rudy's hospital window, as he typically did, he reached over and gave Rudy's hand a squeeze. "You deserve companionship and peace. We all do. But let me just say one thing, and please, will you take it to heart? Do not. Do *not* place the metric of your happiness, your recovery, your wellness, depression relapses on to Sasha, or the situation of having her with you. I know this sounds obvious, but just will you promise me to watch for that?"

Rudy was touched by the words "promise me," something he'd hear from Bee, from a family member, a friend. A simple, genuine, nonclinical request, devoid of rhetoric.

"I promise you and I am grateful to you

more than you'll know. You folks up here —" Rudy choked up.

Dr. Ring patted Rudy on the back, and then set down his tea. "Rudy, it's been a pleasure. Remember that you have more support around you than you realize."

Rudy thought back on his admission, on how he'd been frightened and indifferent and skeptical all at once. He could see now how his initial fear and apprehension came from movie clichés and the pictures people were quick to paint when describing the mentally ill (or an unkempt or homeless person, for that matter — weren't they all the same?). *She looked as though she escaped the nuthouse!* Really? Like a college student or emergency room nurse? Like a professional opera tenor or software engineer or winery owner?

Sure, Rudy remained spooked by the idea of somehow becoming as lost as the patient who floated through the halls of the locked unit — with a bald head and hollowed-out eyes that made him appear like a cross between a ghost and a hard-boiled egg. One morning the gentleman peered through the window of the door of the group therapy meeting on the locked side, blinking in at the patients from both units. The pointed tip of the man's big head, patched with thin wisps of black hair, knocked gently against the glass, as if he wanted to get in, join the others. One of the group leaders would step out to help the patient to the nurse's station. Rudy felt both pity and fear toward the man, and shame for experiencing that tinge of fear. But it wasn't fear *of* the guy so much as anxiety over falling down the same dark hole that had trapped him. Later, a young woman named Cheyenne, who was staying on the unlocked side for a second time — for a lithium tune-up — expressed serious concern for the man.

"Hi, Alex!" she called out, as the gentleman shuffled by with a lockdown group, through the open-unit dayroom to the stairwell down to the garden for air. These patients had to venture out en masse, with a nurse. Alex just stared over his shoulder blankly at Cheyenne, as though she were as incongruous as a clam or shoe.

"Oh, no." Cheyenne looked struck as the thick door thumped shut after the group. "Alex and I were here at the same time before. Over here." She tapped the long table where some of them lingered after dinner, working puzzles, playing games, reading the paper. "He was funny. Totally athletic. I wonder what happened." And by *happened,* Rudy knew that this was likely a chewed-up-by-life event that could have happened to any of them. The death of a spouse, for example.

At night, when insomnia hovered beside Rudy's bed, rudely mouth-breathing and tapping its foot against the bedframe, Rudy imagined himself declining like Alex. Landing back in the hospital on the locked side, suddenly that vacant and lost, his mind an empty parking lot. There but for the grace of Sasha, CeCe, Dr. Ring, and a team of excellent doctors and med students, Rudy was doing better. But he knew he would have to work on himself once home. Every day.

The day before Rudy was to leave the hospital, CeCe came by looking tired, with circles under her eyes cover-up makeup couldn't quite hide. Rudy tried to get out of her what was going on at home, but she was adamant about it. Focusing soley on Rudy's discharge — what the plan would be that day, that week, and in the weeks following. There was an outpatient program Dr. Ring wanted Rudy to attend. Where would that be? How would Rudy get there?

"I'll drive," he assured her.

"On this new medication?"

"It's not new at this point. I'm acclimated

and will be fine."

CeCe took notes in her day planner, and suddenly Rudy felt like her second child for whom arrangements needed to be made while she worked.

"Sweetheart," Rudy bent over with his hands on his knees, looking up at her from below so he could meet her gaze, "I'm going to be fine. Things are looking up. There's a plan. A post-hospitalization plan that the doctors and a social worker will go over with me. You can come and meet with us if you like. But it's optional."

CeCe stopped writing. She looked hurt.

"I mean," Rudy ran his hand over his face, clean-shaven for Sasha, "I just don't want you to worry too much. I'm not medicated to the point of impairment. I'm worlds better . . . In fact . . ." Rudy stumbled. He went over the lines he'd memorized pacing the hall the day before. *Companionship, symbiotic, two souls on our own . . .*

"Sit down." His voice was somewhere between a plea and a command. CeCe sighed heavily. Set her planner on the table before her, took a long sip of tea. She released her head and shoulders into the headrest of the chair behind her, looking relieved to relinquish her take-charge church lady duties for a moment.

"I am going to be fine. I will return to work. And I'm going to continue seeing Sasha. We've become very close while I've been in the hospital."

"Dad," CeCe said apologetically — perhaps she could tell that this wasn't easy for Rudy. "I'm sorry. I am *so* tired. I'm just. I hope you know, my reservations about your getting to know Sasha quickly, my reservations about your becoming close while so vulnerable — they have *nothing* to do with her personally. I can see that she's special. I'm just scared. I'm scared for you. God, I sound like a dumb self-help book. I'm scared for *me*. For my marriage. Which also has nothing to do with you or Sasha. I want to be" — her voice caught in her throat — "good."

Rudy laughed so suddenly and loudly that CeCe jumped, startled. "Darling, I'm so sorry, I'm not laughing at you. That's just. I don't know of a way you could be any more of a good person."

"That's exactly what I mean." CeCe sighed with exasperation. "I don't want to be a bumbling, bossy Goody Two-shoes. I want to be . . ." She was fighting back crying, still unable to speak (Lord, when they got out of here were they still all going to be crying messes?), and Rudy felt angry with his son-in-law for making his daughter feel anything but absolutely great about herself.

"I want to be a good daughter. And a good mother. I want to be a good wife." Her face was pinched and red, as though she might sob, but she regained her composure. "I want to be a good, you know, lighthearted daughter of Sasha's new guy. I want Mom to be proud. I want my husband to love me, my daughter to think I'm fun. The mom who doesn't care that there's cupcake frosting on her daughter's elbows. Sometimes I feel like *you're* the only one who thinks I'm okay the way I am."

Rudy was so touched by this, he stood up and lurched toward his daughter to give her a hug. He had imagined himself to be an irritant to CeCe.

"I *do* think you are *wonderful* the way you are! And I feel angry with anyone who doesn't agree."

CeCe kicked off her shoes. She rubbed her eyes in a way that must be bad for them. Then she let out such a sigh that Rudy was grateful for the relief he heard.

The nurse came in to take Rudy's vitals. CeCe complimented her on her scrubs, her shoes, her hair band. Although orderly and critical of the way so many things worked,

CeCe was always complimentary of others. Demonstratively so. Just like her mother.

"Not sure if there are any harder workers out there," Rudy said, shyly indicating the nurse, Lilly, among his favorites. When she was finished with Rudy, he followed her and the cart out into the hall.

"My daughter is so tired," he told her. "May I ask you for a favor?"

"Shoot."

"You know those blankets from the warmer . . . ?"

"Let me bring Cecilia one."

And in less than a minute Lilly returned with one of the warm, nubby blankets that was an armful of comfort. Then she handed Rudy a cold can of ginger ale and a straw.

"I owe you one." Rudy turned back into the room. CeCe's eyes were closed and her legs hung over one arm of the chair. Rudy unfolded the blanket and enveloped her inside it. CeCe sighed again, even more deeply. He popped open the can of ginger ale, unwrapped the straw, and set the drink before her on the hospital table.

"We'll be landing in Honolulu in approximately five hours and fifteen minutes," he told her.

She sipped the ginger ale and closed her eyes again.

He tucked one of the pillows from his bed behind her neck, pushing it down so that it was level with the top of her ears and hairline, offering her the best neck support.

Rudy then took hold of the blue hospital curtain, which was pushed back and gathered along the ceiling at the head of his bed. He tugged it around to the window, creating a wall of privacy between them and the door. CeCe's eyes remained closed.

"I have a proposal to make," Rudy declared, knocking the edge of his small, institutional glass with the tines of his fork.

"But of course." Sasha was nonplussed as she dove into her mashed potatoes. Tonight they were eating two hospital dinners. You would not think hospital salmon would be good, but it was among the nicest dishes. And Sasha was of the same opinion as Rudy: Food made by anyone else started two steps above the live-alone diet of toast and cereal for dinner.

"Now that I am leaving the hospital, I would like us to start dating. Officially."

Sasha laughed, her pale pink cheeks blushing a deeper rose color. She waved a hand in dismissal. "I have husband. *At large.*" She winced a little, took a bite of salmon, and looked up and above Rudy's head thought-

313

fully. "A husband with a girlfriend and baby who is nowhere to be found. Whose name is on my mortgage, who occasionally finds a way into my bank account but who will not come home. His cell phone number is same and I call and I call and leave message and I am so aggravated I don't call anymore. I don't want him to think I am heartbroken and want him to come home. His girlfriend can have him. I want to sell my house, which is on the verge of selling itself via the bank if Gabor doesn't show up and sell it with me and allow us to divide our property. Limbo." Sasha set down her fork.

Rudy wished he hadn't interrupted her from eating her dinner.

"That's exactly what I talked about with my doctor today: limbo. Hercules's hydra. A quagmire of snakes. As soon as you cut off one, another rears its head. Which is why you have to stop attacking the snakes one at a time and cut the whole thing off at the neck."

"And what about missing snake? Missing alcoholic ne'er-do-well husband?"

Rudy cleared the dishes from Sasha's tray to the radiator. He flipped the paper place mat on her plastic tray and gave it a wipe with a napkin. He lay out a fresh napkin and fork. Then he opened his nightstand drawer and produced a tiny gourmet grocery store cake that CeCe had brought for him.

Sasha's eyes filled with tears when he placed the little cake between them, facing her. It was chocolate with thick fudge chocolate frosting and a cream layer within, with two pink roses adorning it. Chocolate was her favorite. Rudy had learned this when the word *cocoa* came up in their crossword puzzle, which he always pulled from one of the morning newspapers and saved to do with her. The word *cocoa* had led to a dream discussion of desserts they loved, the good news being that they both had a sweet tooth.

"This is very nice," Sasha stammered.

Rudy could see she was working to regain her composure. Like CeCe, she clearly did not like to weep in front of others. Her tale of Stefi had been an anomaly she seemed a little embarrassed by. Maybe he shouldn't have pushed her into a serious conversation now.

"Sasha, I do not want to push you into anything. And I don't want you to pity-date me."

"What is this 'pity-date,' Rudy?"

"I mean, don't feel like you have to say yes because I have a crush on you and I'm in a mental hospital."

Sasha's look became grave. "Rudy, there is nothing I want more than to be 'official.' It is just . . . I am married woman with many complications."

"A full set of luggage with carry-on and steamer trunks?"

Sasha nodded and giggled.

"Me too. The cure for that?"

Sasha shook her head. "Ah, if only we knew."

"Cake." Rudy cut a slice, placed it on her plate.

She made sure to get all the frosting as she ate. Licking her fingers, she agreed to come over and cook him dinner when he got home from the hospital. "That is a start," she declared.

"When I was a young man," Rudy told Sasha, "I wanted to get married, but had no idea, no plan, for what to do after that. I let Bee make all of our plans. Now I'm figuring out what *I* want — and the first thing that I want is a dinner, at my home, with you.

"I made you this." Rudy opened his nightstand drawer and produced the small, decoupage box that he had made in the occupational therapy room on the unit. "It's not fancy or expensive, but it's heartfelt and it's all the colors that you like. It reminds me of you, and I feel cheerful whenever I see it."

Sasha gasped. Her face flushed pink again. "Beautiful, you made?"

"Occupational therapy. Decoupage!"

Sasha held the box in two hands and looked up at the ceiling. "You know," she said. "You've already given me so many gifts." She raised one hand, counting out with her fingers in the air: "Music, laughs at dull job, confidence, happy stories of happy marriage, dogwood tree name!" Her hand was splayed out with five items. She giggled. "This is beautiful. I love it." She pulled the box to her chest.

To give her a moment, Rudy stepped out to the kitchen to make her fresh tea with milk and sugar, the way she liked it. The hospital hall smelled of warm chicken and lemon-lime cleaner. It smelled of comfort and institutional walls at the same time. Rudy was excited by the notion of learning all the other things she liked — more of the small things such as Chopin waltzes and desserts with marzipan. The list would grow. A list of all the things he could do to add to her happiness. In this way, Sasha was like Bethany — simple things brought her pleasure. And when it came to these small joys, she was demonstrative, irrepressible. This song! Those trees! Yet both women were quick to gently tease Rudy — to not let him get away with buffoonery or bluster. Was it all right to draw these similarities between Bee and Sasha? He decided it was probably okay. Because awakening one Wednesday morning to find your wife dead beside you under the duvet proved one, and perhaps *only* one, adage: Life *is* short. This was perhaps the one tired maxim that rang true through the thick layers of dark, depressive dreams and murky, choking days of grief. And when it came to how you would possibly live out the rest of your days without driving off a cliff, some things became clear: Finding love isn't about finding someone at the right time. It's about finding the right person, regardless of the time. Once we're a certain age, we know these things, don't we? There are no checklist test drives, rebound relationship rules, or appropriate periods of mourning. We aren't meant to be punished with scratchy black Victorian garb buttoned up to our chins. Even CeCe didn't have the energy or heart to lecture her father — who loved her mother as much as she could ever love anyone — about the possible pitfalls of dating Sasha.

Rudy returned to the hospital room with a fresh cup of hot tea for Sasha. She had taken her hair out of its ponytail and brushed it. Her tresses lay fluffy and bright around her face. She cradled the cup in her hands.

"Does Cecilia know?" she asked Rudy shyly. "That we are becoming 'official.' "

Rudy nodded. "She can't wait to meet you."

22

At work, Sasha rested her hip bones against the warmth of the watch case. She didn't want sleepiness to envelop her during the late-morning slow period, so she opened the glass and rearranged the watches, moving the more expensive pieces toward the front. The first of October was close enough to holiday season to do so, their manager had said. He implored them: "Make your case burst with treasures shoppers would love to find under the tree!" Silicon Valley certainly relished status symbols. The store's decorator would dress everything in holly and gold, silver, and ruby-red glass balls to complement the felt. "We want them to spend, spend, spend!" the manager chirped at Sasha.

Sasha was a conservative shopper, but this year her discount would prove useful for holiday gifts. Sasha was so happy to have significant others to shop for this year:

Rudy, CeCe, and CeCe's little daughter, who Rudolph had said was delighted by just about everything from pigeons to cardboard boxes.

Now Judy, Sasha's sometimes lunch partner, wandered over from Clinique. Their special had just ended. "Silicon Valley now has enough mini mascaras to fill a landfill," Judy had said the day prior. By today they'd cleaned up the aftermath of the rush. Now came the lull.

"Hey," Judy told Sasha, "there are a couple of cute men over in the Suits Department. Well, one guy's in Suits and the other guy is in Shoes, I think. Want to take a walk around to meet them?"

Judy was bold. The last time they'd made such rounds, she had done Sasha's makeup first.

"Land you a guy, help you sell more watches. Can't hurt!"

Sasha didn't wear a wedding ring, and no one at work other than Rudy knew about Gabor.

Judy was kind and funny, but her topics of conversation didn't extend to Chopin. Sasha had been worried about the makeup makeover, given that Judy's routine included a thick layer of foundation — a mask Sasha couldn't imagine using. She begged off that layer, and as she watched in the mirror she was pleased by the pale peach and very light bronze blush and shadow Judy applied, followed by light brown eyeliner she smudged in such a way Sasha would never be able to replicate. Last, she made Sasha open her mouth as she applied a nude pink lipstick, which had required lip smacking, followed by a sheer gloss. Sasha even purchased a few of the products later with her discount — a luxury for her.

"C'mon — let's go for a stroll."

Sasha politely declined. "I'm so tired," she explained. "I've been visiting a friend in the hospital most nights." She paused. "And, I am dating." She didn't mention that the dates had all been *at* the hospital.

"What? You didn't *tell* me." Judy reached across the watch counter, the sleeve of her white Clinique lab-coat uniform making little static pings on the glass. She squeezed Sasha's arm. "You have a *boyfriend.*" Judy clapped and did a little jump. There were streaks of tester lipstick on the top of one of her hands.

Sasha nodded and smiled shyly at the watches. Judy giggled, waned, and winked conspiratorially as she sidled back to her station, bubbling with happiness for her friend.

It was true: Sasha was a girlfriend. A welcome status, given that she was no longer a mother, and hardly a daughter, given her parents were gone. She was hardly a wife. Her one brother, who lived in England, had a new family, and it was too far and expensive for either him or Sasha to travel all the way between the west coast of America and their little village. Besides, the new wife wasn't that welcoming.

Yet being happy worried Sasha. Even on the sunny warm days of September in Palo Alto, she imagined the ice that had taken her and Gabor down, broken her back, broken her spirit. Something about that incident might rise up, invisible and dangerous, to hurt her again. To take something else away. Stefi had been torn from her. Gabor was gone. Maybe Rudy would be next. Come home from the hospital, mix up medications, and die in *his* sleep, as his poor wife had. She returned to focusing on the watches, moving her favorite Swiss Army Watch front and center. For now, she was a girlfriend, she told herself. A girlfriend who was happy just to play gin rummy.

"Dad, don't make her your *project*." CeCe was getting over a cold, and her nose looked pinched and raw. The dry hospital air probably didn't help.

"I don't intend to! She is my *friend.*" Rudy straightened his covers and pillow. He couldn't wait to get home and sit in a chair, instead of this bed, and sleep in a bed that didn't move. "Lady friend," he added softly, immediately regretting these stodgy words.

CeCe blew her nose. Her weeping during hospital visits — a great relief to Rudy that brought them closer — had given way to the seasonal cold, and now she seemed plain run-down and distressed. To Rudy, it seemed like the first time she had truly succumbed to the pain of her mother's absence.

"Whatever." Cecilia sighed with resignation. "*Lady friend.* Oh my god."

"Well, I don't know!" Rudy raised his voice, startling CeCe. She sat up straighter in her chair, ballerina neck posture. "I haven't dated since I met your mother in college. And I would like to point out — as you rush to judge my social life — that most of my dates have been in a hospital! Other than one dinner I made for her at home, and a food court lunch we shared. And these have all been with a woman whom I am genuinely interested in, whom I was already friendly with at work. Your mother knows about her! Knew about her. I told her about her. My friend from Hungary in

Watches. Our mornings in the crazy circus of the first floor of the department store. Sasha has been nothing but kind to me, and now, as her friend, I want to help her get rid of her good-for-nothing husband so that she can get on with her life, too. You think life in a new country is easy? When you've got a mortgage and the family court system to navigate? You, more than anyone, know that age comes with complications."

Rudy raised a finger as he made this point. Suddenly he felt verbose, as if he were badgering his drained daughter with a lecture. He folded his hands in his lap.

It was early — the time between occupational therapy and dinner and visiting hours — but the nurses had become lax with Rudy, allowing his quiet, low-maintenance visitors lots of leeway.

CeCe slumped back in her chair, sipped cranberry juice from a hospital carton. "I'm sorry. Spencer keeps pointing out how judgmental I am. And the weird thing is, I see it now. But I don't mean to be. I'm oblivious, I suppose." She folded her arms across her chest, burying her hands under her arms. Usually this was to keep herself from ripping at her nearly bleeding cuticles.

"Don't apologize," Rudy told her. "You have every right to express your opinion.

You lost your mother."

"I'm an adult, Dad," CeCe reminded him. "With a family. At least for now."

The nurse came in to give Rudy his four o'clock medication and take his vitals. The antidepressants no longer had side effects. The mild antianxiety medication made his dreams steady, instead of turning into repetitive nightmares of that unthinkable morning. Plus, the daily goals on his white-board had escalated from "SHOWER" (on that first day in the hospital) to proactive tasks, such as "RESCHEDULE DENTIST APPOINTMENT."

Rudy had spent some time planning how to help Sasha extricate herself from her marriage. But now he wondered: *Was* his plan to help Sasha a patronizing *project*? He'd started a list of tasks he thought he could help her with, which included: cook hearty dinners, find divorce attorney, help her sell her house. Then Sasha could quit one job. Was this intrusive? Was he attacking Sasha's "Hercules's hydra," instead of his own? Yet he didn't want to date Sasha while watching her work two jobs to the point of exhaustion, deal with a deadbeat husband, America's legal system, and the sale of a home. As a white, male American, who didn't even need to work at this point, he had a leg up. And, after all, it was he who had gotten the rest at the hospital. It couldn't possibly have been a reprieve for Sasha to visit him so generously.

Besides, his own list was fairly short — just grief, really. And cleaning out his wife's things. Being there for his daughter.

At the hospital, some patients befriended and tried to help others solve their problems. "Remember," a group leader told them, "it was always easy to give advice. Meanwhile, we become unavailable for our own challenges."

But then in another group, they discussed having a plan in place when it came time to leave the hospital. You were supposed to line up a doctor, therapist, and day hospitalization program — a nine to three weekday routine of group therapy, lunch, and activities. *Crazy School,* Rudy thought. A young social worker handed out sheets of resources.

"The hardest part is asking for help," he gently told the group, pushing his slightly bent wire-rimmed glasses up on his nose.

Rudy didn't subscribe to this platitude. Having landed in bed like an injured rhino just before his in-patient hospitalization, he believed that for those living alone the hardest part was *getting* help. Getting toast.

Rudy had spent an entire day in bed trying to will himself into the kitchen to make a stack of toast.

Until recently he'd felt alone in the world without Bee. But he hadn't been left behind. He'd punished himself. Isolated himself.

Now Rudy was free to leave the hospital and try to start fresh. CeCe had to attend a school event for her daughter the next afternoon, and Sasha had volunteered to pick up Rudy.

The next day Rudy's pulse began drumming in his chest and throat in the afternoon. Later his limbs trembled and one foot tapped the floor, as he stood talking to Sasha, not feeling still enough to sit down. It wasn't Sasha that made him nervous or the ride arrangement. Something — *everything* it seemed — in Rudy's body was pointing toward a fear of leaving the hospital.

CeCe called as he was packing up with Sasha, and asked to speak to her. From Rudy's perspective, she didn't seem to let Sasha get a word in edgewise. A few seconds later, Sasha handed the phone back to Rudy, and he apologized for what he imagined were minute-by-minute orders issued by his daughter.

"Like police a little." Rudy could tell that Sasha was suppressing the giggles. He laughed, letting out a big cleansing breath that seemed to slow his heart rate. "But nice, not mean. And, you know," Sasha mused, "CeCe is very easy English-speaking person to understand, because she is so direct."

Rudy agreed. There were certainly no vague requests or instructions from CeCe. No nuances to decipher.

"She is the most literal-minded person I know. My daughter. Bethany and I used to say we couldn't imagine where her funny little personality came from." Rudy chided himself for bringing up Bee. But he and Sasha had discussed her quite a bit, along with Stefi, and Gabor. Still, he worried that now Sasha might feel excluded from his family. His family history. Oh, who was he kidding? He was a bachelor with a grand piano and too-big house who was fifty-four going on seventy-five.

"Ah, but this is a good thing, you know," Sasha observed, apparently unfazed by the mention of Bethany. "Do you know the hardest thing about learning English? Those sayings: 'That's the way the cookie crumbles.' "

"Aphorisms?"

"Yes, aphorisms. A rolling stone gathers no moss."

"A penny saved is a penny earned," Rudy shot back.

"A bird in the hand is worth two in the bush?" Sasha flipped a piece of her hair up over her lips, thinking. "Crazy, this. Means what?"

"Well —"

"Everything happens for a reason," Sasha added.

"That's a platitude!" Rudy corrected excitedly. "They're the bane of clichés. Especially if you're grieving."

Sasha tilted back her head, her gray eyes gazing up at the ceiling as she thought for a moment. She looked at Rudy.

"Definitely," she agreed, squeezing each of his shoulders. "What doesn't kill us, only makes us stronger. I say no!"

Just like everyone else, Tessie, Rudy's discharge nurse, seemed to find Sasha a delight. The latter wore a gray cashmere cardigan over a white T-shirt, her blond hair pulled back loosely into a ponytail. The gray sweater brought out the lovely blue-gray of Sasha's eyes. She wore blue jeans, white socks and loafers. It always thrilled Rudy to see Sasha in her jeans. Not in a sexy way, but because he was seeing her — a co-worker, after all — in her casual attire. Wearing the clothes in which she was most comfortable and most herself. It made Rudy feel closer to her. A kind of intimacy he wasn't sure he could even explain to anyone without sounding silly.

The three of them stood in a row, using the radiator cover as a table, as Tessie spread out and went over Rudy's discharge papers. Essentially, he just needed to initial a few spots, and follow the directions for when he got home, starting with a stop at the drug-store by his house for his new meds, which Dr. Ring had already phoned in. The partial hospitalization program (PHP) started in two days, giving Rudy a day at home to rest and acclimate.

Then came the embarrassingly strong recommendation that someone stay with the patient his first night home.

"I'll stay —" Sasha started.

"I'll phone Ce—" Rudy said.

"It's just that first night —" Tessie explained. "To be sa—"

"Guest room?" Rudy asked Sasha.

"Sure," Sasha replied.

Rudy felt his face flush red and warm.

Tessie stood behind Sasha and smiled her broad grin — moon face, straight white

331

teeth, waist-long brown hair tied back in a braid. "You'll work it out, I know," Tessie said, diminishing the big deal of these two adults sleeping in the same house.

Rudy nodded in agreement. He tried to act casually, decided that he'd tell Sasha once they were in the car that she shouldn't feel obligated. Even if CeCe couldn't come, he'd be fine.

Tessie helped Sasha and Rudy load his duffel bag and other items from the room onto a small hospital cart, before ducking out of the room.

Sasha took the helm of the wheelchair, seemingly happy to push him, despite his chagrin. He was not an invalid!

The floor secretary bid them farewell from behind the tall nurse's station. She stood to wave, a flash of bright pink fingernails as they passed.

"Oh, your wife has come to take you home! How nice!"

Rudy felt his face redden. "Friend," he corrected her, calling out over his shoulder. He felt embarrassed for Sasha. Saddled with this old wheelchair man! He was glad to be facing forward, away from Sasha and Tessie, so they couldn't see his mortified face. They paused at the double doors beyond the nurse's station and Tessie punched the big silver square button beside the doors, and they slooooowly swung open automatically. But then Sasha pushed the wheelchair around in a U-turn, so that both she and Rudy faced the front desk — the unit secretary and other nurses gathered there now. Tessie continued past them on down the hall.

"Meet you at the elevators," she called out.

Sasha pushed the wheelchair a little closer to the nurse's station, then stopped. Rudy smelled the clean, green-grass-and-citrus scent of her perfume as she leaned forward over him toward the group gathered there. A delightful tickle of her hair brushed his warm cheek.

"You are correct!" Sasha called out, holding a forefinger in the air. "*Girl*friend." With that, Sasha spun the wheelchair back through the double doors toward the bank of elevators.

As they drove home to Rudy's house, Sasha followed his directions, but he noticed she seemed to already know the way. She pulled into the driveway, parked, and clapped her hands with a we-made-it smack, and winked at Rudy. As he climbed out she scooped up the thick folder of his paperwork along with his medication from their store stop and ferried them into the house with them. Rudy hadn't wanted it to be like this at *all* — him an invalid, Sasha a nurse! So he concentrated on picking up his stride, taking care of business.

After carrying in all his reading materials, his computer, and a small bag of other belongings, he started a grocery shopping list. He was going to cook dinner for Sasha every night. It was the one thing he could start right away that might lighten her burden.

But then Sasha announced: "We have everything we need for dinner tonight," as she lined up his meds on the kitchen counter. "A stroganoff, it's mild, and a salad and sorbet. Plus I'm going to heat up this crusty French bread, and we'll have it with butter to make the meal more hearty."

"But I wanted to —"

"You need to put on some weight, sir."

"And you," Rudy poked Sasha in the side and she giggled.

He felt buoyant. He imagined she might be experiencing that pleasing feeling of *actually* being able to help someone. A capacity he'd yearned for since the paramedics hauled off Bethany.

As Sasha turned on the oven, Rudy peered into the refrigerator to check what sort of petrified, atrophied, and moldy disasters might lurk within. To his surprise, the refrigerator had been completely cleaned out, wiped down, and filled with fresh groceries, neatly arranged on the shelves. All the dribbles of widower take-out spills and pots of unfinished heated soups he'd been too lethargic to clean up — gone.

"My daughter sure is organized, isn't she?" Rudy whistled. "Runs a tight ship."

Sasha agreed with a hug, the softness of her cashmere sweater brushing what he imagined to be his too-rough cheek. But Sasha squeezed him tighter, the strength in her arms surprising him. Soft *and* strong. She released him, pushed his shoulders back to have a look at him, smiled approvingly, then kissed his bristly cheek. Together they fixed a snack of cheese and crackers and bubbly waters, and shuffled to sit in the living room.

After they'd removed their shoes and set their feet up on the coffee table, they talked about the hospital, Sasha's job, and how she didn't like the temporary piano player nearly as much as Rudy.

"He plays so mechanically," she observed between bites of cheese and crackers. "And *so* serious. Like a robot."

Rudy felt puffed up by this news. He

stood, bowed comically, and crossed the room to the piano to play her favorite Chopin piece, flipping aside imaginary tuxedo tails. But just as he settled in on the bench, he jumped up and swept a large framed photograph of Bee off the center of the piano. He loved the picture, the black-and-white film offering a timeless appeal — as though Bee might still be alive, as though she might walk through the door wearing the wool sweater they'd bought her in Ireland. Yet how would Sasha feel with Rudy's wife staring at her warmly, as if to say, "Enjoy the piano! Have a drink! I'm on my way home!" He frantically looked around the room and finally settled on stashing the picture on a bottom bookshelf.

When Sasha realized what Rudy had done — that he had moved Bethany's lovely photograph — she padded to the bookshelf in her stocking feet, lifted the frame gently — careful not to smudge the glass — and settled it back among a cluster of other family photos atop the piano.

"It's a beautiful photograph," she told Rudy, sitting beside him on the bench.

He made a show of scooting over, but barely moved, because he loved Sasha's closeness.

"She's so pretty," Sasha said. "She was a

wonderful wife, Rudy. I know, because I was in terrible marriage. She will always be in your heart."

Sasha thumped her fist on her chest; just beside a chain with a gold, heart-shaped locket that Rudy knew held a tiny picture of Sasha's daughter, Stefi.

Sasha rested her head on Rudy's shoulder. "You know," she told him, "this is not a deadline to stop honoring Bee."

III

23

It was late October now — almost Halloween. Rudy had been home from the hospital for nearly a month.

His first night home, Sasha had stayed with him, sleeping in the guest room, which had its own bath, on the other side of which was an office that had been CeCe's room growing up. Rudy was relieved by Sasha's decisiveness, choosing the guest room, and placing a framed photograph of Stefi beside the clock radio.

"May I see?" Rudy had asked, standing on the threshold in his stocking feet, and pointing to the photo. Sasha smiled and brought it to him. Her daughter was the spitting image of her, only with brighter hair — so blond it was almost white, pink satiny ribbons braided through her pigtails. She held a giant turkey drumstick, and the snapshot looked as though it had been taken at a Renaissance fair. The little girl was laughing — her mouth wide open, exposing tiny white corn-kernel teeth. Something chocolaty smudged her cheek. In photographs of people who had died, Rudy felt that he could see the motion within them that day or moment. Stefi's head tipping back in laughter, little legs kicking in the air as someone held her around the waist.

"Nutella." Sasha looked over Rudy's shoulder, pointing at the smudge. "Her favorite. Sandwiches, on a banana, spoonfuls from the jar."

Sasha's hand brushed Rudy's thumb. He wanted to hug her. He knew Sasha was being transported back to that day. The hot, dry fairgrounds, the smell of face paint.

Indeed, Sasha remembered the bees buzzing around the meat kabobs in the heat, sawdust kicked up above Stefi's little fringed suede bootlets and sprinkled across her calves and knees like cocoa powder. Gabor, several beers into the day, was still jolly, making Stefi laugh as he lifted her into his arms and swung her in a circle. "You are the princess, Stefi, of this entire kingdom. You are the keeper of all the Nutella in the land."

Stefi nodded vigorously. "I am! I shall be generous," she declared. "And share it with all my people!" She and her girlfriends at school had adopted this pattern of speech from the imaginary worlds they inhabited in books and movies. Like a cross between Chaucer and a Disney princess.

"I like this photograph," Sasha explained to Rudy, gently setting the frame back on the night table beside the double bed.

"It is of Stefi, but it is also of a happy day," Rudy guessed." Happier California days. When you were a family."

Sasha nodded. She sat down on the bed, which was covered with a quilt Bee and CeCe had made together for one of CeCe's Girl Scout badges. It was to include pieces of fabric from throughout CeCe's life. "Who saves all their kids' clothes?" Bee had lamented, frantic to find enough cloth, cutting into a plaid shirt of Rudy's. "Hey," Rudy had protested, "I still wear that."

"Not anymore," Bee had informed him. "I'm billing it as part of a Halloween costume that CeCe once wore as Ellie Mae Clampitt." Bee measured and cut four diamond-shaped swaths out of the back of the red-and-white shirt. "Or maybe she went as an Italian restaurant table."

"Hey, that's *Dad's,*" CeCe pointed out with disapproval.

"You want this badge?" Bee asked her daughter. CeCe nodded seriously.

"You want to sew a quilt?" she asked Rudy. Rudy shook his head vigorously, grateful for his wife's ingenuity.

After CeCe no longer wore her Girl Scout uniform or sash, Bee cut out the part of the sash bearing her badges and sewed it into the quilt, about eighteen inches down from the top and in the center, so it stood out for all to admire.

Rudy scooted beside Sasha on the bed. She took her hand in his. "Happier days behind us. Happier days to come."

"Yep," Rudy agreed. He kissed her cheek, the warmth of which made hime close his eyes and breathe in the sweet, slightly vanilla, slightly orange smell of her hair.

The following morning, Rudy got up early to discover that the door to Sasha's room had blown open. He peeked in on her for just a moment before pulling the door closed. Her spray of blond hair across the pillow filled him with a hope he couldn't possibly have imagined that first night trying to sleep in the hospital — the room a sterile black cavern of loneliness. When he passed by the guest bathroom, he felt foolish for being so excited by the sight of her toothbrush, tube of toothpaste, and bar of Clinique soap. A hairbrush entwined with

344

blond hairs. He sensed possibility. In that day. In his life.

And then it was time to be alone for the first time in weeks. Rudy remembered standing in his entryway, trying to convey to Sasha it was no big deal she was going back to her place, back to her jobs, leaving him in sweatpants and a Stanford sweatshirt that had been CeCe's. After he kissed her on each of her cheeks and she responded with a kiss on the mouth, after she refused to let him walk her out to her car and carry her small bag, after she closed the door, Rudy had been able to keep the smile on his face until he heard the door's click. Then he felt his face droop, heard the depression scratching at the windows to get in. He tried to be present, focusing on what he would fix himself for dinner, realizing that this would be his first dinner alone in a month. There would be no tray of varied food groups with Sasha or hospital pineapple upside-down cake or *Jeopardy!* on TV after dinner in the dayroom.

He had shifted from foot to foot, wondering what to do with his grief. For he had stuffed it under the bed when Sasha returned with him from the hospital. Now it was sliding down the banister. *Alone, are we? Here I am! What's for dinner? A loaf of loneliness? Let's play the piano — a little song called widower!*

Oh, fuck off, Rudy thought. He wasn't one to swear often, but sometimes he used his own R-rated version of CBT to ward off negative thoughts. He'd been skeptical at first that any of the piles of handouts brought home from the hospital would help. That his confuddled brain (a cross between confused and befuddled, he'd explained to his new therapist) would remember any of the hospital tricks. On some days his stay there remained as a blur of meal forms to fill out, circles of lost faces in group, and the bright blue expanse of sky above his hospital bed window. But the breathing exercises, the replacement thoughts, the distraction exercises — they had actually worked that first day home. There was nothing to lose, he'd learned. He had a dark inner world separate from Sasha's, one which he had continued to slay on. He was a brave knight. A CBT musketeer.

The autumn was Sasha's favorite time of year in California — she loved the way summer might linger all the way into November. Some days might be as warm as seventy degrees Fahrenheit — with roses still blooming in the yards — yellow ones tinged with red and peach, spotted and bumpy, imperfections from the cold nights that were coming on. Sasha loved these less-than-perfect flowers, which were always far more fragrant than those bought at a store or florist's. California roses bloomed into the fall. Back home in Hungary, there might be warm days, but the sun would have vanished by now, leaving the world like a black-and-white photograph. Above the houses and concrete apartment buildings, gray clouds would thicken and billow into coal smokestacks of gloom.

Sasha loved the long line of gingko trees along Rudy's street. They had turned uniformly yellow now, so that when the sun hit them in the afternoon they looked lit from within, like rows of candles. At home, the leaves all would have fallen from the trees, leaving bare branches like arthritic fingers clawing at a bitterly chilling white sky. The concrete buildings, the frozen yellow-brown grass that was lumpy and unforgiving when you walked across it — so easy to turn an ankle. The world there was raw and depleted, and the change of season depleted one's spirits. Rainy days arrived by November. Longer nights meant longer and longer drinking hours for Gabor. (But it wasn't home anymore, was it? Maybe Sasha would take Rudy to see Hungary one day. But surely she could call America her home now.)

While these delicious two or three extra months of almost-summer were remarkable to Sasha, what she didn't particularly like was this American holiday — Halloween — that brought children swarming to your door. When Stefi was little, Sasha and Gabor had dressed her up and taken her from apartment to apartment in their first place in Fremont, before they bought the tiny house in San Jose. At the apartment building there were just enough people who knew them to collect a few little treats and have them fawn over Stefi's costume, as a ladybug or princess. Remembering this, Sasha was consumed with a wistful sadness, but she would be strong. Strong for Rudy. Strong for *herself.*

Halloween was their first holiday together.

Rudy had stressed that morning, for the third time, that they could turn out the lights, just leave the bright garage floodlight on over the driveway so no one tripped and fell, and step out to eat and see a movie. Sasha sighed deeply and shook her head. She considered this seriously — playing hooky from Halloween sounded both wonderful and like cheating.

Holidays had always been opportunities for Sasha to make little celebrations for Stefi. She could buy an inexpensive kit to carve a pumpkin to look like a kitty. Letting Stefi scoop out the pumpkin innards with her bare hands until there were strings and seeds in her hair and she laughed and laughed and rolled on the floor until they had to put her in a warm bath and to bed, and finish the carving kit on their own — Sasha and Gabor. A couple. When they had first arrived in California, Gabor was happy, and he barely drank. He was reliable enough to either give Stefi a bath or finish the fine carving of the outline of a cat's whiskers through the thick skin of an autumn pumpkin.

Sasha insisted to Rudy that she would be okay handing out candy with him. He warned her again — with excitement in his voice this time — that a lot of kids came to his house. "Your bum will barely get the chance to skim the seat of your chair before the doorbell rings again." He and Bee had always loved this about their neighborhood, especially after Cecilia outgrew trick-or-treating, and especially once she went off to college.

Even if it turned out that next year their tradition would be dinner out and a movie on Halloween night, Sasha wanted to do things with Rudy in as normal a fashion as possible this year.

They were each afraid that their grief would seep into the other's psyche — like algae that eventually choked out the oxygen and killed the decorative carp in a pond. Too thick. Eutrophic.

And so they had a huge bowl of candy at the ready, and many bags with which to refill it. While it was still light out, Rudy grilled cheeseburgers on the barbecue on the back patio, serving Sasha on a tray in front of the TV — a World Series baseball game, which she insisted she enjoyed. The hamburger was the best she'd ever eaten, she told him. Brown on the outside and juicy in the center, with lettuce, tomato, and pickles. Potato chips and carrot sticks and coleslaw. They each sipped from beers. Sasha let out a huge sigh as she licked the foam from her upper lip. The thing she liked about the baseball game was that she could follow it in a basic sense — balls, strikes, bases, outs, home runs — but she didn't have to concentrate on it carefully like the plot of a movie. Her mind could wander. She wished the holidays — even Easter, with the stores' baskets and flavored lip balms and stuffed bunnies, socks and sweets which

she had loved for filling Stefi's basket —
were over, and it was early summer and no
one was coming to the door.

There was the crack of a baseball bat, the
ball shooting straight out of the park and
into the packed crowd in the seats along the
San Francisco Bay. The fans cheered. Rudy
and Sasha cheered. Then the doorbell rang.

"The littlest ones come before it's quite
dark," Rudy said, wiping his mouth with his
napkin and getting up from his tray to head
out into the front hall. "You enjoy your supper," he told Sasha.

But Sasha didn't want to hide in the living room like a stowaway or mistress. She
followed Rudy into the hallway, touching
his elbow and putting on a smile as he
scooped up the big wooden salad bowl of
candy.

Their first customers were CeCe and
Keira — Kiki, who was dressed in a little
white lab coat.

"Scientist?" Rudy guessed.

"EnTOmoloGIST," Kiki declared, pointing to the spiders that had been attached to
her pockets, kicking up her little hiking
boots, and showing off her *real* magnifying
glass. "It's a kind of scientist who likes
bugs," she explained to Rudy.

"Oh, right!" Rudy agreed, slapping his

forehead. "And studies them. Maybe you will one day.

"Only my granddaughter," Rudy whispered to Sasha, giggling as they headed to the kitchen for cider and Kiki's miniature hamburger (protein, Rudy insisted!) and cake donut holes — a ritual before trick-or-treating. Kiki loved cake donuts more than candy.

"Always up to her elbows in dirt," CeCe called after Sasha and Rudy en route to the kitchen. "In the classroom, in the yard. We've got an aquarium ant farm that terrifies me. I'm sure it's only a matter of time before those ants get into the kitchen and bake a cake."

After their little supper, Sasha went with CeCe and Keira to trick-or-treat on their street. She wondered if she'd ever get used to marching up to strangers' front doors and ringing the bell.

Halloween had been an unexpected pleasure, even though Rudy knew the lead-up had given both him and Sasha some anxiety. Halloween meant the holidays were coming. Without Bee. Without Stefi. Although these would be his first holidays with Sasha. Assuming she'd join him. For everything. He hoped she'd join him for everything. He got so anxious and worried by the idea of the coming holidays that Rudy stocked up on ridiculous amounts of candy, eating it in the evenings like a nervous squirrel. *Move in with me* — he'd rehearsed this plea in his mind a million times; it came to him all the time, like a song you couldn't get out of your head. But he didn't have a follow-up speech to back up the fact that, without a doubt, this was what Sasha should do.

They'd started sleeping together, the first time Rudy carrying Sasha from his living room when she'd nearly fallen asleep after dinner and a movie.

"All we have to do is sleep," he'd proclaimed. But Sasha had other ideas. It was like swimming. Swimming in a stream, swimming in a pool, swimming in the ocean. His scalp tingling from the cool water, his arms and legs loosening, toes touching the bottom, coming up for air, grasping each other's arms. Laughing.

In the morning, Sasha revealed that she was wary of invading Rudy's former marital bed. That evening he went out and bought all new bedding. He washed and dried everything and made up the bed fresh. From then on they were lovers, bedmates, cemented best friends.

■ ■ ■ ■

Rudy and Sasha went for walks, built fires, and cooked dinners at Rudy's place.

"Move in with me," Rudy finally blurted, the second week they'd shared his room. "Sell your house, live here for real. Marry me, move in with me, go to the rest home with me."

"Polygamy illegal!" Sasha pinched the extra bit of flesh above Rudy's boxers.

He sucked in his belly, shot out an arm to flex his fist for her. "I will crush other husband. I am number one husband." He reached for a sip of water beside the bed, offered some to Sasha. She drank, sat up, and pulled her nightgown over her head. "Oof, must get ready for work."

"And that's another thing," Rudy declared. "You choose, but I vote that you only work one of your jobs. Especially since you're selling your house. And I've got more than enough of what I need for one person — enough for two."

Sasha turned to him. Her eyebrows lifted as she pushed her fluffed hair out of her eyes.

"This is real life," Sasha said, raising her forefinger in the air and pointing it at him.

354

"Real life, big move."

"Is that a yes!" Rudy was as excited as a kid. He knew life's complications. They both did. *You've got this,* Bee had said to him his first day at the department store piano after the disgrace of losing his job. He had *not* lost his job, Bee had insisted, once again. He'd been downsized, with a very good package, like so many other workers in the valley. It had nothing, *nothing* to do with his worth as an employee, let alone as a person.

Sasha nodded so slowly it could have been interpreted as some sort of neck stretch for a crick.

"We've got this," Rudy told her, touching his forefinger to hers.

She hooked her finger around his and gave him a real nod.

"We've got this." She drew him in for a hug, his stubble rough against her sensitive skin — a familiar morning sensation she'd quickly grown to love. Hungary had always been home in her mind. From the time she'd moved to America. Gabor had been a winding, too-narrow road, clinging to a cliff too close to a sheer drop to the ocean. To that icy sidewalk. Like Highway One down the Big Sur coast, which he had driven frighteningly fast, a day in which she feared she might die, and honestly wondered if it would be a much-needed release from this man. But Rudy. Rudy was home. This was Rudy and Bethany's house, yes. She realized now, however, why it didn't matter that it had been Bethany's home for so many years. Because to Sasha, Rudy was home.

She had heard this in an American song or movie — a person proclaiming that another person was home. Maybe in one of those cheerful show tunes. At the time, Sasha had found the notion plain silly. Another cookie-crumbles saying that she didn't get. But now. Now she felt the truth of this and realized that it wasn't a distinctly American feeling, but universal. A phenomenon for everyone, yet probably a sense of companionship few got to experience. For the first time since Stefi's death, Sasha thought, *I am lucky.*

The next week, Rudy and Sasha chose a real estate agent. The agent seemed to sense that they were both floundering a bit when it came to making a plan, so she took over. She happened to have a young couple new to the Valley who needed to rent a place for six months until spring, when she would put Sasha's house on the market. She would rent to the young couple for a slightly reduced price, in exchange for some light renovation: painting the walls, landscaping.

As they sat at Rudy's dining room table going over the Realtor's plan, the Realtor said to Sasha, "He's blushing and you're beaming, so I'm guessing your plan is to move in together." Sasha giggled and Rudy coughed, and then they all sipped their water.

Next Rudy and Sasha met with a divorce attorney who drew up papers with which a process server would attempt to serve Gabor. Sasha was given a copy, too, on the off-chance she would come into contact with her husband. The attorney insisted that all she would have to do was hand Gabor the papers. Rudy scrutinized the lawyer's bill — which included a charge of $90 for leaving a voicemail. "We break down our hourly rate," the lawyer told Rudy.

"Mmm-hmm," Rudy replied agreeably. "I see you also round up, and have made repeated phone calls to a number we told you was no longer Gabor's employer. At ninety dollars a pop?"

"I'll take one off," the attorney said. He didn't say the firm had made a mistake. These lawyers never said they made a mistake. There was an attorney in Rudy's poker group and the words "I was mistaken,

I'm sorry . . ." had never crossed the guy's lips.

"And you capitalize on others' misfortune."

"How about I remove the charge for the other call, too?" the attorney conceded, as though he were doing Sasha a big favor.

"Nah, leave it," Rudy told him. "I want to be able to show people that you guys charge ninety dollars to leave a voicemail."

The attorney stood, straightened his expensive pinstripes. Rudy took Sasha's hand as they stood, too. In family court, your own attorney was somehow on equal footing with the opposing counsel and the judge. The lawyers, judges, and bailiffs all punched in to work together every morning. Rudy had learned this in the short time he had spent researching, interviewing, and hiring an attorney for Sasha. He knew from working with attorneys on Bethany's estate that they could be overcharging to the point of billing you for their mistakes. From what he could tell, the family court system was a capricious cross between a Gogol short story and a Bugs Bunny cartoon. And so he felt this was the one thing in this situation that, as a native English speaker and Californian, he could help Sasha with.

■ ■ ■ ■

Sasha quit her job cleaning the locker rooms at the club, giving a week's notice. The ladies at the club — the women who attended regularly and some of the instructors and personal trainers — all of whom used the cushy locker rooms and formed overlapping friendships, got Sasha a cake for her last day. A friendly, artificially tanned woman made a healthy pomegranate-lemonade punch that was delicious. They chipped in and paid for another maid to work that day, and tipped her for cleaning up after their shindig. A few of the club members whispered to Sasha that she had been "our favorite" housekeeper.

They also chipped in and bought her a beautiful silver bracelet that you pinched together to expand and collapse. The top of the bracelet was woven with a braid of gold, too. Sasha couldn't remember the last time she wore a bracelet. Bracelets bumped up against the counters and buckets as she cleaned, and against the watch case as she demonstrated her wares at the department store.

The morning after her last day working at the gym, Sasha awoke in a silly mood —

giddy from being released from her cleaning job. She and Rudy talked and snuggled and had coffee and English muffins in bed.

She spun the bracelet from the ladies at the club around and around on her wrist, showing it to Rudy yet again.

Once she had put on the bracelet, she did not take it off, not even in the shower or in bed. Every day it reminded her of the celebration of her moving on in this struggle to stay afloat in California.

24

One day, Rudy opened the door to find an agitated, sandy-blond, mustachioed man, wearing a navy T-shirt with some sort of logo involving a bulldog, and blue jeans. His feet were clad in well-worn sneakers, one with the laces untied and about to fall to the ground.

"Can I help you?" Rudy did not push open the screen door.

From over his shoulder, Sasha said, *"Gabor."* Her voice was not raised, but she'd moved further behind Rudy, clutching a handful of the fabric of his Oxford shirt at his waist, as though wanting to become a part of him.

"Who's this baboon?" Gabor asked, poking a finger into the screen door at Rudy.

Sasha knew Gabor meant buffoon. He called anyone he thought to be a buffoon a baboon, insisting that this was the correct word for what he meant. While Sasha had taken English classes eight out of the ten years they had lived in America, Gabor blustered through with irrational confidence, confusing nouns in such a way that made Sasha giggle, which in turn made him simmer with anger. Carpet instead of blanket. Carpets for covers. Sasha's vocabulary soared past his once she began working at the store, and his anger and hubris turned to cruelty, teasing her drunkenly on her "Fancyee pants English speak."

"I'm Rudy Knowles." Rudy pushed open the screen door. "This is my home, and I suggest you come in, as you appear to be drunk and angry."

Sasha could not imagine why Rudy was inviting him into the house.

Gabor lifted a leg comically high and, getting tangled in the loose shoelace, stumbled and lurched through the door into the hallway. Sasha led Gabor into the combination kitchen and family room at the back of the house.

In moments, it was as if no time had passed. Gabor began a familiar circular argument: It was Sasha's fault that Stefi had drowned.

"I would have *saved* her!" Gabor punched his chest with his fist. "*I* can swim."

"The only thing you're swimming in is

vodka." Sasha collapsed on the love seat in the family room and massaged her temples. "And shhh. Hush. You are making a scene." She had wanted Gabor to appear for so long, and now all she wanted was for him to vanish. New girlfriend, new baby, divorce, goodbye.

"Oh, a scene," Gabor said, mocking her. "At fancy new boyfriend's fancy house."

"Gabor, you have a girlfriend and a new baby." It occurred to Sasha that she did not know the sex of the baby or its age. She wasn't jealous of this new girlfriend or the baby. How could you resent a baby? She just wanted her life back — and this new life, too. Was that greedy? Gabor wanted whatever he didn't have, unless it was vodka or beer.

Sasha *could* swim. Gabor *never* came with her to Stefi's Saturday morning lessons. And once she got the job at the fancy California club, the one free staff class she'd signed up for was mommy-and-me swimming lessons. "Watch me swim!" Stefi had begged her father at home, doing the breaststroke on the kitchen floor before her father. But Sasha knew from experience that there was no point in reminding Gabor of any of this now, especially in his current state.

Right now, Sasha wanted to go swimming.

To dive down to the bottom of the ocean until she couldn't hear the drunken voice of her husband. She wanted the water to be clear and thin, not thick and murky and heavy and green-gray. She wanted to swim to the bottom and pick up a rock that was smooth in her hand. Then shoot to the top, water rushing in her ears. Pop through the surface and spray water out of her mouth and throw the rock as far as she could. She wanted to take Stefi back to mommy-and-me swim class, save her from drowning. *She* could have saved her.

Gabor sat beside her now on the love seat, erupting in spurts and fits like the geysers they'd seen at Yellowstone.

"Yes, I have son. But I miss my daughter. I miss my daughter!" Gabor's voice was getting louder. The tone-deaf repetitive rants of a drunk.

You left us, Sasha wanted to remind him. But it had been a relief. Instead, she said, "And what would be her school lunch? Hunh? When you forgot to pack her lunch or give her lunch money? Would she eat leaves while other children unpacked sandwiches from home?"

"I want . . . I want," Gabor sputtered.

"You want whatever you don't have."

"You think you're so smart because you

have job." Gabor lowered his head, trying to meet Sasha's gaze, as she sat bent over, clutching her head. "I want to get job. I want to be working. You think I don't want to be working? I want two jobs and boyfriend with fancy house."

"Listen to yourself. You want a boyfriend. And two jobs. Okay. I'll introduce you to my HR manager at Nordstrom."

"Yes, I want to sell devil's timepiece jewels to bored rich people."

Laughter burst between Sasha's lips in a spitty gust and then she was crying. There was no arguing with a drunk. There was no arguing with an ex.

"I want to eat coffee and cake in break room with my girlfriends." Gabor's red-eyed gaze shot around the room now. This was how the let's-find-more-booze march started, looking around the room as though there might be a tap in the wall. "I want to get out of this computer engineer hell with no work. I want them to stop hassling me, unemployment office. I look for job! I want to get out of this place! I want to take Stefi and go home, like we never came to this place! I want to braid her hair!"

Sasha's laughter gave way to tears. That had been the one thing Gabor could do — braid their daughter's hair. Both a single braid down her back, and pigtail braids, parted neatly with a comb. He had never actually driven or walked Stefi to school or packed a lunch. But he had braided her hair, and Stefi loved it when he did. He made her giggle and laugh, her fine, blond-white hair slippery and straight; Gabor saying, *Hold still.* Then he'd tickle her and she'd giggle and squirm and he'd repeat, *Hold still!* Finally, they'd get down to business, Stefi holding her head still — with sweet, almost grown-up straight posture — her face assuming a serious look. When Gabor was finished, Stefi loved to examine her hair with the hand mirror in the medicine chest mirror.

Look, Mama! she'd insist.

Sasha knew that grief boiled within him, as it did her, but she hadn't had the luxury of not working, of being an unreliable employee — drunk or sober. And now Gabor acted like it hadn't been a sign of strength and perseverance to keep going. Still, Sasha thought, standing behind Rudy at the refrigerator now as Gabor carelessly rooted through the shelves, no doubt looking for alcohol. She did not want to let Gabor go just yet. She needed to give him the divorce papers to *really* get away from him.

She followed him to the kitchen island,

where he had taken a seat, cracking open a beer he'd scored.

"Gabor. I want my daughter to come with me to work on Take Your Daughter to Work Day," she told him in a low stern voice. "I want my daughter to ask me to tie her shoes again. I want my daughter to beg me to sing one last verse of a made-up song to her before bed. I want my daughter to correct me on my English, and to give her ten kisses for every time she does, smart girl *whom* I love. I want my daughter to have maple syrup on her chin so that I can lick my thumb and dab it off. I want my daughter to start piano lessons. I want to have to remind my daughter to practice her piano scales, to pull up her kneesocks, to be nice to old ladies."

Sasha collapsed at the kitchen table weeping, her arms folded across her knees, her head resting on them, the slight scratchiness of her sweater making her want to shout. Rudy rubbed her shoulder. She could hear Gabor back at the refrigerator, taking out the wine she and Rudy were going to finish — a special bottle from their tri-tip dinner the night before. Gabor probably couldn't imagine the fact that someone — two people — wouldn't finish a bottle of wine.

"Fancy," she heard Gabor say.

"Help yourself to a glass," she heard Rudy say. His voice was calm, not unkind, but not bright or inviting. Don't offer Gabor more alcohol! She supposed Rudy was just trying to placate him.

"Let's all have a talk," he tried reasoning with their unwanted guest. Unwanted, yet they'd waited so long to locate him!

Sasha nodded into her lap. She felt as though she might never be able to lift her head again. Still, she sat up straight, yanking tissues from a box on the table. Turning to Gabor and Rudy by the island in the kitchen, she realized that Gabor was probably even drunker than she'd realized. He slid a bottle in a paper bag from his beat-up brown leather jacket and took a swig from it, telling Rudy suddenly that he didn't like fancy yuppie wine.

"Gotcha," Rudy said, pulling a medium-sized glass from the cupboard and dropping a few ice cubes into it. "May I?" he asked Gabor, reaching for the brown-bag bottle. Gabor allowed Rudy to pour him a drink from his bottle, which Rudy then set on the counter, and Gabor quickly pocketed again.

"One moment," Rudy said, excusing himself as he stepped over to the little built-in kitchen desk, which housed a small computer and some shelves and drawers. Rudy pulled out the manila envelope with the divorce papers in it.

"Sasha has something for you," Rudy said, lowering his voice so that it was grave and gravelly.

Maybe Gabor suspected trouble, because he drained his glass, set it on the counter by the sink, and said, "No thank you. Actually, I should be going." With that he lunged toward the door from the kitchen to the garage. He must have thought this was a back door to the driveway or carport, as it had been in Sasha and Gabor's house. But as he opened the door to the garage, the automatic lights blinked on. Still, he stumbled down the two concrete steps, closing the door behind him.

By the time Rudy reached the garage, Gabor had climbed into Rudy's car. While he didn't have the keys, the locks in the car thumped as Gabor snapped them down.

Rudy clicked his keys so that the locks popped back open.

Gabor clunked the locks shut again. Sasha had always had two children, really. She took the manila envelope of divorce papers from Rudy. He stood in the doorway and watched her as she clomped defiantly down the two concrete steps from the kitchen, lurching toward the car in her clogs. She rapped on the window of the car, then twirled her fist round and round in the air.

"Roll down the window there, mister."

"He doesn't have the key," Rudy pointed out, just as Gabor opened the door about eight inches.

"You order the burger and fries, medium Coke?" Sasha asked.

Sasha was scrappy and resourceful, *and* she could be very funny. As this part of her personality had emerged, Rudy felt almost quixotic for having imagined her — perhaps from her love of Chopin, and the delicate watches she handled daily — as a damsel in distress. As delicate as the ballerina that popped up out of CeCe's childhood musical jewelry box with a little pink tutu. This wasn't really how he thought of her, but the image appeared now to chide him as he realized how brave she was, how proud he was of her for her bravery.

Sasha produced the manila folder from behind her back. "This came in the mail for you." Gabor reached for it, seemingly encouraged by the official look of the front of the envelope. Maybe he thought it contained a check for unemployment, or disability. Sasha stepped up to the window, speaking into the glass, as Gabor closed the car door and the locks clunked shut again.

"For you. From Santa Clara County Court. I want a divorce."

"Health insurance," Gabor only said.

"You can COBRA. By law, you can COBRA. But you better get your own job, because it's expensive."

"You are Cobra!" Gabor yelled at the window, stabbing the glass with his stubby square forefinger. "You are snake, witch, kill our daughter."

"That's *enough*!" From behind her, Rudy bellowed the words. "Sasha, come here, please." His voice was kind, not bossy. She turned from the car. Her husband had locked himself in her boyfriend's car, but at least she had managed to serve the deadbeat with divorce papers.

"Useless process server overcharging attorney," Sasha said, clearly shaken as she passed Rudy and stood partially behind him on the threshold into the kitchen and family room area.

"Gabor, you can stay in the car as long as you want, until the police get here," Rudy said loudly and calmly — like a pilot on a rocky flight describing the details of the situation to the passengers. "I am going inside to call them now. You may get out of the car while we are waiting for them to ar-

371

rive . . . I'd appreciate it if you not vomit in my car, but my suggestion to you is to get out, and go on home now." Rudy rolled up the garage door so that Gabor could scramble out.

Sasha backed into the house.

Gabor opened the door, threw out the manila envelope, and locked himself in the car again.

Idiot, Sasha thought. This was what always got him — and them as a couple — into trouble. His illogical, stewed thinking when drunk. He had a perfectly good escape, he had a new family. A divorce would surely be appreciated by the mother of his baby. He was broken. Not a broken soul — more like a broken-down appliance.

"Go home, Gabor," Sasha advised.

Rudy took Sasha's elbow and encouraged her to go into the house and sit down.

"Listen, Gabor," he calmly called into the garage. "You can throw away those papers, but you have a court date to appear, and you have been served with the papers. It's not difficult and it doesn't have to be acrimonious. All you have to do is show up and we will do the paperwork. Don't make it harder. Take it with you and go. You don't even have to read it. Just look at the date and be sure to show up."

"I will sue *you,* piano player dime store!" Gabor shouted.

But Rudy had already turned from him. He closed the door to the garage just in time to see Sasha, who had clearly heard Gabor, spit a sip of red wine she'd taken straight over the kitchen sink and onto the window.

"I'm sorry," she said, starting to cry.

"It's okay," Rudy said, turning her from the sink to give her a hug. "You missed your sweater. The window's easy to wipe off."

Sasha collapsed into him, breaking into sobs.

"You are strong," Rudy told her. "Against all these odds, you are strong and good."

"I am not strong," Sasha said, standing up and turning to splash her face with cool water from the sink.

"Well, you don't have to be," Rudy replied. "You know, the doctor at the hospital asked me *who* I was being strong for. He said, 'We are too strong and we snap in the breeze. You ever see palm trees in a really big storm? In a hurricane, even category five — the worst, they bend all the way down, like giant feather dusters sweeping the ground.' He said it was one of the most remarkable things he'd ever seen. This uncanny resilience we somehow muster."

Sasha seemed to take heart with his

words. Rudy appreciated her strength. Yet wanted to alleviate some of the relentless stress that pressed into her always-sore back.

The police came sooner than they'd expected. When they opened the door to the garage, Gabor was gone. The police hovered over Rudy and shone their flashlights into his car, as they made sure the car had not been vandalized. It had not. And along with Gabor, the big brown envelope of divorce papers was gone.

25

Bethany knew by their second date in college that she would marry Rudy. And she was hardly a romantic! In her English Lit class she found the doomed heroines in Edith Wharton's novels much more authentic than the happily-ever-after wedding church bell tales of Jane Austen. It was after Bee and Rudy seceded from their group of dining hall and pub friends and ventured out on their own that they finally embarked on what you could call a proper date. They went out to dinner in town to a Thai place with white tablecloths and delicious food, topped off with a dessert of mango and sticky rice with coconut milk and coconut ice cream. Rudy had given Bee a choice of restaurants for their outing, paper menus collected ahead of time, so that she could choose the restaurant. He was a foodie even back then, but never a food snob. He always loved admiring others' preparation of food, and feeding friends, as much as he enjoyed eating. Not pleased with the restaurant's wine list on that date, though, he had called ahead and asked if he could bring a bottle and pay a corkage fee. Bee was impressed that Rudy had worked this all out ahead of time. She learned over dinner that Rudy's mother had died rapidly of pancreatic cancer the previous year. This experience seemed to plunge him into the grown-up world ahead of others his age, and explained how he did seem the most mature in their college group of friends.

"So fast," Bee remarked, on how Rudy's mother had only lived for a few months after her diagnosis.

"There really are no symptoms before it reaches stage four," he explained, "next thing you know your mom's in a hospital bed in the living room."

Bee's eyes welled up for this sweet boy.

Rudy scooped more noodles onto her plate. "The pancreas should get its shit together if you ask me."

Next thing, Bee cracked up, spitting out a bit of her Thai iced tea onto her plate. "Oh, that is *not* funny," she apologized. "I just . . . you rarely curse!"

Rudy blushed. Then he started to laugh because it was so awful it was funny and he had clearly been so angered by his mother's senseless death and they were both laughing and crying at the same time and trying not to choke on their food.

"I love you," Rudy told her.

They slept together that night. "I put out on the first date," Bee giggled in the years to come.

"We'd known each other for months," Rudy reminded her.

They had. Study sessions and long group gabs after dining hall dinners, with cups and cups of coffee. All of them procrastinating on their papers due, singing Monty Python's "Bruces' Philosophers Song."

"EEEEEmanual Kant was a real pissant." Rudy, with a beautiful voice, Bee couldn't help noticing, would get them started, and they'd all stay until the dining room closed and they were kicked out.

On their second date Rudy made beef Bolognese for Bee, explaining how the little bit of milk you added to the browning meat helped break down the fat and give it a sweet, nutty taste.

They slept together again that night, and talked until dawn. Rudy was the most completely authentic human being Bee thought she'd ever met. Serious, funny, patient, happy, even if prone to dark moods, always complimentary to her, way too hard on himself. A bundle of contradictions that somehow made her feel comfortable, relaxed, and safe.

Well into their marriage they sang the philosphers song in bed. They also continued to play a silly game they'd invented in college, lying tangled in the sheets after making love, staring up at the ceiling and stating:

"If I get hit by a bus . . ."

"Play 'Wish You Were Here' by Pink Floyd at my funeral."

"Play 'Shine on You Crazy Diamond' at mine."

"If I get hit by a bus, the $200,000 in cash is hidden in the walls in our cabin in Tahoe."

"We don't have a cabin in Tahoe."

"Oh, right."

"If I get hit by a bus, please get remarried," Rudy said to Bee one night when they were in their forties, lying in bed, listening to the cars splash by in the rain-soaked street below their bedroom window.

Bee rolled over and kissed him. "Have you noticed how few buses there are these days, anyway?"

"I mean it." Rudy drew her closer, kissed the lace of her camisole, the top of her head.

"But not that guy at the bagel shop. I don't like the way he looks at you."

Bee pulled away from him, pinched his nose, which he hated.

"I have a secret celebrity crush on Bill Hader. I'm going to marry him if you get hit by a bus."

"AGE INAPPROPRIATE!" Rudy declared.

"Yessssss," Bee said. "And very cute and hilarious . . ."

"He can't sing," Rudy declared. "And I bet he can't play the piano." Rudy's tone took a more serious turn. "Seriously, I'm not kidding. If anything happens to me, don't wait around forever. Remarry, promise?"

Bee rolled over and he spooned her. "Just not that jerk who admires the garden so enthusiastically when you're out there in your tank top, weeding. I see how he looks at your beautiful arms!"

Bee gently elbowed Rudy in the gut. "If I get hit by a bus, promise me you won't be too hard on yourself," she said softly.

"Don't you worry." He lifted his wife's hair and kissed the back of her neck in the place where it was especially soft, and a little damp. "Besides, you're going to outlive me by years. Statistically proven."

26

Since Sasha first began staying at Rudy's house, they had taken longer and longer walks together around the neighborhood, and up into the surrounding hills, where Sasha was delighted to see deer, and rabbits. It helped Rudy work out the hospital kinks, and helped Sasha curb her jitters.

November had arrived and it was raining. One morning there was a particularly big storm: the rain gutters plonking, a few roof shingles flying on to the lawn. When the storm let up in the afternoon, they ventured out for their stroll. The sky darkened, though, and it began to rain harder. The leaves clogged the sewer drains, and water pooled up in the street. They had bundled up in raincoats and hiking shoes. Rudy brought along two huge golf umbrellas. It was nice to be outside and breathe the cold, moist air, watch the steam of their breath billow before them. Rudy crouched down in the street and began to dig at the leaves clogging the sewer drain.

"If I had a shovel . . ." he mused.

Sasha crouched down with him, and together they cleared a path for the water to run into the drain, as they tossed leaves and muck onto the grass at the edge of the sidewalk.

"Yuck! Cold!" Sasha laughed. "Stinky!"

Rudy laughed. Sasha laughed harder, gulping and coughing.

"Why are we laughing?" Rudy asked her, rain dripping from the hood of his raincoat onto his nose, then his chest. They were out playing in the muck. He was sticky and warm under all the layers now and looked forward to getting home to a quick shower, dry fire, and glass of wine.

Sasha pulled a package of tissues from her pocket and handed a wad to Rudy. They wiped off their hands. Sasha rinsed her fingers again in the cold, cleaner flow of water. "Ayeeee!" she cried. She used the last bit of tissue to wipe her hands, then buried them into an old pair of woolen mittens from her pockets.

"I would like new gloves for Christmas," she announced.

Christmas. Before Rudy met Sasha, he never could have imagined Christmas again.

"We can pick out together," she said, "with my discount."

"You are practical to the point of being unromantic," Rudy told her. They were on the sidewalk again. Sasha picked up a huge, perfectly shaped orange leaf. She put it in her pocket where the tissues had been, careful to keep it flat.

"Besides," Rudy said, "I might like to shop at a *different* store. I'm not sure I want to see Dinner Theater Darren and the whole crew." There was no crew, really, just the headless mannequin, and the worry that the sadness that had haunted him those months playing at the store after Bee died might return. Might wrap itself around his head like one of those nearby dramatically wide and long cashmere pashminas, until he choked.

"Suit yourself," Sasha said.

They walked in silence, making one last loop around another block, until they'd reached the house. Rudy never called it *his* house anymore. It was *the* house. Where he'd hoped Sasha and her kitty, and even her own grief, would feel at home. He'd swiped, blown-up, and framed a black-and-white photograph of Stefi and Sasha that he had loved at first sight. She kept it in a box of her things, though, and he wasn't sure if it had been out on display back at her house. "Trigger warning," he'd said when he presented her with it, adding that they could hang it or shove it in the attic crawl space if it was too sad. Sasha wept, but chose the former option. It now hung in the hallway, near a photo of CeCe as a girl, sternly running a strawberry lemonade stand at the foot of their driveway.

The holidays — *Christmas,* he thought — and then his birthday, December 30. Back when Bee was alive, when Rudy's landmark fiftieth birthday had been approaching, he'd obsessed over it so much that he started to think he would turn fifty-one that year. After she died, he felt one hundred. He hadn't even thought about his birthday this year. He realized now that he hadn't been able to imagine his birthday without Bethany. He hadn't really believed he was going to live that long, get that far. It wasn't a suicidal tendency. He didn't think so. For a while there, he just didn't think there was a reason to get out of bed anymore. Next thing, he was in the hospital. CeCe was there, *crying.* And then Sasha. And then he was sitting up, playing cards. They still played gin rummy some nights. Tonight when they got home — it was five o'clock already, nearly dark — Rudy was going to build a big fire, and have cheese, crackers, and wine with Sasha. Then he'd pull out the coq au vin he'd started in the morning, put it in the oven, sit down with her until it was time to heat the bread and toss the salad. Someone for whom to cook and eat with. That was not something you could put in an anti-depressant pill. CeCe stopped by for dinner many nights now that Spencer had moved out, so they all could eat as a family. Keira even took her bath and put on her pj's before she and her mom left because she would fall asleep in the car before they got home. Rudy and Sasha had the pleasure of reading her stories after her bath. CeCe repeatedly told her dad how much these evenings helped her.

"You know," Sasha said, as they sloshed across the street, waving hello to a neighbor who was attaching a plastic green accordion water spout to his rain gutter. "You know, after you left the store, it was like they really missed you."

"Oh yeah? What makes you think so?" Rudy saw the notes floating across his sheet music, smelled the cloying, too-strong smell of old-lady perfume the saleswomen spritzed as samples for wary oncoming customers in the aisles near the piano.

"Because, I forgot to tell you. That PA

system. For maybe a week after you were gone it kept calling your name, like they expected you to be there. I *told* them you were in the hospital. But still that *lady.*"

"Really? So I'm not *completely* crazy." Rudy laughed, but under the layers of raincoat and pullovers, he cringed at the thought of going back there. He'd quit that job and started a part-time butcher counter gig.

"I called them for you," Sasha said, "then told them in person. Still, she called you for another day or two." She shook her head and smiled, her gray eyes developing that mischievous twinkle. "I liked hearing your name. It made me miss you less." She kicked some leaves in their path. You could smell both the effluvium of rotting leaves and the crisp newness of autumn air. Wood fires and waxy Duraflames.

Sasha stopped on the sidewalk, wiped a browning, webby acacia leaf from her sleeve. She firmly held Rudy's arm, stopping him. She cleared her throat, which was always a sign that she would be trying her best to speak without an accent.

"Rudolph Knowles," she beckoned. Her sultry monotone was perfect. Hundreds of hours behind the watch counter, and she had it down to a tee. *"Rudolph Knowles."*

She raised her eyebrows suggestively.

Rudy bent to kiss her, to shut her up. Both of their faces were wet now, and the rain was coming down in earnest.

Sasha laughed, pulling quickly away from his kiss, holding up a hand to stop him. *"Rudolph Knowles,"* she repeated. Her breath billowed from between her pink chapped lips. She broke into laughter and took off running toward the house.

Rudy followed, his boots squishing and clunking, as he broke through a shortcut over the grass by the curb. Soon his boots' sogginess slowed him. And Sasha was fast! She'd been on the track team in high school. She had medals. She'd shown him one in a box of things she'd opened but not yet unpacked. There was so much more to learn about her.

She turned and looked over her shoulder, breaking into a final sprint to the front porch, laughing and bending with a cramp but still running.

Rudy thought, hell, maybe they'd take a hot shower together when they got home. *See I'm* not *a fuddy-duddy,* he wanted his new poker buddies to know.

"I'm going to beat you," Sasha shouted over her shoulder.

At the front door she flipped down her

hood, and Rudy watched it fill with rain and a few falling leaves.

"Calling Mr. *Rudolph Knowles.*" Argh! In that perfect butterscotch-sauce silken monotone. He would catch her, throw her over his shoulder, tickle her until she had to stop.

Sasha reached the front porch, stamped her feet, placed her black mittened hands on her hips. Rudy tried to catch up, crossing their driveway, and then their lawn, where his boots made a sucking noise in the muddy grass. Sure, he could navigate an attorney's bill and home inspection report, but in some ways, he would always be a few steps behind Sasha.

Sasha waited for Rudy, swiping at her runny nose with a tissue from her pocket. Steam clouded up from her mouth as she teased one last time, *"Paging Rudolph Knowles!"*

ACKNOWLEDGMENTS

I have an embarrassing number of people to thank for helping me get back up on my feet and finish this book. First, so much love and gratitude to Lisa Pongrace, who will sit beside your hospital bed and work on a crossword with you in crayon. (No sharp objects!) Many, many thanks to writing partners Eileen Bordy and Vicky Mlyniec, to savior Jane Ganahl, and to cheerleaders Karen Eberle, Kim Ratcliff, and Julie Culleton. Special love and thanks to Dorothy, Sam, and Owen Chin.

Thank you to editor Tara Parsons for rescuing me with lovely guidance and to her whip-smart editorial assistant, Isabella Betita. And for the bang-up job by copy editor Rick Willett. Much graditude to the folks at Gallery Books for their open arms, generosity, energy, enthusiasm, and smarts: Kate Dresser, Molly Gregory, Michelle Podberezniak, Diana Velasquez, Meagan Harris, and Jennifer Bergstrom. Always, deep thanks to Linda Chester and to Gary Jaffe — who brings daily cheer to the many tasks of publishing.

Love and thanks to Greg Solberg, and always, always, to Frank Baldwin, champion of writers.

To those who contributed to a Go Fund Me that my agent Laurie Fox (the most generous person I know), Patrick Miller, and Jen Listung kindly set up for me, I don't even know how to thank you. All I can do is give to others' causes and to the arts whenever I'm able. The donors include: Catherine Taman, Scott E., Julie Righeimer, Jane Moore, Mary Patrick, Amy Poeppel, Kathy Seal, Ken Crichlow, Vivian Ruth Sawyer, Nora Escher, Peter Coughlan, John Williamson, Maggie Jarrett, Allyson Tilton, James Beer, Bj Fishman, Jenny Clarke Caruso, Tanya and Chris Orman, Gwen Clarke Fujie, Jean Escher, Annie Young, Frank Baldwin, Lis Bensley, Shannon Calder, Christine Silverstein, Mark Ebner, Jennifer Stivers, Crystal Nichols, Michelle Richmond, Ben Hess, Izabela Menezes, Pirie Jensen, Tom Parker, Shelly King Schuur, Mae and Sam Mlyniec, Catherine Hartshorn, Curt Anderson, Janet Hancock, Mary Tougher, Sheila Himmel, Jana McBurney-

Lin, Sarah Chue, Francoise Vincent, Julie Espinoza, Shani Gilchrist, Sherri White, Julie Knight, Jane Green, Linda Bonney Bostrom, Jane Boursaw, Amy Hatvany, Janis Cooke Newman, Cheryl Strayed, Karen Bjorneby, Mary Vellequette, Heather Young, Linda Sexton, Jennie Shortridge, Ellen Sussman, Vicky Mlyniec, Eileen Bordy, and Kim and Jimmy Ratcliff. I'm so grateful for the generosity from these friends, readers, and fellow authors. I look forward to sending you treats, meeting with some of your book clubs, and reading the above wonderful authors' new work. To the anonymous donors, please know how grateful I am for your kind generosity. It meant the world. And the rent!

Shout-out of love to my family — my brothers Robbie, Jeff, and Kev; lovely sisters-in-law Sarah, Jean, and Theresa; Sam (!) and Jenny; Wyatt and Crystal; Jeff and Emily; Natalie and her brood; and my beloved artist uncle Gene. Thanks to those surrogate family folks for sticking with us nutty Winstons.

In loving memory and with thanks for his help to Lance Cowell, with special luck and love to his widow, Judy (an ever-helpful friend), and beautiful daughter, Sarah. Sarah, you are a gem.

At Stanford Medical Center, thank you to Drs. King and Birnbaum, and to all the nurses, especially Ali, who could keep you calm in a category 5 hurricane. All these folks are unsung heroes.

I miss my loyal office assistant Popoki every day. Without him, there's no one to print blank documents with their bum.

Finally, thanks to the first people to make me laugh after coming out of the hospital in 2013 — Dave Hill, Tom Scharpling, and Jon Wurster, and to all the lovely FOTs. If you laugh so hard you spit iced tea on your kitchen wall, things must be looking up.

ABOUT THE AUTHOR

Born and raised in Hartford, Connecticut, **Lolly Winston** holds an MFA in creative writing from Sarah Lawrence College, where she wrote a collection of short stories as her thesis. She is the author of *New York Times* bestselling novels *Good Grief* and *Happiness Sold Separately*, which is being developed as a film. Her short stories have appeared in *The Sun, The Southeast Review, The Third Berkshire Anthology, Girls' Night Out,* and others. She's contributed essays to the anthologies *Kiss Tomorrow Hello* and *Bad Girls.*